THE WRONG HONOURABLE AGENDAS

Amyas Cullen

A catalogue record for this book is available from
the National Library of New Zealand.

ISBN 978-0-473-34963-9

Book production DIY Publishing Ltd
Printed by About Print Ltd

THE WRONG HONOURABLE AGENDAS

Amyas Cullen

This is a fiction of an Island Administrator
who struggles between law and justice
amidst the darkness of carnage

Dedication

Who made my 1 get into 6.
Chrissie,
Hayden,
Joyce,
and
my long-suffering Barb.

CONTENTS

1.
The Migrants

A TEPID OCEAN SEETHED wafer thin over his enormous pitted back, hardly even disturbing well-fed seabirds momentarily perched precariously. Phosphorous eddies split down framing his bulk in symmetrical patterns spiralling to oblivion.

He lay there quietly in the dark, in the all too rare calm. Together and alone.

His texture broken by crustaceaned pockmarked scars from long ago fought battles. He feared nothing now. He was that big.

Membranes constantly fed him data from miles below, from miles around, the depths below whose raw pressure would crush man's pitiful body, from cold that would snap-freeze surface creatures, to the blistering heat from the black billowing plumes deep below in the mountain ranges. Now all just a walk in the garden. He knew it all from ages of travel and inherited genes.

He sensed the rhythmic thud of ships' propellers too distant to concern him. An accompanying irritating gnat scream by small craft were all too common. Perhaps he might get the satisfaction of swatting them as he recalled his past.

He guessed every creature must have its share of parasites. That was nature. Signs he was close to land, he no longer needed. Though he set a generous pace, some weaker ones were now tiring so he would settle here for a few days and nights to consolidate the pod before the final push.

His instincts told him that this season he had plenty of time.

Most importantly he communicated with the pod nearby constantly while he herded them to the summer grounds where food would be plentiful, where it was time to wean and cows ready and wanting to mate and laze for a while, to shrug off challenges to his authority, to grow fat for the lean seasons ahead.

High above, man's inferior imitation of thin metal and rivets coursed towards the same destination. Passengers inside held the same agenda.

The aircraft jerked on automatic pilot in a decreasing triangle of still distant black earth, the craft and the GPS satellites far above. The movements imperceptible to the crowded passengers most of whom slept; a few hardy ones at the back slurred loudly indulging in drunken grievances long forgotten by everybody bar the defeated.

Snapper sat back in his seat, his eyes dried out and irritated by air conditioning. He rasped his tongue over the roof of his mouth seeking out moisture. But there was none to be had. A stale linger of red wine with his meal perhaps smelt more than tasted. Never destined to be vintage and par with his meal, he decided.

He lolled his head sideways envious of those passengers genuinely asleep. Still, there was nothing to be done about that now. His seat remained stubbornly indifferent to his large frame.

He gazed upon the American woman asleep beside him. Her strength of character not even in the shadows of her chair. Her mouth completely fallen, open stumps of teeth scattered like drunken tombstones, her body sagged at every angle, her defined bottom lip hung like a broad-leaf kelp. Snapper only just knew she wasn't dead by the occasional noisy laboured flappery inhale. Never noticed her breathe out. He imagined her silently inflating beside him. He wondered idly if she was about to explode.

Through hooded eyes he surveyed as much as he could before leaning towards her slipping a hand gently inside her still-fastened seatbelt. Just as loose as the start. He was satisfied now.

"Can I help you, sir?" A statement more than a question.

Startled, he fully awoke embarrassed. "No, thanks, but perhaps you could tell me the local time. I seem to have missed the announcement." He sought strength to look up guileless.

High above he saw two large dark oval pearls looking down at him laughingly. The whole head surrounded by a manicured round blurry dark rich brown halo. Make-up immaculately practised applied. Professional cheerfulness emanated. Very island doll-like, he thought.

"Well, it is just before dawn. We will see the islands soon enough then the flight plan is usually to fly over the mainland and land from the opposite side. We can check the island's time then." She smiled.

Her smile brought out her personality. A slight smear of bright lipstick over strong white teeth made her magnificently human. Before he could say anything she had ghosted off.

He returned to his examination of the cellulite oscillating beside him. A single silver strand ran from her bulging tapestried neck. Did she know it was there? Maybe he should save her embarrassment and pluck it now. Shards of silver traversed the length running an endless race, tempting him. Maybe, though, she was proud of it. Some eccentrics were like that. He wondered.

He was just in twilight when he felt the thin cover being tucked into his sides and feeling all the security of an infant, he slept likewise.

Snapper woke with a start. Whether it was the aircraft or something in his mind he couldn't be sure. He pushed the cover aside. One little nap left him more refreshed than the hours of sleep he had attempted.

He felt a casual eye pause lingering from the huddled form. He cast a solitary eye back. She winked at him. Personality had gelled together all her individual parts into a powerful woman. "You know you snore? Like a girl?" she chuckled.

"No!" Snapper considered. "Nobody ever told me that."

Sounds of life reverberated disharmony throughout the plane. Mostly from the back.

She peered towards the commotion that seemed centred over a giant. He filled two seats and minions ran servitude around him.

"I could have had him, any time, in my youth," she smugged at Snapper.

"No doubt about it," he agreed.

She looked at him accusingly. "Now I am older with layers of more than sedentary fat. Sometimes I pay for it, you know?"

"Just indulgence and why shouldn't you?" he supported.

"I don't see that you would have to."

She looked away, unsatisfied.

Snapper gestured to the hostess beaming in return. "Say! Who is that big boy at the back?"

"He is the 'game breaker'. Magnificent body. If in doubt, give him the ball. Doesn't take no as an answer at all well!"

"Guess that what makes him the sportsman that he is," Snapper observed and turned back to the window.

"But it's just a game."

"But the game is everything." Snapper ended the conversation.

Outside black was not so sheer. Others on the plane now were waking. Sensing the end of their travel their volume of concerns lifted. In the confines of their carriage, passengers feeling secure since the beginning of their flight now irrationally doubted at least one item had been lost. Patience with young ones, their own and others, every single one lost in the hubris.

Snapper always thought this the worst time of any flight. Perhaps he could have taken a cruise.

The hostess worked her way down towards him checking and soothing as she went. A distant glimpse of recognition raised his spirits. Perhaps his imagination? She had been taught and practised to be personal. Still he wondered about an opening gambit if there indeed was something to be nurtured. He watched as others chanced their moment while she professionally laughed them all off.

In the end he decided 'nothing'. Nothing was never an embarrassment.

"How are you now, sir?" she asked.

"Fine, thank you."

She hesitated while tidying up passenger comforts refuse. "I noticed you travel very lightly. Just a yellow carryall. You are not just another tourist?"

Snapper winced. This was an aspect he had overlooked but too late now. At least she read nothing into it. Time for a little practice. "You are right, of course. I am returning home after many years abroad and it seems most of the clothes I left behind so long ago still fit even though no longer fashionable. Is it obvious?"

"No!" she blushed delightfully, slightly. "We crew bet on passenger occupation. Whoever gets the most wins heaps at one of the bars."

"Do you have a problem with any of the others?" Snapper was keen to help. Now he had got one back.

"Well," she conceded. "Those two are tricky. They hardly talk. European passports. Spend most of their time poring over their papers, calculators, charts, huddle and calculate some more. We are sure they are not married or in any sort of relationship. Not much more baggage than yourself." She discreetly singled them out.

Snapper saw she was right. They did act out of the ordinary. Oblivious to everybody else on the plane. "I would say they are professional gamblers. The island is having an enormous jackpot in lotto that would attract from far afield." He did not convince himself, never mind.

"Thank you," she beamed at him and moved on with her labours.

He received a nudge from the neighbouring elbow. "I think that is land out there!" Others thought so too and the plane leaned over slightly. Snapper hoped it was the pilot, not the weight of passengers.

In another world scene outside a minute signet ring etched against black velvet. Far to the right lay two exclamation marks. Most passengers now focused as the plane drew ever so painfully slowly closer to the outline.

Now surf outlined a dark pulsating blob. Small lines of dew grew into spider webs of light but still even at this distance there were no features around the lagoon. Evidence the shores had developed ribbon first and gradually moved inland, quality land held quality light. Dots gave way slowly to signs of civilization.

An announcement was made that though the island was visible the plane would traverse in a wide arc and it would be some time before passengers disembarked. Snapper confirmed this to himself. There was no time given or orders and suggestions for arrival. He sat back.

Myriad lights converted to streets, factories and communities with little to no sign of early resident activity.

'The Marks', two exclamation points, grew larger without revealing features. They looked sinister and their reputation was enhanced by all of the island invaders.

What the Lapita started, with European settlers using the two isles as penal colonies, as did temporary administrators during the world wars and postwar. Now their history is folklore and still as a means of adjusting the young fallen by the wayside. All generations of all ages hated them.

The morning greeted the plane in its wide arc and painted the island into its full colourful postcard features before the start of the humid heat; below factories in the middle of suburbs paved a clear path, the only thing left to be done. The trip now done, the aircraft began its final approach.

While most scrambled disorderly leaving keen to absorb new experiences, Snapper sat back pensively. His companion long ago clambered over him anxious to keep to her tour itinerary.

Time was Snapper's itinerary. He reached up for his overnight bag and headed after the others.

Customs was the usual casual island approach. The security of the departing countries and the isolation of the island provided blanket cause against problems even with this crowd.

Snapper passed over his passport and travel papers. Without looking up the security started in monotone repetition, "Anything to declare?" Without pause for an answer, "Here for the football? Tourist centre in the middle of town can help! State's biggest lotto on Friday. Whales expected next weekend." Now he paused mentally checking off his list.

He looked up. How big the queue was now? It has been a long, long shift!

"Accommodation's at a premium." He looked up to Snapper at last.

"It's not a problem," Snapper reassured him.

"Three buses have already departed. There will be another in fifteen minutes and so on until all passengers have been accounted for." Snapper felt dismissed.

He stood in the automatic doorway. He felt a twinge of

disappointment. Long gone was the broken shell path leading to the aircraft from a single building. Gone were the palms and views of the ocean and island peninsula; gone too were all the kids who came to watch the twice-weekly doubled engine propeller plane lurch around. Gone was the overwhelming labouring engines, forcing you to close your eyes, gone was the static announcements impure but with pride and enthusiasm with an occasional squeal from close feedback through the system, replaced by the computer hum and swish of its precise communications. Gone too were the powerful fuel odours.

Now were modern buildings equal to any other Snapper thought could be found unique to any country.

The morning smells exclusive to the island brought back memories. A tear welled up in his eye. He brushed it aside and aimed for the bus. At least at this late stage there was no demand for seats. He decided a good old island breakfast would lift him.

2.
Of Mice and Men

In the coolish gloom of the pre-morning the city slept peacefully. Without sound the small group's pre-adolescent shadows flickered along the manufacturer's pitch roof. The movement equalled their fears for although the dark covered them with a blanket of security, their confidence only extended to as far as they could squint. Mischievousness increased their senses.

They looked down through the big windows to the black of the large machines set out in a mosaic pattern below. The soft tar of the wide guttering between the skylights threatening to tug off their shoes and squish up between their toes like some primordial ooze gave confidence of walking at heights. Splotches of dark red skinned rust islands floated haphazardly against the dark roof. Testament to futile maintenance.

"So, Gus, you think you would like to be in charge?" came a hiss. "Perhaps you should lead!" He shoved Gus forward.

Gus twisted in astonishment to his leader. "What? No! That is not on my mind at all! We all know you are the boss!"

"That's right. I'm in bloody charge!" Simon replied. He gave Gus a heaving rough shove as he twisted in response.

Gus spread-eagled over the window looking up at them. They all watched in silent horror as stretch marks raced from the glass sills to centre and the eagle-spanned outstretched body. The inevitable result tumbled out in slow motion with surprisingly very little noise other than a tinkle of glass giving a perverse light overture. Gus and windows and frame disappeared into the depths.

The splodge landing of overripe fruit brought home to each reality and gave them control again.

"Oh Jesus!"

"I don't want to be here!"

"Are you alright down there?"

"Oh! My God!"

"We will get help!"

Simon glared at them silent in thought. Inward he evoked a kaleidoscope of emotions he was scarcely able to control. He could not believe he had the courage to implement his dream.

Elated at his own bravery, trepidation at what lay ahead, concern he may not have thought everything through, a little frightened of his commitment, he had mastered and above all he was now in charge.

He looked at the bunch cowering in front of him. It was all so good. He would have to split the group. No problem.

He would be free of his father at last! A few more beatings perhaps then he would be gone from this arsehole, and shit hole, of an island. He had the world to conquer and he was determined to do so by his own efforts and not bully others like his father. He had broken the cycle they had preached so much at school. But Simon had always been perturbed by the lack of emotions at the preach of freedom.

Then he decided no! He didn't want to break out like they said. That would be too easy. What he wanted was a role reversal. In his turn he would rather 'look after' his father in his old age.

Now that idea appealed to him. He knew he would dwell on variations.

"Come on. There is nothing to do here for him. I mean you can't even see him! Now you, Gene!" Simon hit a small quivering heap beside him. "You come with me. You others go down the side there. It's a bit dark but you will be safe enough."

He watched the others leave thoughtfully. The twins were beyond help he saw. Such wimps! Adam was always in the shadows looking after little Tommy. I don't know why we tolerate him. Now Adam may be the next problem. Never to the forefront but always watchful and loyal to the end for his friends. Possibly an asset or just as likely a liability. Never mind that now.

In the gloom below, Gus could only distinguish outlines and hear voices. He tried gingerly to move but he was pinioned over a machine as securely as a butterfly on display. He found no voice of his own either!

Don't leave me! He willed the others to stay. He tried hard to make out their shadows against the night. As they left, worried silence disturbed him. The night insects should have started their chorus by now.

I would have thought Adam would have stayed; the idea passed through his mind then he concentrated on helping himself. He had had to do a lot of that lately. He had developed muscular and tall, all bulk. Older generations he noted treated him with caution, several mentioning how he resembled an uncle he had never seen.

Women he associated with his mother had begun to pay him with growing regard. It was all so strange. There was nobody to confide in and no explanations.

He mused over the trouble he would be in when he got home but he knew his mother would be all comfort and concern and affection crying his name over and over as she had every time he got into a real fix.

Strange that he could not feel any pain, he thought, and his breathing took real effort. He groaned quietly.

In time Gus realized he was dying. Sudden real bitter hatred erupted at friends who deserted him.

He wished them all dead!

Dying was a lonely thing. And not by old age. Then he wanted more. No, that was not enough! He wanted them to suffer before they died. Suffer badly! Gus wanted them to know that this was their end just as he was experiencing. How would they like that?

He felt still disappointed by Adam. The black of the night conceded surrender to the day though the sun had not yet made an appearance.

Gus listened hard. Whose footsteps could he hear in the distance? Here! He was over here. If they were searching for him why didn't they come closer? For Christ's sakes! He struggled to move or make a sound to get attention but the machine pinned him solid.

His efforts tired him immediately. He slumped and closed his eyes still listening to the steps. His life slowly dripped onto the floor sounding of slow deliberate steps in an ever-increasing circle of blood.

The red mottled floor now matched the red mottled roof.

He heard a distant roar and lights of angels, the whistle of wings closer and closer overhead, filled the whole sky. Gus blinked and life disappeared with his manmade apparition.

He missed the tinkle of broken glass and plaintive call of his friend as he broke in. Adam held his hand for a short time just standing there weeping. "I am so sorry, old friend! We were all queued behind you. I just don't know what happened." Finally even Adam left.

Simon allowed a smile to himself as he reached ground. He had cultivated Eugene with the play on his name and Gene's video camera was essential to his finance plans though Gene was not.

"What's that?"

Eugene looked up in terror.

That's right! Smile for the security camera, thought Simon. My old man will test his influence to help me but, son, you have nobody 'cause you are nobody. Still the police are not fast and I need you, well, your video camera anyway, for a couple of days at least.

I know, as he thought things through, Jane is an inspirational solution. She would do anything for him including being 'friendly' to Gene.

Simon looked down contemptuously. I bet you cream yourself just over her tits. Still, as long as I achieve my goal. Simon had a parting thought. He had better check her out. Make sure she was clean. Don't want to be stuffed up by a poisoned chalice now, do we?

He looked around satisfied, and they too headed home.

❊ ❊ ❊

In the great hall housing all his cars Cedric daintily picked off a perceptible mote. Then he polished the black of imaginary swipe his first action had created.

He disciplined himself against further buffing. He held great affection for his BMW as he did with his Range Rover, his other cars, bikes and his other assets. Ruefully he included his wife.

Satisfied, he saw the reflection of his slightly bulbous nose; the black didn't reflect his greying and receding mottled forehead. Looks were not part of his family but wealth was, and wealth stayed longer. His was the third generation and he had always been conscious of being reminded how riches and power only lasted three tiers. He was determined to prove this wrong.

He and his twin had been born with other assets such as a fine intellect, utter determination, plus arrogance.

Cedric felt for his brother and the death of his brothers wife. Perhaps Cyril should have his car instead of that late-model Nissan. One thing they did not agree on was standards. Cedric always felt if you had wealth, flaunt it, whereas Cyril didn't laud it at all. Cedric shook his head to himself in wonderment.

Wealth also brought happiness and whereas he spotted his wife and promptly bought her, he had been happy. On the other hand, Cyril always used his position to court various women before his wife. Now his Elsie was dead.

Cedric had always remained faithful, not through conscience but practicality. Sex used up precious time that interfered with his scientific medical research. And now in this hour of grief he saw his opportunity to gain worldwide esteem. An unknown infection had taken Elsie and Cedric was motivated to triumph, maybe international personal status.

Wealth and intelligence allowed him his own facilities. Security was always paramount and he had personally screened his small dedicated staff. He continued to carry out his personal checks.

Although he always gave them full credit he made sure his name and enterprise was mentioned. None had betrayed him to date. He was confident because he paid well.

Now it was all total personal opportunity! His paranoia ran full licence. He increased his security. Allowed all the staff possible special leave until it was over, conditional on them staying in contact in case he needed other expertise. Expensive but worth it!

This was a once-in-a-lifetime personal chance. He would share it with no-one!

He opened the doors to watch a golden sunrise over the placid morning waters. Even in adversity life was good.

3.
Milestones

Snapper stood idly outside the café ruminating disappointment. His tongue picking his teeth over his casual brunch. The café used to cater for individuals but today it caters for the masses and the taste quality declined accordingly, as though he was expected.

What to do first? He watched tourists snap pictures and bargains while the shop catered for heaven, staff trying hard not to show as much by burying themselves in labours. What else would you expect?

Groups of kids stood scruffy much as he had on street corners watching the world evolve, a contempt towards social community spirit passed generation to generation.

The First Citadel Bank ought to be his first visit. Better to get his finances sorted first.

Again the front presented solid dependability beckoning customers, enticing them by façade. Cathedral windows viewed busy but happy staff with customers inside. What happened to the old days when any account was based on solid reputation? Perhaps he was getting older, Snapper decided, cynical as he ambled up steps allowing the front doors to open automatically and digest him.

He filled out the prerequisite forms at one of the personalized counters. He didn't hesitate in joining the shortest queue, the 'Learner' sign a beacon of less professional service but likely more personal.

He smiled widely at the learner's returning acknowledgement, still yet unburdened by conviction. "Just want to open an account and make a small deposit?"

"Sure, I can do that," she looked relieved. Snapper was beginning to warm to her already.

"I think it is all in order," he beamed at her. "Take your time. I am in no hurry."

She meticulously scanned the sheets. "Mr Baukor, this deposit is considerable. I will just get a senior to assist." She pressed an unseen button.

A youthful well-dressed confident employee ghosted in and appraised the situation at a glance. "The amount is unusually specific, perhaps some special purpose intended, ah? Perhaps if you just pop into this cubicle to our left, allow us some privacy."

"Perhaps not!" Snapper beamed at him equally. "Miss … is doing just fine and it's not complicated. Thank you, anyway." There was nothing warm in his smile.

The rebuff was not taken well. The advisor ghosted away.

"Rose, you can call me Rose if you like." Rose flushed by challenge and adrenaline.

"That would be nice. My name is Alby," he replied.

"This is a substantial amount to deposit, and for a current account. So precise! I am sure that I know this does not best serve your interests," Rose looked at him questioningly, scanning for confirmation.

Snapper's smile gave her that. "Your best will do just fine." He waited patiently.

"Well!' she said, after repeatedly ensuring all particulars were correct. She didn't want errors especially now! "Here is a temporary ID and bank access cards until the start of business tomorrow when I can give you more permanent records."

"Are you trying to make a date with me?" Snapper felt a warm glow at her blush and delightful discomfort.

"If you like!" Snapper liked her mastering the situation. Rose was turning out to be a real pearl.

He smiled again and waved his farewell.

On crest of the street corner opposite, Simon clapped his hands, getting the attention of those lingering around him. "It's worked! The camera picked up everything through the side window and he is loaded, or should I say, was." His elation sickly infectious!

The group laughed in group triumph while privately wondering who else would be bold enough to enter the bank and make the withdrawal. The time portal from the teller going to lunch and the security downloading was precise but sufficient.

"Fuck you all! I'll do it myself." Simon could read their minds. They always thought so small.

He gently uncoupled the large photo lens attached to the camera front, which he took for himself. "Look!" he tried to placate them. "It's a victimless crime. The bank will repay the money. It's not as if we are stealing from him. Now that just wouldn't be right. I wouldn't ask any of you to do that!"

They watched Snapper amble down the road. "He don't look filthy rich to me," one of the twins observed. "What would Adam say?"

"Yes!" continued the other. "Perhaps we should wait for somebody else."

"Get out of my way!" Their leader resigned himself to possessing all the bravado, upset at the mention of another. He wondered himself where Adam was as well. He stepped confidently towards the bank. Still, the stranger looked familiar; though he was sure they had never met. Here goes. "He won't be filthy rich soon!"

In a small space of time he re-emerged, unable to contain his elation. The others rushed to see what treasures awaited.

❊ ❊ ❊

Snapper later returned to the square to retrieve his bearings. The tourists mingled, the kids were gone. Maybe this café had something to tempt him. The tempo of commerce had not altered.

Rose positively hurtled towards him from the bank. "This is terrible, terrible!" she cried.

She was cut off abruptly. "Nothing can be so bad on such a fine day. Just tell me what it is!" Snapper didn't want to make a scene.

She hesitated. Didn't he understand how pressing it was? Her body tried its best to convey urgency, completely unread. She searched for gentle words, diplomatic words.

"Come now." Snapper led her to the café. "A hot drink or maybe a cold drink can put things in perspective." He beamed in support.

"Perspective! Yes, that is what I need, yes," she garbled on while her companion preened her with little tut-tut noises.

Snapper waited until she had her drink but she still looked shaken. "Well! Everything was fine when I left. You seemed happy enough, so what happened at lunch?" he prompted her.

"Lunch. Yes. Lunch! When I was at lunch someone pretended to be you and took some of your deposit," but she looked at ease now it was out. "I am so sorry!"

He shrugged. "Rose, it's only money. We can replace it. I thought it was going to be something important."

"I don't know how they did it. They just knew everything. You didn't talk to anyone, did you?"

"Nope!" Snapper cheerfully reassured her. "Look, let's go to the bank and you and I can handle whatever needs to be done. You did such good work this morning I am sure it can all easily be fixed. Besides you are faultless. Now you must not share any of the blame, should you?"

"No! But I feel so bad." He was a strange man she decided but sweet enough. Others would be devastated and publicly abuse her being the front-line staff.

This guy looked as if he had broken a tooth in his comb. Perhaps he was right, perspective and all may all work out. The bank would be the place to go.

Rose led him to the bank. Snapper could tell they all knew from the apprehensive looks, the evasive manoeuvres and their body language. Snapper could feel his temper.

This was one time for him to bury it well. He would be satisfied with a view of the security tapes and records. And if he was satisfied so would be the bank. No fuss was a win-win result.

❈ ❈ ❈

Cedric viewed his white-coated troops with pride. "There are only a certain number of possibilities. You can choose. Whichever is right will get bonuses. Others will be paid double the holiday allowance until this is over. You see there are no losers, as per the norm.

Who wants first stab?" He knew it would be Bobby.

Bobby stepped forward. "I will go with blood and clots." So predictable. Others followed inspirations as if by script.

Finally a trio left looked uncomfortable. None said much either socially or at work but they were the brightest of the lot, always worked together and essential to other projects.

Tim raised his eyebrows questioningly. A leader this time though there was no discernible leader within the group. "Anecdotal evidence suggests a VD strain."

Cedric nodded his assent. It was not his thoughts but he didn't want to share anything unnecessarily.

"Yes!" Al was always last. "Aerial borne." His was a statement more than anything. Cedric bit his tongue. Al was never right but he was extremely thorough and useful personality in commitment to time-eating tasks no other wanted that still had to be done. This time Cedric was happy to give him his lead.

❊ ❊ ❊

The taxi driver lurched his car over the road. Same volumes of abuse and venom ribboned from the street after him. He accepted such a daily ritual. This was a time of plenty. He scanned his mirrors looking for the best passengers. What would his luck be today?

He was startled by the sudden lurch of a bulk climbing into the back. A quick survey was disappointing. Of all the tourists around he scored a local and this one looked near penniless. He remained unimpressed.

Snapper leaned over. "You are for hire?"

"Yes," came the reply but the clear inference was not for you. "Where are we going?"

A short trip might be made up for and he could guess how long before he was touting for business again.

"Oh, I don't know. Let's just have a ride round. A scenic tour if you like. I'm in no hurry."

"That's fine with me." The driver's tone spoke volumes.

"Just drive around the blocks in a figure of eight formation."

Snapper looked but could not sight the kids. "How about up the knoll? Turn right at the car yard. And past McCarthy's."

It was probably too soon for the kids still counting their haul with backward glances and questions about their getaway. They would soon be confident and swagger back for a little reward to spend, each. Time did not factor.

"Man, how long have you been away? Old man McCarthy died ages ago and his sons died in the store fire not long after. Those streets have been revamped more than once, but I think I can locate you there!" The driver glanced back again but his passenger was distracted. "Say! The meter's ticking over, you know!"

"Better pull over for a minute then." The driver was at least positive about this; at last, as he did so, this crap fare was over!

Both men peered silently at each other. Snapper levelled his shoulders and sighed. The taxi driver just knew it! No money! He had better come up with something original, the driver thought, or his passenger ought to have a preference for hospital food. He waited.

"I think you and I are of the same kind," Snapper started. The driver gestured his fare to go ahead. "Have the same drive. Let's talk turkey!"

"I guess. Right," the driver acknowledged and paused. He was lost while he was certain his fare was taking the piss out of him; poor understanding thwarted any challenge.

Still! The driver knew he was cursed. All these golden times as he looked at his passenger and here he was stuck with what? Some dithering old simpleton reminiscing on what no longer was reality. Bets are he has no more money either, not that he needed any really, but. He snuck another look. What was the old dick writing? A letter of complaint, of course! He decided enough was enough. If his fare mucked him around then he was out of it!

The driver pulled his car away into light traffic.

Snapper looked over. "Do you know this address? It used to be the outskirts of town." He handed forward a note. Instinct told him the taxi driver was always one more step ahead, at least. But look at the scruff!

The driver snapped it up and shoved it hard against his pocket, hesitant to even look at it. Finally glancing down he recognized the address. Who would have thought it?

He pretended indifference. Judging by the state of the note, his life's total possession. "Not the outskirts any more for a long time now. There are more affluent areas and scenic spots to visit."

"No!" Snapper replied. "Just take me there and keep the note. I don't have change," Snapper apologised.

"Nor I so early in the day!" The driver peered at his fare. Great! I will be lucky to profit from this. Lucky indeed!

"Let's not worry about it then."

Despondent by fate the cabbie looked down. Now what could he do? Green colours caught his eye. A hundred-dollar note. American! His day positively brightened. He looked at the figure in the back with fresh regard.

"I think that you and I speak the same language," Snapper observed. "Let's keep on going, ah?"

Holy mothers! Suddenly this fare was so profitable. The taxi lurched forward positive; he had gone from pauper to prince. He wondered whether to explain the overpayment to his fare. He needed to think more about it.

4.
Crossroads

Snapper produced another bill. The driver finally felt obliged and commented this sudden income was far in excess of his margins of profit. But his taxi was waved away. A warm toot farewelled his new best friend.

Snapper looked up and down the main street. Everything was the same yet different. Smaller, he decided. His last perception had been as a youth.

He examined the small bleached cottage, patched grass, higgledy-piggledy flower beds. Patchwork, if you wanted to be charitable. Typical of the owner though. Restarted everything repeatedly, finished nothing. Time taken from the previous attempt allowed a colour fad or regrowth accentuating time.

Standing with his hand leaning down on the small gate held by its one and a half hinges, Snapper knew this would be his last chance just to walk away. Equally he knew he would not, so with his other hand hiding in his pocket Snapper sighed and followed his path to the door.

Knocking on the door he heard footsteps and loud voices competing as to who should answer the door. Anybody else! Sounds of muffled steps were now more adult than he recalled.

Two dreamy reluctant eyes appraised him. He looked directly back. Down ran from the front of ears and small scars from picked spots dotted a fine complexion. Snapper waited as attitude in the eyes mellowed. Recognition shine at last and the door flung wide welcomingly open.

"Uncle Albert!" A ruckus's fanfare now announced his arrival to all the inhabitants. Another fine complexion materialized. Large brown eyes familiar with strong thick antenna lashes popped in flickering in adoration, in wonder and awe.

An old familiar voice resonated from the pit. "Don't talk crap! Boy!"

"I think that must be my invitation to come in." Brother and sister swept each aside in an honour guard of glee indeed. Ben's outline hid changes of age; the character the same. Lisa merged into the outline.

Immediately Snapper sensed her as he stepped into the kitchen. His old vulnerability returned. How many times had he tried to replicate this moment with substitutes, synthetics blended with memories. Now he knew what compelled him and he was sure if he could bottle some he would be so rich.

She smiled at Snapper warmly. "This place is a mess," she apologized.

"I know how it is! There is so much to catch up on. Years and years in fact. But you two look fine. Are you OK?" Snapper had instantly mellowed.

"Yes," Ben replied for them both. "Are you here for long? This is so unexpected. You could have dropped a line, you know? You should have. Out of the blue like this."

Snapper moved attention to the kids. "Look at you both nearly all grown up."

"We are grown up!" said the boy indignant. "But watch this! I can still do your trick." He toyed a coin between his fingers. "I have practised!"

Snapper took the coin and in one deft movement from his pocket two harsh heavy coins appeared. "One for you and your sister. But you look after them. They are pirate's doubloons."

"No! Uncle! You are teasing us," the girl chuckled shyly. "Dublin is a city. You can't fool us any longer, you know?"

"I know, still …"

He was cut off by Lisa. "You have been in contact with your family? So quick after the death of your nephew? They will be pleased indeed. We are so sorry!"

Snapper looked up from her children. "I know nothing of any

family tragedy. The family made it clear when I left my contact was to be less than minimal. I have honoured my part. Do you think they know I am here?"

"No! Not unless they have seen you … and recognized you. You were always so bloody-minded, you know? This is how this all came about," Ben explained. "Your Gus fell into one of the factories. He was turning out to be a lot like you, you know? You want us to speak to your family, your parents at least, or brother?"

Snapper pursed his lips. "I will see them all in due course, of course. But at the moment I am looking for somewhere to stay. Is the old flat available? I do realize it is short notice," he apologised.

"Let me just check?" Ben ambled awkwardly out of the room.

"If you didn't know about this, why are you here?" Lisa spoke at last. The kids hovered.

"To see you, of course. Old times, you know!"

"Old times should stay old times."

"I know, but it doesn't hurt to treasure them."

Ben peered back towards the kitchen. He was worried now and didn't want to be overheard. He had dreaded this moment. He thumbed a scrap of paper as if rosary beads. Finally plucking up all of his meagre courage he read the number a few more times before he dialled. Nobody could touch him over the phone; it was after that filled his mind.

"Hi!" that American twang resonated harshly in the earpiece. Didn't sound a threatening villain he feared. Ben still didn't want to upset him.

"Ben!" No small talk. Ben wanted this over as soon as possible. "The man is here wanting his flat."

"Is that so? I haven't heard about this?" The American was surprised.

"I think he came straight here. We have always been good friends and supporters, you know."

"OK. His flat will be ready for him within the hour. You can take him yourself, can't you?"

"Yep!" Ben agreed straight away.

"Good, very good," the voice chuckled. "Say, do you know if he has time for a game of golf?"

"Don't know that he plays."

"Sport of kings, you know. If he doesn't play I can pay for a few lessons. And you have mail."

"Sure," Ben agreed. But the phone had already been hung up. Ben shook himself. That hadn't been so bad. He didn't know why he had worried. He returned relieved and pleased to be with his visitor.

"Look! I don't want to be rude but it has been a long day and I am really wanting some sleep. I thought maybe we could all go to the club tomorrow afternoon some time and I can catch up with everyone there at the same time," Snapper was saying.

"Sure," Ben replied. "Um, you don't play golf, do you?"

"Just have a cup here, spend some time with the kids and we can take you round straight away," Lisa suggested, implored, ignoring Ben.

"Fine with me," Snapper agreed and sat back relaxing. Christ! I have only been here two minutes and offers come in, he thought to himself. It's going to be *long* brief stay.

❊ ❊ ❊

The two brothers preened each other. Identical jet black suits with bright white shirts: they looked like a couple of crows, ugly birds, small appraising scrutinizing black eyes for lint or the smallest imperfections.

Cyril sighed. "This is a tough time for me, brother."

"I know!" came the reply. "But I can help you through it." Cedric reached into his pocket careful to minimize creases. "Here, take this phial and rub a little of the contents under your eyes about an hour before. Its evaporation will have you crying like a baby. You, ah, did have some insurance, didn't you?"

"How dare you! I value my wife as much as you value yours, you know. The insurers will not need your magic to make them weep." They both giggled at the thought.

"I can always count on you. You have made all the arrangements."

Cyril placed a heavy manicured hand on his brother's shoulder. "It is costing a pretty penny. I tried for a much cheaper casket and arrangements! So melodramatic! I offered him a cut you know but he was having none of it. It's still all insurance."

"Self-righteous prick! You make him stay poor." They giggled some. "I guess all the usual dignitaries will fawn around as well."

"A little gastroenteritis could occur, you know." They laughed at the prospect of others' acute discomfort. "Perhaps we could ask for refund or damages."

"Introducing a little chlorophyll seems right."

"Don't give the little shits too much credit." They laughed again. "I'll think about it. It's all free anyway, of course!"

"And we get a free ride in the back away from the mourners. Pathetic! Not even a donation asked. Another opportunity lost on him. Speaking of free rides, you are not bringing that bitch of a mistress are you? You know she only wants you for your — our — money." Cedric was getting serious.

"Fuck me! Why did you go and spoil the atmosphere? Of course she's after what she can get. Aren't they all? You are upset 'cause she got to me first. And she is good, bloody good. My knob is still really sore!" Cyril remonstrated mock indignity with suffering.

'So she won't be coming. Good, I can't stand her!" Cedric looked at his watch. "Now you have made us late!" he cried. "We have no time for another drink! I suppose we had better be where we are supposed to be. Company." He leaned over and opened the door to his brother's Nissan with such precision it must surely be tainted and ambled back to his own car, a discreet distance away.

"It's going to be a long day," Cyril agreed.

❋ ❋ ❋

High above the town centre an enormous desk shone brilliantly yet dwarfed by the large room.

Magnificent rich red streaks in the wood buffed by years and generations of hard work with tender care mirrored well on the big man seated behind.

Cheap plastic in-trays tiered by slender stainless steel rods incongruously out of place. Well-worn scruffy paper files anchored it all down by weight.

Morgan leaned back filling out his equally luxurious chair waited on the small figure in front of him. "Apprise me of the last twenty-four hours' events, chief! Give me the bad news first. We don't want to end the morning on a bad note, do we?"

"Mostly run of the mill, boss. We have security footage of the events leading to the boy's death. Group of kids. Maybe five or six. Got a couple of good shots but it is what is in the shadows that are of interest. Should be able to identify them in the next couple of days and bring them in.

"Another rape of the same, not involving any of the tourists that we know of. We are not yet any closer to identifying him. That remains my highest priority. The Rev will be agitating as soon as he hears, of course. So expect him to come calling!

"A few drunken disorders, all minor considering the numbers in town. Just as well because we are really stretched.

"Put up the couple of UN inspectors about the deaths. Going to the latest's funeral this afternoon. I still have a tight hold on the press. It couldn't surface at a worse time. But just goes to show the old girl was as rich as, so it is not just the poor as an excuse this time. Will you be going?"

"I don't know. Those brothers are far from my favourites and I don't want to be seen condoning the pricks," Morgan conceded. "Rupert! What else? Give me something positive! When are the whales due?"

"Within a week, boss. Do you want to set up your own fast service judicial circus?"

Morgan nodded. "It will be easier dispensing with tourists as well as the inevitable dickheads! Any other concerns?"

"You know my feelings about the lotto."

"Yes! I bloody well do. And how stretched you are. So go about your business but stay alert." Morgan dismissed his chief. He kept his worries to himself. It seemed it was going to be a long day.

5
The Day Dawns New

Snapper lay back still. A small edge of trimmed hair on the back of his neck pricked and scratched against damp on the pillow beneath. Comfort felt old familiar surroundings, familiar sounds and smells, waged against an interloping sense of another person's personal touches. Staring up he could not see them but he felt their substance and once the knowledge was there it was not to be rid of.

There was nothing for it. He would have to get up.

He peered lazily over to read the blue illuminated time of his clock. Already after eight. He would make his own breakfast. No such substitutes in town. He raised himself. Should he try to plan the day or just let it whirl around him? He aimed for the buses to the town square first. That was sufficient!

❊ ❊ ❊

The new widower groaned. Cyril sighed loudly again. "Back to routine. Thank God that is all over. Thank God I have you, brother."

Cedric reacted. "No! It's not all over. It's up to me to find how you are now alone and I am determined to do so!"

"Wow! I don't know what that stuff you gave me was. I am still a little tearful, for God's sake."

"Find someone else." He was ignored. "You want me to buy you somebody? Somebody nice."

"Thanks, Cedric, but I can't take charity."

"Charity starts at home. I remember that. You should too."

Cyril laughed. That was better. "I don't need charity. Especially yours!"

Cedric pressed him. "Get rid of that slut you have tagged onto. She is nothing but trouble!"

"Actually she has been very helpful indeed," Cyril defended her. "I have been neglecting her of late and …"

He was cut off. "Has she been neglecting you?"

"No! Not at all. In fact she's extremely accommodating."

"Good! There is nothing more to be said then, is there?"

"No! I suppose not." Cyril sighed again. "I guess you are right. You usually are. It is time I moved on."

"In that case we had both better to get back to business. You really should buy yourself a decent car." Cedric tried yet again. "Just even look at them!"

❀ ❀ ❀

"A car's a must!" Simon presided. "What do you think, Ross? You are the best driver of us all."

The group immediately relaxed when Simon released his grip. Ross thought as the others waited. Something powerful but not immediately noticeable, still a power symbol. He thought of the scorch marks on the reserve of past drivers and how many had not made it. The reserve's notorious Black Hole consumed so many over-confident.

At last. "There is a BMW at the 'Top of the Hill'. Not a late model, of course, I know, but should meet our needs." A pause. "Any other thoughts?"

They all looked to Simon. No other opinion mattered.

"That's a good choice! A bloody good choice!" Simon finally agreed reaffirming his leadership. He never got sick of that. They all ambled hurriedly towards the car sales.

There was no real hurry. The car yard had been a haven for kids as long as anyone could remember. And 'Honest Pete!' had began the careers of many quality mechanics over the ages.

❀ ❀ ❀

Snapper stood in the long hall of the administration building. Aisles and signs everywhere. He shook his head. He only recalled half a dozen offices when he left. Back then everybody knew everybody's business anyway.

Implied opulence courted him as he walked down the great hall. Pictures of dignitaries and national favourites peered haughtily at him. Those he knew of were no such thing in real life. He supposed dress attire implied co-operation.

The administration's second in charge had a double doorway, of course, and Snapper smiled. Security's pretty lax. Then again nothing ever happened here while holiday mode left most staff absent. He pushed open an outer chamber door.

Inside was a massive round desk matched by a massive round woman. "Can I help you?"

"Morgan!"

"The boss is busy this morning, already behind with his appointments. I can get you in to see him maybe late next week, if you can tell me what the subject matter would be?"

Snapper didn't wait. "If he is already behind then I am not being an inconvenience," he beamed to her as he brushed past. "I can get to see him now, thanks anyway." He gave her a conqueror's smile as he entered the room.

"Hi!" he greeted two occupants. The boss sat passively behind his desk. If he was surprised he didn't show it. His underling leaned against the corner of his desk. A tall thin flamingo streak, his suit hanging as if from a coat hanger, was startled.

Morgan leaned back, his hands clasped behind his head a sigh in motion. "Snapper! As I live and breathe!" He raised himself and tottered forward to stand in greeting, nudging his assistant aside away from his desk.

Snapper approached with relish for an emotional embrace.

A smaller round weather storm bustled into the room. "Hold it right there!" from a protective mother reckless of possibilities. "Security's right behind me! And you are toast, buster!"

Then Liz stood staring, sizing. Watching two giants in greeting face off each other. They seemed to her as two prehistoric bulls competing over mating rights. Perhaps her. She imagined the two turning, bearing roughly but kindly to her overwhelmed intimate body. Her massive bra started to pinch. She could feel moist.

The two did get her attention. Had she inadvertently said something, swallowed something during her fancy? "Sorry!" she said. "Sorry!" But she was not regretting anything. Never had in her whole life. When her husband wanted a 'big' woman she happily obliged and multiple envelopes now adorned her body. She was still happy and so was he. Now her figure and a large grey 'V' combed back in her equally well-rounded hair increased her presence.

"Bob!" Morgan took charge. "Note the time it takes for security to get here! The useless bastard!"

Bob swallowed vigorously. His Adam's apple a throat's trombone practice.

"Sit in my chair, Lizzy Lee!" The large blob squeezed herself in a blush of self-conscious lubricant.

Silence.

"Snapper, meet my team. This is Bob. My adjutant does everything for me, says nothing, never sleeps apparently, a real pearl of a find." Bob fidgeted acknowledgement.

"Elizabeth Leigh, my personal secretary cum everything, God only knows how many secrets she has stored away." Lizzy was modestly downcast.

Snapper nodded to her. A polite but firm knock on the door interrupted and a slight figure diplomatically moved in.

He sized up the cluster of people. An instant vehement hostility towards and received from Snapper was almost tangible. "Sorry to interrupt. Silent alarm, you know. I have taken the liberty of cancelling it."

An old tanned ruddy face under a cap covered forehead, rubbed red smoky eyes that determinedly unfocused rested on silver hair and precise silver moustache, the ends tobacco tanned. A gap in large front square teeth, once one ground down by prolonged excessive pipe use, similarly stained. Sleeves half rolled up industrially in contrast to military precision. The tone and speech clipped.

"Alright, chief. This is an old friend, Snapper! No harm done."

He looked at Snapper. Smoky red eyes gave no welcome at all. "How do you do?"

"How do you do?" Snapper returned.

The chief reflected back momentarily. He had been overseer to an African state born of multiple tribes collected together by a stroke of an English pen another continent away. Still in his time he installed and kept peace and justice through the strength of his personality until he missed a shipment of guns. A village wantonly decimated was the result. He had armed four or five volunteers and eventually chased down the band. In a moment's lack of his attention his volunteers obliterated all the offenders.

Their explanation being surely that was why he had given them arms to add another chapter to their blood-soaked history and now they would need to defend themselves from the inevitable repercussions.

He saw the full futility of his job and without a word shot all his volunteers and had driven away.

Now on these paradise islands he had encountered civil criminal elements but there had been no serious cracks in the society's veneer. He now smelt evil that permeated the room like an old friend. "Call me Rupert if you like. Perhaps, if I could check your passport?"

Snapper shrugged as he handed it over. "What's been happening anyway? A real sports extravaganza. Tourists coming out your eyeballs. This is great, isn't it?"

"No! No, it's not!" Morgan sobered the conversation. "Bob was just going to update me. You may as well stay and listen in." He liked to have more than one stance. He looked quiet at his chief. Sometimes a luxury, he thought, sometimes a necessity, sometimes useful.

Snapper had not finished, however. "I thought all passports were checked to accommodation addresses and copies kept."

The chief was unmoved. "Only accommodations of over a limited capacity and then only for a limited time. As a matter of fact most are computer screened when they check in. Then again I take a random sample check, when I feel inclined!"

Bob swallowed again. He was uncomfortable at all this

impromptu. Due procedure had been casually cast aside without regard. Still, he was only an employee and he knew better than to protest.

"Right, skipping the usual minor misdemeanours we still have clamped down on a health risk that has caused fatalities of some local women. I received the two WHO officers to help oversee things. They seem very obliging.

"Picked up security tapes of some young offenders. Can identify two, I wondered if you want to preside?"

"Why?" Morgan asked.

"Keeps them out of the court system. To carry on, another violation last night. He must be pretty fit!"

Morgan looked skyward. He gestured eyes at Snapper. "We have a serial rapist for a small while now and no leads. He is labelled 'Gentleman' because he causes a minimum of violence. Provides lubricants on occasions, no evidence of excessive force and comforts them afterwards. Still, we have no leads. He wears a mask we suspect disguises a defect. Don't know how he picks his victims and witnesses yet to come forward."

He shrugged his shoulders in despair. "Well, Liz, it's going to be a long morning so cancel my appointments and usher in the indignant as soon as. I just don't know what to do!"

Snapper looked sympathetic. "If there is anything I can do, just say so?"

"Are you sure? I can't ask of a person just arrived." Morgan looked at him hard.

Snapper opened his arms wide generously. "Come here, old friend. A brother in arms I cannot refuse. I don't know how I might help but you know if I can I will assist with a minimum of inconvenience!"

Morgan embraced him simply. "Thank you, thank you so much!"

Liz looked on in awe. Here were two giant friends now leaning on each other's shoulder, heads down, supporting each other, helping and cementing their friendship.

She saw teardrops fall sparkling from one or both. Nobody

could tell them apart. And she was moved by them both.

The chief looked on bewildered. He would just have to be patient, wondering. Nobody saw Liz slip back to her desk.

Recovering he spoke, "Here comes the little purple weevil now! Scuttling across the road!"

Morgan peered out of the window in mutual contempt. "With his shadow. How I would dearly love to take the wind out of those sails."

"Carry on, boss?" Bob felt he needed prompting.

"Nope," Morgan sat down. "Let's weather out this storm first."

The chief shrugged his shoulders. Snapper not knowing what to do shrugged his as well.

Liz knocked discreetly on the door. "Rev Long is on his way. Do you want him to use the front entrance?"

Morgan nodded.

"Thank you." As she turned, "The Rev Long for you." She announced his entrance.

"Morning, Minister! So good of you to call unannounced. But if one minister cannot make time for a fellow minister, what is the world coming to?" Morgan hated the purple colour worn with shards of black as if a badge of honour. An island shell carving looked plastic, disgusting him, aggravating him the more. Worse, his own brother simpering like a personal reverend's cloud behind.

Rev Long could not resist himself either. "Minister in name only! My parish looks for God. Yours serve to God! Damn me for taking his name in vain!"

"What exactly are you here for?" The chief was intolerant.

"One of, no, I should be correct, yet another of my parish suffered great anguish and social stigma at the hands of one person you are unable to identify, let alone apprehend!"

"This has not been made public yet. So how do you know so much, so quickly?" Morgan retorted. "Perhaps you are the one with the inside knowledge?"

The priest was untested. "Most of your citizens see me first as the best viable alternative to yourself. What does that tell you?"

"It tells me that you live in dreamland. I was voted in by a healthy majority, have done for years. But if you are a viable alternative perhaps I should look into it!"

Long carried on. "Your own brother here, Louie, has been comforting my flock as if it is some compensate for your responsibilities. You don't know what a service he has been to this community." He at last settled back a bit and noticed the stranger. "Who might you be? A detective perhaps? A good detective?"

"Afraid not." Snapper pointed to Louie hovering in the background behind Long. "Tell him who I am, quiet one!"

Louie spoke unconvincingly. "That is Snapper! I didn't know you were back. You missed your family's funeral."

"I have already paid my condolences. Not my funeral!" Snapper turned to Morgan apologetically. "I must take my leave. I have a very important lunch date but I will be at the old club later tonight, if it is still there?"

Morgan nodded. "You may not recognize it!"

As Snapper's large frame disappeared, red eyes following, the chief asked anybody, "Who the hell is he?"

Bob continued to swallow vigorously.

Morgan prompted, "Tell him, Louie, go on, brother, tell him what everybody else knows or think they know!"

"Well, um," Louie spoke slowly indeed. "Not much to tell really. A couple of school kids were killed in a fight situation. Snapper, or Vincent as he was then, was a suspect though nothing was ever proven. He did state he was there at the first time with a girl. The only, um, explanation he ever gave was that something must have snapped.

"And the name stuck. After that there were more fatalities of the same nature. The police and general would euphemistically say 'they were snapped'. So everybody looked at Snapper, being the common denominator. The only vague connection was the deceased had all been school bullies. Um, eventually everything got too much and he left. The fatalities stopped at the same time, so coincidence or what?"

"Thanks, Louie," Morgan beamed at him. "You put that in a nutshell, and now he's back!" 'Long can leave,' he pauses, 'by himself!' Long is happy enough to depart.

The chief chimed in. "Thank you for all that but now we have things to do. Business to conduct, et cetera. If anything turns up we will let you know first," he reassured them as he gestured them out.

"Interesting tale?" Morgan asked himself, alone.

"I have his passport!"

"I asked you to screen one of all arrivals and have done so how many times for months, years and longer and you screw up!" Morgan was upset!

"Let's be fair here on my staff. They are totally under-resourced and your bod has no criminal record. Why? It is in their role to detain strangers?"

"Your role should be a scrotum on a eunuch! OK, we can't go back, I suppose. Better get your funeral garb dry-cleaned and set up your own office at the morgue!"

"I'll have him tailed constantly just for you, at great expense to me, and I will have you informed!"

"That will have to do for now." Morgan was back on track. "Liz! Get in here!"

The door opened; a large body filled the frame. Liz's voice from behind. "Conrad from the Citadel is pressing!"

Morgan looked at him pensive. "I have a few spare moments as it happens. Well! Banker, you do not visit all that often at all. How can I be of service to such a distinguished citizen?"

"Did you know Snapper has emerged?" Conrad sweated freely.

"I've heard rumours. Have you seen him?"

"No, I have not personally! However, today he made a deposit exactly equal to the funds you made me freeze plus interest to date, to the last cent! A coincidence I think not!"

The chief stepped in. "Perhaps if you could see your security footage we can resolve this immediately?"

"Ah!" Conrad wilted a little. "There is a problem with that. It seems security needed it for something else and it got damaged."

Morgan mimicked, "A coincidence I think not! Look! If you want our help you had better come clean. The only thing that causes a bank concern is loss of money!"

"Well! No complaint has been received so there is no loss as I understand it," the banker defended.

"What do you want?" Morgan could smell dubious.

"Protection, of course! You promised me protection if he ever came back. You said he could never come back and now he is here amongst us! Raising flags!"

"Conrad! You were acting under my instructions. I doubt you would be a target. In fact, I should be. However, the chief here will assign you a guard most of the time. Not all of the time, we are just too busy, you understand?" Morgan worried, but he tried not to show it. "You have told me everything, haven't you? I can't do a lot if I don't know everything!"

"I will have to be satisfied, won't I?" but the banker was far less than satisfied. He stalked out.

"Liz! Get your arse in here and it is not for dictation!"

Liz coyly entered, prepared for the worst, which she knew was never that bad, but protocols had to be followed.

"This time you are in deep, deep doo-doos!" Morgan started.

Liz smiled inwardly. The boss's turn of phrase meant she was anything but. She wondered why she had been summoned.

"You just can't let anybody in willy-nilly," she heard Morgan say. "How can you run a place like this? Perhaps you need to be reminded you can be replaced!"

Desperately Liz searched for the real subject. It had to be the stranger! "It's your old friend! He just took me by surprise! Barging in like that. Who is he to take such liberties? Such disrespect for this institution. How?"

"Shut up!" the chief had other things on his mind. "For God's sake. Well, he won't be hard to find. He is, after all, a big fellow. As you are, boss."

"That is my point. Liz, describe Snapper for the benefit of the Chief."

"Well, Chief," Liz thought back hard furiously. "He was a big man, quite old, no disrespect intended, moves really well, probably a very good dancer. I wouldn't mind finding out. No identifiable distinguishing characteristics though."

Morgan explained, "That is the problem in a nutshell. Chief, he is non-descript. He blends in with everything and he is not stupid, so go and find him!"

❋ ❋ ❋

Outside, Snapper squinted in the bright sunlight. The air-conditioned office no longer masked the heat of the morning.

A police guard casually watched him and others. "'Scuse me." He stood just as tall as the officer. "Where can you get an old-fashioned car around here?"

"Top of the Hill."

"Is that still there? Who runs it now? It has historical value, surely."

"Still there last time I looked. Lot of businesses interested in that site. The old man died not so long ago and the son owns it now. Might have some historical value once it's gone, I suppose."

Snapper agreed. "Thanks. I suppose I can walk up." He whistled happily. Not a flicker of recognition but he felt that to be a brief interlude.

The boys hoarded around the BMW convertible mutual pride bursting from their shirts. Small flaws shrank before their eyes, appealing features grew. It was a fun machine and they visioned many parties of the car, maybe even often sex alone or otherwise in the back seat. That is what they all thought.

A check jacket overpowered, made them shade their eyes. "Interested in this car, are you? Well! A pretty interesting choice. I know it has a few scratches and dings, but that is part of its colourful history. Owned by 'real' men, you know." The jacket started his patter.

He learnt from his dad each broad generation wanted to know only particular themes. Didn't matter how you dressed things up, or even what was said. Buyers only listened to what they wanted to — if you got it right! Life would have been boring but as his son he liked easy challenges and these kids were just ripe.

He started to wind things up. "So like any hero the scratches mean this car has survival instincts. What it has learnt on its way to the top is up to you to find out! But I can tell you all this. Those marks are ones of respect to all other drivers. The dark and silver streaks, more bruises and scars, you now? Drivers will hold you in high regard. And as for the womenfolk, well, you just take your pick and remember you do not have to stay once the appeal has worn out."

"Yep! It is a panty-dropper alright!" Ross voiced everybody's thoughts making them uncomfortable yet proud and united.

Simon smiled with and at the others. His scheme was working better than he could have imagined. He knew now he was in charge and the fat wad of bank notes in his pocket reinforced his view. "What do you think, Adam?"

Adam didn't have to think. "You are a genius. No doubt about it. Even Tommy here is over the moon."

Yes, little Tommy. Simon thought, hasn't shown a cent of what I have given to him although he always had plenty of gratitude.

He would have to think about how he would fit into his greater scheme of things. He was certainly disposable but how to profit by it and not offend Adam, his new best friend.

"Ah! I see Eugene isn't here," Adam observed. "You know he is spending more time with your girlfriend. In fact the little prick is getting positively possessive!"

"Yeah, well, don't worry about it!" Simon replied. He thought, she's not my girlfriend. What was it his dad told him? That's right 'You can lead a horse to water but you will never drag the bastard away until he's finished.'

"Let's go and buy a car!" he headed the group off to do just that. Ducklings obediently followed a checked jacket mother.

Snapper wandered in around the entrance moving aimlessly aside.

The BMW full of kids swirled round the courtyard. "Isn't he the dude who bought us our car?" came from the back.

"So it is! Give him our thanks, guys," Simon agreed.

Snapper nonchalantly peered at the screaming giggling faces as they shot past. He paused to look around then saw his target submerged amongst crap in the far corner.

"Top of the Hill," the salesman greeted him. It looked as if this was going to be a good morning.

"Interesting check jacket!" Snapper observed. "You might make a sale yet. Just let me look for a minute. You might even make a dollar!"

"Sure, sure. After all, this is the Top of the Hill," he announced as he backed off. But only so far.

Snapper liked everything he saw of the old Valiant Regal. The wide cracks etched across rich brown leather seats. Stains on the safety straps. Original carpet and mats, not in original condition. Good tyres and only surface rust. He ignored the extras. Large floodlights angled from secure attachments to the front grille. Signs of an extra horn hinted from under the bonnet.

He ignored the price tag, faded as old as the car. "Want to make a sale?"

"Sure, sure. After all, this is the Top of the Hill, only the best here!"

"Let's talk turkey in your office. It is getting hot out here."

"Sure. Take it for a test drive. Take your time. Air-conditioning may even still work. If it doesn't, I will make a good reduction."

"That's not necessary," Snapper smiled at him. "After all, you are only trying to make a dollar, right?"

"That is so right," the salesman purred. "I am only trying to make a dollar, an honest dollar. So rare these days." This guy was going to be easier than the kids.

"Well, then, let's go to your office. Have I got a deal for you, if you are really only trying to make a dollar," and he permitted the salesman to hustle him towards the office.

❀ ❀ ❀

The kids patrolled their new turf in their new car. "Better put in ten dollars," Ross suggested as he drove.

"No! Damn it! Fill it up!" Simon decided. "I can pay. Then we can divvy up the rest to yous."

"What do you want, Ross?"

"Wouldn't mind testing it out. Put it through its paces if you can stand for it."

"Oh yes!" they all agreed in eager anticipation.

❊ ❊ ❊

Morgan turned to Bob. "I want you to take Holly to the club for me tonight."

"Sorry, boss, no can do." Bob spoke reluctantly.

"No need to apologize. In fact, I want you to take her to tea. That is not a request. You understand me?"

Bob sighed. "Yes, boss, I would love to take her. Your credit card, of course?"

Morgan raised an eyebrow. "You have been acting strange lately. What's the matter?"

"Nothing, boss, honestly."

"Bullshit! You are fidgeting a hole into the bloody floor. You don't have the hots for my wife, do you now?"

Bob was all fidget now. "What a question, really."

"What are you saying? Holly is not attractive?" Morgan smelt blood.

"No! I am not saying that!" Bob retorted.

"So then you are saying you are attracted to her?"

Upset, Bob became verbal. "Of course. When were you last seen in the company of an unattractive woman? Stop putting words in my mouth and hand over your card, for God's sake!"

"OK, then." Morgan was satisfied. "As long as you know your place."? " He groped down and flicked him his card, making a play at reluctance.

6.
Dining Out

CEDRIC JUST COULD NOT concentrate himself to concentrate. He paced up and down his life long demands of staff to report results denying them progress reports now left him frustrated. He loathed such practices in others and now with WHO's officials here to take his credit without any effort on their part made him just boil. He who had been the model of patience could sense his big chance physically slipping away. He felt physically sick. Perhaps he could cull out the most unlikely. No, he knew that was not an option, not yet anyway; he would have to be so very thorough to taste success.

Still, who would he choose if he could? He favoured Tim, the outsider. Tim had produced startling results. More appealing to Cedric, he was on the outer. Tim was considered cold-hearted and ruthless. Tim's opinionated nature decried others' sense of ethics and sensitivity for victims earning him his status. Plus his moonlighting was tolerated only because of his charity work, even though his work usually turned profitable.

He appealed to Cedric!

Perhaps he should take a break and call on this brother. That was always a light interlude. Plus he was free now he had ditched the bitch. He rang Cyril for lunch. Cedric decided he would even pay without protest.

❄ ❄ ❄

The BMW roared around suburbia; upsetting residents brought temporary pleasure. Simon wanted to lower their profile considerably. "Let's go to the reserve and see just what our car is capable of." He was very careful to say 'our'.

Silence.

"OK, then," he continued. "Perhaps we should spend a little of our money. Nothing flash, mind you, just one or two little treasures. If I see you with gold teeth I will strike gold," he warned.

The others nodded their agreement. It all made perfect sense and Simon had been right so far. Especially since the factory.

"What about you, Tom?" Simon picked on the wimp of the group.

"No money left!" Tom was not even concerned. "Gave it all to Mum. Because of her health, you know," he explained.

Simon looked at him. He felt envy. His family would not have even entertained the idea. At the same time he felt sympathy. He knew Tom's mother was on her deathbed, and she meant so much to the boy.

Touching. "Let me buy you something just so you can share in the group buzz?" Simon invited him.

"No, it was my choice,' came the reply.

Simon shrugged his shoulders. Well, he had tried.

❀ ❀ ❀

The Clear View hotel bars were buzzing. In fact, the whole town was buzzing. Miranda watched others with limited curiosity. There was something missing somewhere. Always had been! She had never been caught up in such excitement before. Always a missing edge. Some small defect of her own no doubt, she concluded reluctantly.

She habitually avoided eye contact as she scanned the bar. Hers was a genuine beauty withstanding time and she read admirers as others did the weather. Sometimes she wished to be like the others and she had tried. She had been with rich and poor. Dominant, and subservient, she had been there too. Searching still.

A massive young giant sat himself down. Miranda was not interested at this time. "I am waiting for a business meeting," she dismissed him.

But he was having none of it. "Do you know who I am?" he demanded.

"No! You don't move in my circle of friends."

"I am the 'Game Breaker'. I am in demand."

"And I am waiting for business to be conducted." She realized he was going nowhere. "Perhaps when my business is finished ..."

His team-mates came and dragged him away not fully compliant.

She heard rather than saw a chair scrape. "Evelyn Thwaites? Evelyn Miranda Thwaites?"

She surveyed the bulk blobbed in front of her. A big build covered by bigger clothes. Disillusionment was oblivious to others, not to him. Any other time she would have dismissed him promptly. "Yes, tell me you are Snapper?"

"Correct!" he acknowledged.

"You are not what I was expecting. What is your business then?" He showed no personal interest in her. Was she at last losing it?

"I do know expectations. I am a project manager, if you like?"

"Project?" She smiled. This was good. "What is the nature of your projects?"

Snapper smiled back. "Human resources. I help people or individuals fulfil their potential. I understand you wish me to assist an individual?"

Miranda felt her pulse. She did not like to think she misread people. Snapper had wiped a large chunk off her confidence. "Yes! That is so. But he needs to know why."

"Completing one's education is so important. That is only one of many aspects our project team specializes in." Snapper nodded wisely in agreement.

"I would like to be part of the team. Purely on a voluntary basis, of course. But I have a strong desire to see this project through to the completion." This was full of promise. As had promises seemed and so permanent in the past. Miranda knew they all resulted in nothing.

Snapper shook his head. "No! That is not part of our corporate strategy."

"You stupid old man! Get out of my way!" The sportsman was back.

"Perhaps later. Right now this is only business. I have no other interest." Snapper tried to placate him.

"Fuck off!" The giant was having none of it. "I like to see what I am getting and I am getting to see what I like."

"I said when we are finished. Whatever your business is is no concern of mine." Snapper was equally persistent.

The team came and dragged the noisy giant away most reluctantly indeed.

"Perhaps if you have your candidate's memorandum we can take it from there." Snapper wanted out but not noticeably.

Miranda felt grieved. "I have done all you asked! And it has cost me plenty with little to show so far. Perhaps you could show a little hospitality?" she complained.

"No!" Snapper wanted progress. "It's cost Cyril heaps but not everything yet. You have to appreciate I am talking about a high community profile indeed to a complete stranger and safety comes first. Let's continue our business elsewhere. Maybe upstairs?"

Both got up. Neither answered.

People ambled round the lobby. Old-style lifts slow to arrive, fast to fill. Snapper waited patiently holding his companion back from the first available. When he was satisfied they moved towards the opening lift doors.

"Fucking bitch!" The playmaker had kept an eye on them. He clasped an enormous hand holding the door open.

"Get out!" he commanded. All the occupants evacuated smartly indeed. "Not you two!" He rolled his eyes towards his new prize. "And you, old man. Try to do the dirty on me. There is a price for that and it is very nearly time to pay!"

Miranda felt her chest heave fighting for composed breath. Now will tell her if all she has heard about Snapper is accurate. Maybe, just maybe, this is what she had been missing. So intriguing.

The doors rattled closed. "Right!" the giant menaced Snapper. "You should stay in your own league, dad."

In a quivering voice and downcast lips Snapper whispered, "I think you may be right after all."

The player gazed disbelieving. This was heaven! Really heaven.

Some old bitch simply panting for it, and all to himself. She will be panting for something else next. Just the way he liked it. His opposition cowering in the corner, on or off the field he crushed all oncomers. This was perfect. He enjoyed a winner and the winner takes all. As he had relished in the past. Should he keep a memento? he wondered. All the time in the world.

Now for the old man. Look at him! Well, he hasn't pissed himself yet. An arm or abdomen. Perhaps spare him his old head. Eeny, meeny, miny, moe.

He lazily reached forward. His hand grasped air. Wow! How did he miss that? The old man was lucky but now his luck had run out and he had nowhere to go. He stood back to time himself better.

Snapper stood up arms swinging.

What the hell was this? thought the giant. Trying to defend himself. What a laugh! He swung into action with a deep growl.

From nowhere he felt a strong finger probe deeply into his shoulder. A familiar ache of stretched tendons of sporting injuries, but surely not here? Here in this crappy hotel lift?

His arm felt leaden. He strummed pins and needle fingers across the flesh of his thumb as much as he could only do. His fingers fattening although they didn't look it. It must have been a lucky shot!

He broke from his self-concentration. Confident, he watched in slow motion the same probe into his other upper arm.

And what had happened to the old simpering wimp? He was the same outline but self-assured, dominant. He could see the woman too had increased her excitement. How had their roles got so wrong? The old man had developed into a real threat. How did he miss it?

Snapper's voice was different as well. "Where is your room?" he heard.

"Room? I don't have a room," he replied. Snapper ignored him completely.

"Third floor, for the rest of this week," the woman answered in a thick and husky voice.

Snapper pressed the button for three floors. Snapper turned to the giant. "I need compliance. Am I going to get it?"

"Fuck yourself! You will be dead meat soon enough!" came the retort.

"Yes!" Snapper thought aloud. "I was hoping to avoid all this. Never mind." He prodded bulk repeatedly very painfully until the devastated sportsman automatically winced at his tormentor's approach.

"Before we get out I hope you know your place?" Snapper asked.

The big guy nodded simply. Now the woman was looking at Snapper the way he was used to receiving attention.

Well! The old bitch could have the old bastard. She simply wasn't worth it. Same as in sport, you crushed the opposition especially if you could end their career, if not you waited for the next encounter and thought new strategies, winning strategies, final strategies.

He stumbled out of the lift moaning softly. He hated this in himself! It showed softness and therefore loser and therefore time to finish the job.

A plush cream speckled carpet laid for this event was decorated with the Island colours and shells designed to point in whatever direction you chose. Already many feet had blurred the centre line and a wake of spillages carried up the hall.

Same as washing a rally car in the middle of a stage. What a waste of time and money. Visitors' regard certainly took a holiday with their owners. Snapper felt disappointment.

Loud sounds from an adjacent room covered any noise they made plus. The giant willed just anyone to come to the door. Willed with desperation survival imparts. Deep down he knew all the occupants were centred on one thing: self indulgence. He could smell sex wafting through the door and he knew of their pills perhaps in a communal bowl, and drinks required to sustain such an effort. Despite himself, he could feel himself become aroused!

Miranda unlocked and opened the door wide to her room and stood aside while Snapper prodded their victim to a large bed. "Say, you could teach me that! Some of that, all of that, actually?"

"Face down!" Snapper commanded coupled with a swift jab to the back propelling the helpless torso onward. He turned to the woman and squeezed her shoulder.

Instant pain swamped her but was gone before she could gasp.

Only warm fuzzy sensations remained. "Christ!" she managed.

"Well," said Snapper, "you should know what you want others to experience."

"Show me on him?" she indicated towards the lump on the bed. She had never felt so, so hungry.

"If you go down this road there is no turning back and ultimately to your life and lifestyle," Snapper warned.

"Do you want me to pay to plead?"

"No!" he protested, tearing the shirt off the prone form on the bed. "Press here very gently. Perhaps with only a fingernail, and only for an instant. He will feel pretty much what you have felt."

Miranda leaned forward to the precise spot and lingered with her finger. She would savour this moment, she knew. This was real power! At last her life was complete!

The body on the bed arched violently curved, frightening her. She stepped back in reaction while the sportsman slumped with a little whimper.

"Christ!" Snapper growled at her. "I said just for an instant! You lingered on purpose. All I wanted you to do was to immobilize him!"

"Sorry. I am learning, you know!"

"So am I!" he retorted, still angry.

"Um, what else? I mean, what is the worst that can happen, anyway?" She was all concentration now.

Snapper sighed. "You will kill him, that's what! The death of anybody steals their dignity, no more dreams, no courage, no fears, just nothing. And it is not as you know it. There is no dramatic music, no death scenes, no background, just a last sordid breath. You have to treat such people with the dignity they deserve. They deserve not to know that their time has come.

It is both unnecessary physical and mental cruelty. I am more of a tradesman. If you are not strong it will affect your lifestyle forever and likely shorten your own life. Think before you say this is what you want."

Miranda, without pause, replied. "Tell me about those moves. You must have been taught them somewhere?"

Snapper shook his head, changing the subject. "You have the details of your candidate I asked for? Let's get on with it then."

"Sorry! I completely forgot about that!" she replied, delving into her bag. "I have completed all you have asked although not all of it seems relevant."

Snapper riffled through the pages browsing. "I need a few minutes to absorb all this. Can you entertain yourself for a precious few minutes?"

"Well," she insisted, "you will have to show me a few spots!"

The figure on the bed was showing signs of movement. Snapper bent over offering him a pillow. "If you bite on this hard, it makes time go that much faster." Any reply was stifled.

"Here," he sighed. He made little crosses on the body, which twitched at the slightest of touches. "Here, here and maybe a bit over there. Now don't press hard enough to leave an impression. You don't need to and the coroner likes straightforward work."

Miranda flexed her fingers. "I do not remember anything like this on the school curriculum. Now go and sit down and read, will you?"

The body writhed and squirmed constantly. Miranda held her fingernails in growing enjoyment. She had never realized people had so many pressure points. And she had only just started. She called over her shoulder, "Are you sure I cannot help you? You know Cyril has always been happy to pay premiums for good-quality work."

Snapper looked up. He paused. "No names in front of witnesses. Even the St John ambulance staff learn some points to make sure they are not to be easily fooled. I will tell you what I can do. You can stand in his field of vision at the front of his car. He should recognize you and have time to put two and two together."

Miranda gazed at Snapper. Despite obvious risks she felt herself warming to him. His professionalism impressed her and importantly he was so thorough and self-assured and most importantly he was free as a bird, seemingly immune. Perhaps some time on his shirt tails and the world would be at large.

In contrast every time she spoke Snapper felt she was a convenient commodity. Expendable but a good foil against his adversaries. The chief came to mind. There were other possibilities. Miranda was a fast learner and keen, but was she a listener?

It must be fate, karma, call it what you like, she decided. She felt compelled to contact Bob just to thank him. Though they had never met and it seemed to her Bob had never actually met Snapper, Bob was understanding her language and requests. Three strangers and it had all come together so well! She intended to make every effort to please.

Snapper stood up and stretched himself. "I have to pop out for a few minutes. Can you look after him until I get back?"

She nodded with the widest smile. "We will be just fine."

Snapper nodded back and peered out the door. Pausing only until he was sure that nobody was in the hall and didn't seem likely to be, he quietly closed the door behind him.

As silently as he left Snapper returned, seemingly immediately. Miranda was bent over the head on the bed.

She stood up as she heard him. Full generous breasts shone from a cascade of tears as large ripe fruit ready for picking. Her nipples great orbs covering most of the globes.

Snapper was startled by the scene. How could something horrendously repulsive be equally so overpowering attractive? He cast aside urges welling up intruding his thoughts.

"Well?' Snapper asked at last.

"I was just giving him what he wanted! He asked to see what he was getting, and now he knows."

"I'm not worried about him. It is time to move on, if you have finished here."

"Just let me show you my favourite!" She jabbed down. The body on the bed levitated ever so slightly and slumped with a wheezy sigh. "Shit!" she said. "That is a disappointment! I wanted you to see my prowess."

"I think I have," Snapper responded. "He's dead. Never mind, I can fix this. In the meantime are you perhaps interested in golf? I have a round or two and I've been looking for a substitute."

Miranda dismissed the body. "Oh well! Since you ask OK but I have never played the game." This was a new step and she did not want to trip!

"Right! I will just make a phone call." Snapper looked pleased.

He punched in numbers on the room's phone and waited until a voice could be heard answering.

He spoke in a high tone, breathless. "Rod, I am down in the bar. They are having a genitals competition. You should see this guy, more than three ordinary men, and now look at her get up." He paused. "Oh my God, my good God!" and he hung up.

Miranda quizzed, "Rod? Do you know the whole floor?"

Snapper smiled at Miranda. "No! It is the message, not the messenger. If you find a twenty-dollar note, do you look to see who lost it or do you just take it? Patience, my dear. Now I want to roll him over onto his back. You see, after he dies all the blood rushes to the lowest point. In this case I want it to be his back!"

She pulled at an arm. "This is useless!"

"Let me," and Snapper rolled him over. "You see because of his state there is no co-operation."

"How do you do that?" she asked amazed.

Snapper suggested, "Well, you might work in an old folks' home for a while. Not one of these rich places, one of the impoverished ones, and you quickly learn how to move bodies around. I want to move him next door but one." He held his head up. "This is what I have been waiting for!"

Outside just down the hall a door slammed and a disappearing clatter of running feet could just be heard.

Snapper looked out. "Good! Good! Come on, let's move him. I just want to get a sheet from next door and all will be a lot easier."

Miranda worried. "They will be back?"

"No! Not for a while. You see the moment has gone and they will be in search for another. There will be plenty to choose from, I expect," he reassured her.

"What about the door? Do you have a key?"

"Nope." Snapper was smug. "There is a small plastic tie stopping the door from closing and none of them will care or check when there is something better at hand."

They dragged at the two corners of the now anchored sheet.

❋ ❋ ❋

As the evening bathed the islands in multi-colours, Morgan hesitantly put aside the file he had been pondering over; interminable details were fading into the back of his brain.

Tomorrow would be time enough. The bustle of the cleaners signalled the end of another day. Only relief at the club was left for him. He glimpsed a shadow in the doorway. "What is it, Liz? Go home!"

"It's the chief, not Liz, boss!"

"There goes my evening! What is it?" Morgan tried to imply his day was finished. Wasted he felt.

"There's been a fatality at a hotel. The Clear View hotel. A top sportsman, in fact, so I thought I should just bring it to your notice. Doesn't have to ruin your night."

"Is Snapper involved?" Morgan cut to the chase.

"Could be," the chief conceded. "Our tail lost him at the elevator."

"Lift! You mean lift! How could they lose him if they were so close?"

"Don't have all the details yet, boss."

"Well! How did he die?"

"Initial opinions say sexual exhaustion. Room was used for group orgy. What a way to go! Lot of evidence of drugs but being such an athlete I doubt we will find any evidence of drugs. Stains on his sheet suggest a herd has run through it. We are still looking."

"Anything to tie it in to Snapper?"

"No! Well, not overly. He was last seen with the victim but not in charge. As witnesses go there were literally hundreds in that bloody hotel. Do you want me to pull him in?"

"It's up to you but don't do him any favours. Anything unusual about the case?"

"Just a few anomalies that don't point to anyone. The carpet in the room is plush indeed. So one would expect a lot of footprints or impressions but there are none in the room or in the hall outside."

"OK then, thanks, keep me informed. Do you have Snapper under surveillance at the moment, before I head off to the club?" This time Morgan had had enough.

"Very lightly, in fact he was heading in that direction anyway! Good night, boss."

❀ ❀ ❀

The well-lit club front held the veneer of the original construction. Large rooms inside spoke of many additions.

First inside was a warm greeting room backgrounded with constant chatter of pokie machines and bar conversations. A doorman stood greeting all newcomers as if for the first time, though at this stage there were very few first-timers.

"Evening, Cad," Morgan greeted him.

"Evening, sir, your wife is already here in reception with a young man," the doorman beamed at him.

"Is that gossip?" Morgan smiled at him.

"Oh no, sir! Just updating you. You know how I feel 'bout gossip, sir," he replied.

Morgan shook his head as he passed.

Snapper watched Morgan's back as he arrived. He stood at the entrance and gazed around.

He reflected in front of the old man in genuine affection. How little he had changed. The eyes just as bright, maybe the hair was thinner and lacking life but still had a wispy curl. He recalled there was more to life about Cad.

"Hello, old friend!" he greeted Cad with near reverence.

He winced at the resounding slap across his ear he never saw coming.

Like everything else Snapper saw deterioration setting in. Perhaps because he had been away the differences stood out. Progress meant regret, not better.

He thought back to the reserve. He had sat in the natural semi-amphitheatre where families sat on the wide tiers and dined. Where natural singers with deep rich voices sang favourites all, for kids, classic favourites and island history, where everybody roared out the choruses. Here all families knew each other in a place absent of animosity. Where men drank and drove families home without incident.

Then a movie production had used more than half a dozen cars for a chase scene down the slopes, and repaired all damages plus donation, but had not stopped youths replicating the scenes.

All vehicles were not successful and ended halfway down plus some fatalities tearing into the tiers was no deterrent. Trail bikes had overtaken the car's role. Now an idle bulldozer rested from cutting tracks to the Black Hole where car bodies were unceremoniously shoved over the edge. Now families stayed away, youths menaced whomever they could and worse after sundown.

Cad smiled at him. "You are still a slow learner. I don't know what I saw in you, do you?"

"No!" Snapper laughed. "I don't know why I took your offer up." He thought back to his youth.

Vincent back then had been just a student. Quietly working hard as a labourer in the family's construction business building his strength all the time transporting materials and tiring constant physical work.

At school he was quiet, shying away from exposure both academically and schoolyard rough and tumble. His one passion was for cars, and driving and engineering. And he found heaven at a used car sales lot with a kind owner.

He was totally fascinated by the one and only one Lisa. He adored her hair, longing to touch silk strands, her complexion; eyes and laughing lips filled his mind. Those eyes could see right to his soul with his struggles and torment. He so wanted to hold her close and just to be with her. Besotted!

His mother stood him up. "I am always so proud of you. Is everything OK?" she always asked.

"Fine!" he always replied. "Everything is sweet."

This time he meant every word. He could never consciously lie to his mother but on reflection that is what it amounted to.

His mouth was dry; his heartbeat loud, his attention to himself immaculate. He looked down at the mass of scratches, bruises and scar tissue generated from his job. Not many he worked with had a full number of fingers and like him blackened nails.

Vincent pulled his sleeves down hard least she think of him as an unfeeling oaf. Now in the absence of her boyfriend he escorted her to where he did not recall. It was his big chance to make inroads.

But he remembered everything else.

They were walking over common ground to the car yard and he had sneaked his arm around her. He raptured over her smell and touch. How could anyone be so lucky?

His stature, confidence and self-assurance was somehow transformed into being a doting idiot. If he realized he was beyond caring.

Oblivious to the world outside he first smelt the strong sweet cigarette and alcohol odours; their scuffed footsteps slowly interrupted his moment. Three toughs still in school uniforms crossed their path. Their timing couldn't have been worse. Any other time would have been a better alternative. Anger welled up deep inside of him. Nevertheless he worked hard not to do anything to upset his moment.

"Well! Well! Well! As soon as Ben goes his little slut samples the community. Looks like she has drawn the short straw." They sniggered. "Isn't that right, Lisa?"

The other lanky one laughed at the question. "Shut up, slutty! We are here to do you to lovebirds a service. See! You both should thank us. Really you should!"

"See," chimed in the third. "We have taken it upon ourselves to sample Lisa. Sort of community spirited."

"Sure!" continued the lanky one. "Look at it this way. No messy fumbling foreplay, all ready soft and moist and warmed up, and no rejection, no headaches either. Isn't that great?"

"Your humour is as pathetic as you are. Now you have had your laugh you move on!" Vincent struggled to get civil words out while Lisa was in earshot.

Aggression overwhelmed thin humour.

"Fuck you!" came an immediate response. "First we'll deal to you and while you are on the ground you can watch us deal to her as well! Who do you think you are now when you have shied away every other time?"

The other continued. "Well! We have the power and we will brand her with our mark so she will know for life who we are. All you bastards will!"

The taller one looked around as he quickly whipped out a knife. Vincent leapt at him. His upswinging arm drove up under the other's chin, crunching his head far back. Vincent never held back any restraint as the taller deflated spiralling at his feet; he was already turning towards Lisa.

She was pushing her weight against the spokesman. "Fucking bitch!" he yelled at her, and giving her a good solid swipe sent her sprawling and dazed.

He felt Vincent's strong hard fingers around his neck and despite his bulk he was being shaken around like a cloth. He found purchase with his foot and they tumbled struggling to gain control.

Vincent saw sheer anger in eyes matching his own, forcing his grip ever stronger. Ever so slowly he dominated but he was of no mind to concentrate on more than one thing. Right now Lisa was his concern. Not only was she in danger but he had let it happen. He squeezed tighter. His adversary deflated as well in his hands.

The third picked up the knife. The rolling broad back one of the largest targets he had seen and he swung with a curled up grin. Now he had the great leveller! How he loved the intimate feel!

None of them saw tall shadows moving quietly amongst them. Picking and weaving, not to interfere unnecessarily until a knobbed malacca cane swung across the knifeman's bridge of his nose and his eyes.

His reflex actions and wailing scream brought the world back to them all.

Vincent scrambled, crabbed his way to the still prone Lisa, crying, sobbing her name, gasping for oxygen.

"She will be alright!" the intruder tried to pacify him. "We will get her home none the worse for it. Fortunately trauma means she will likely remember nothing of tonight apart from your act of escorting her. So you can be whatever you tell her. Depends on your own morals, I guess."

Vincent squinted against the afternoon sun. "Who are you?" He couldn't make out any features. Alarmed and panicked he looked over the prone figures spread on the ground.

The outline chuckled. "You can call me Cad. Everybody does. I was named Theodore Cadwallace. American heritage. Everybody started calling me Theo, but that was too long so it got shortened to Ted and now it is just Cad. Lately, people may think it is for cadaver, I suspect."

Vincent rolled onto his back breathing hard in relief. "What have I done?"

"What any person would do. The question is do you want to pay for their misdemeanours? Do you want to see your Lisa again? To be fair though she will never be your Lisa. Not tonight, not before tonight, not after tonight."

Vincent tried to gather his thoughts. He struggled with foreign concepts, values contradicting those his parents installed in him. "I need to fetch help for the others!"

"Nope!" Cad shook his head. "Not at all. You can only help yourself and the girl. Look at the others. Nobody can help them now. They are or will be dead within the hour. You did that! You and I know, I know all about it. I was watching."

Vincent lolled his head side on. He saw Cad was probably right. One shook momentarily, one hand covering his bloodied face, the other still. He felt a different, another anger rising. "What can I do?"

"For yourself?"

"For Lisa."

"If you help yourself, then you will help Lisa." Cad walked him through. "If you do the civilized thing, you will spend the rest of your life imprisoned.

"Lisa will have to go to trial and I can tell you the defence will be merciless. She will be ruined, on a small island like this, for life, whatever the outcome.

"Both your families will be financially ruined by legal people.

For what? Three little hoods who expect the law to protect them so they can continue their lawless ways."

He made it so logical, so clear, so simple.

Vincent sighed. "Talk to me more."

Cad leaned over him. "Answer these questions. I need to know what you think. If you tell me what you think I want to hear I will just walk away and what I foresee will happen. You understand?"

Vincent nodded compliant.

"I am your only witness! You have personally killed two with your bare hands. How do you feel?"

Vincent shrugged. "I don't actually give a shit about them."

"No! No." Cad was impatient. "How do you feel physically? Nauseous? Sick? Emotionally excited? Guilty? How do you feel?"

"I feel fine. I will feel better when we get out of here. Get Lisa out of here."

"There is first a small obstacle for you to overcome." Cad seemed to muse to himself. "Although the third of the group here cannot yet see he will tell his story to the world for money, as much as he can make, in fact. What do you want to do about it?' He pointed to the mound in the dirt holding his eyes, still bloody fingers over a bloody face.

"Kill him!" Vincent didn't think about it. "He deserves to be with his friends."

"If you do this thing you will be outside society for the rest of your life. Lisa may be safe but you will never get the chance to be with her," Cad warned him.

"Fine!" Vincent decided. "Teach me, what can you teach me?"

Cad answered, "A lot actually. You will be a tradesman. As much in demand as any carpenter, electrician, plumber, lawyer, by people who lack personal means to make their own ends. I can teach you how to love others. You would like that! Ah? You will come back to me whining 'I ache! I ache so!' Because you need to know the emotional need of riches, of power and strength, curiosity, the desire to nurture, for a father, there are so many. I can show you these. But you will learn selective, very selective, because you will be in demand and disease is rampant. You will learn notoriety. Others will compare themselves to you. Some climb mountains, swim lakes just to prove themselves. Idiots will want to prove themselves against you. You will learn selective again but to dispense some of the same as who lie here now. Is that what you would like?"

Vincent looked up at him absorbing his speech. "You are using me!" he accused.

"That is so correct!" Cad laughed at him. "That is society, to be useful. But what do you want to commit to?"

"OK then," Vincent accepted. He was intrigued and began to feel special. "Lisa will be safe?"

Cad shrugged. "Who can say? Life has no guarantees, you know. She will be as safe as you can protect her."

Vincent had to be satisfied with that. He realized he was to spend much time with this funny old man.

❊ ❊ ❊

Now Cad was older, much older and they laughed together intimately at the club entrance.

Morgan interrupted them. "Come on, you two. I need to buy a lotto ticket. I am feeling lucky!"

"I don't feel lucky at all! You want me to have a need to spend my last dollar on this lotto?" Cad asked him. "You had better go inside. Your friends grow impatient."

"Come on, you both. By the time we get there the lotto will drawn, won and spent."

In they went, old friends. A woman in the entrance looked at Snapper quizzically. He reached out to her invitation and she responded, tucking herself under his arm smiling.

Holly saw him next and shook her head. But she gave a warm embrace followed closely by Lisa. Morgan, Ben and Bob felt all apprehensive at the extra time their women's warm welcome had given to Snapper, not knowing why they danced around from one foot to the other, showing cheer, and swallowing their misgivings. Tucking their precious tickets in their pockets.

"You know, Holly," Snapper reminisced, "dinner will be just

fine but what I miss most is a picnic by the sea."

Holly smiled her wrinkled up smile. "Still the little boy. Of course we can. But you men will have to catch lunch or only you men will starve!"

Morgan looked at his watch. "You are late!" he smirked loudly.

"Sorry!" Snapper so seriously answered. "Things have changed so much I got lost and ended up chasing my tail!"

Both men laughed and others followed their infection without knowing the humour.

7.
Cessation Hiatus

THE TIDE FLOWED EN masse, crushing through a narrow channel towards sanctuary, the enormous natural bay protected from the ravaging ocean at large. European colonists named the ebb and flow 'the sluice gates' for its unrelenting violent nature, especially along the narrow stretch of foreshore.

The hills and bays and inlets were dotted together with populations all waiting for the same thing. The pod! Some now paid very well for what had become an annual pilgrimage. Some saw it in their stand as protected heritage. Nowhere else could one get so close under natural conditions.

The whales emerged slowly, distant, unaware of spectators' impatience. Drums, unheard, addressed them, started ancient chants retelling of how the first inhabitants nearly wiped them all out but the great wise king decreed otherwise and now they were gods again, indeed.

Morgan watched from his vantage point of his office. He would have loved to have gone down as close as he could but he was aware others would see this as an excuse to cross arbitrary lines. Such were the trappings of power.

❊ ❊ ❊

Snapper waited in a more isolated cove watching fine grains trickle over his toes and feet. Absorbing his feet gently, outward waves left an extra fine film that tickled his feet. Snapper always enjoyed this moment, his one only guilt-free innocent pleasure. As his ankles gradually submerged he would lift one leg with effort and watch the fluid particles tumble into the void. Stepping aside he would lift his other leg. The process began filling again sucking at his feet.

❋ ❋ ❋

Back in the foothills Simon stood over the others in his, their, car. He still nearly slipped now and then. The coast looked in shadow. "Pathetic! That's all I can say," he scorned. "All that fuss over some fucking fish and then they don't do anything with them."

"Eskimos eat them!" somebody volunteered.

"Well, somebody missed a signpost somewhere!" Simon replied. "Stupid old pricks!"

He slumped back into his front passenger's seat.

"Look at all those flashes!" Ross observed from the driver's seat. "Playing laser strike. Wish I was!"

Simon full of scorn. "They are camera flashes! Idiot! I know it is a bright day but not every camera owner has technical abilities. I mean, look what we have done with just a simple video recorder."

They laughed. How right he was. Adam cleared his throat dramatically.

Simon instinctively turned on him.

Lately he had become more uncomfortable in Adam's presence, but as he was still useful Simon had made no plans for his demise however the Black Hole nearby beckoned, tempting lingering thoughts. "What are you whining about now?"

"Well!" Adam reasoned, "we have just about thrashed the car conventionally. How about we modify the car somewhat?"

Others thought the same but feared bringing up the subject. Sometimes Adam was a real relief!

Simon knew as much. He wasn't making concessions. "How?"

Adam explained for all to hear. "We all know the car already gets too bloody hot even with the windows open. It makes sense to remove the front and rear windows and let the wind go right through. Don't have to break them."

Simon accepted the inevitable but it still had to be his idea. "Well, there are so many of us for a small car. There won't always be all of us. The only person needed is the driver."

"I know a guy who does windscreens. What say we pop the front window and feel the wind on our faces?" Adam pressed home his advantage.

Simon still played hard. "What do you think, Ross?"

Ross wanted to test the car more. "I would like to take it over the dunes! I could, you know!"

"Jesus, no! Those dunes are only for the motocross riders' circuit. Not cars! You will wreck it, you know its history!" Simon privately felt that was a great idea. He wanted to hear more.

"Of course. I know, I could take it down the ridges. I know I could, at the right speeds. The right angles!"

Taking the front window out was suddenly more attractive and was agreed upon. Simon hoped Adam's mate would make a mess of the window but he knew it unlikely. Still, you just never know. Maybe even give it a hand.

❋ ❋ ❋

Cedric paused to watch the sea from his lab's balcony. All his tests were coming up empty. He looked to the whales for inspiration. Indecision sat darkly on him as personal ambition drove him on.

He allowed his current hope to join him. "Well, Tim, it looks like I'm stuck at an impasse."

Tim shrugged his shoulders. He had seen many such occasions come and go and his boss had always triumphed. He thought about reminding him. Perhaps he could promote himself!

Cautiously he spoke up. "I think I am on the right track, boss, but I need what I can't have."

Cedric looked at him closely. "And what is that? Don't I give you everything?"

Tim sighed. "What I really need is a real live volunteer! And if I am right, and I think I am, it will likely kill them. Now what kind of idiot am I going to get on those terms?"

"You mean female? Don't you?"

"Yes! You know of such a person?"

Cedric smiled to himself. "Oh yes! I do know of such a person.

A volunteer. In fact she is such a masochist you don't even need worry about anaesthetics." He watched hope rise in Tim.

Wow! A real live subject without restrictions. Tim was impressed. This is pure research at its finest. "You are joking, aren't you?"

"Yes! Sorry! Just idle thoughts. I was dreaming, sort of," Cedric apologized. Now he had thought it he couldn't take it back, nor did he want to.

The prospect of such heaven gifted for the idea never left Tim either. "You have visitors!" He noted two struggling figures clambering over the steps.

"The last people on this earth I want to see!" Cedric fumed. Their approach so fuelled his temper. "Hello," came a light-hearted greeting at least.

"Hello!" they puffed in return. "Those are quite some steps. You have a veritable fortress here!"

Tim chipped in, conciliatory. "There are easier ways up here, but never mind."

"Sorry!" spoke the elder. "We should introduce ourselves. My name is Dr Gregory and my lady associate is Dr Wylie."

"I am Cedric. I own and run this establishment. Seeing as you have laboured so hard to get here, how can we be of service?" Cedric gave an indifferent display. Tim knew how to read him. The visitors were walking a minefield.

The woman spoke having recovered the better. "Thank you. Let me express our regret at the passing of your brother's partner. In a way though that is why we are here. We are members of WHO interested in the few mysterious deaths that have recently occurred in this nation. Just monitoring, of course. We understand you may be using your facilities in investigating these unfortunate incidents."

"Yes!" Cedric bowed his head in agreement. "Not a pretty issue, especially when it has struck so close to home. Unfortunately, I made only mostly basic summaries to appease the families, you understand. My facilities here are centred on proactive ventures. Though I know the locals place us next to God it is just not so. Most of the place is closed down at the moment; I can give you a brief tour if you are interested?" he invited.

Dr Gregory declined. "That is most gracious. Perhaps you will permit us to, how do you say it, take a raincheck, but for now we have an engagement with some colleagues chasing those blessed whales."

Tim gestured to direct them. "This is a much easier path back." Both locals stood watching the doctors' backs shrink and disappear from view.

Tim spat after them. "Bloody do-gooders! Never trust a physician who lacks personal ambition!"

"What are you talking about?" snarled Cedric bitterly. "They came here to steal, to steal from me. I don't believe it! Bastards!"

"Gee! Boss, I don't know about that. They are only clerks, you know. You have dealt with their kind before, and very effectively." His outburst had surprised Tim.

Cedric turned on him vehemently. "If you are not on my side then piss off! Stealing for yourself or somebody else doesn't matter to me. Haven't I been good to you? Is this how you repay my generosity? Get back to work! I have to think." He added, "Alone!"

"No, you prick! It is I who have been good to you!" Tim never cowered. "And don't forget that!" He stalked off.

❊ ❊ ❊

Rupert swung his way out of his office. An old starving waif looking for a banquet. The more intrepid of his staff looked up. Just as many looked down. Everybody knew somebody's workload was about to increase. They were all so far beyond their limit they wished the thunderstorm of work on anybody else.

"It was my pleasure to have been totally embarrassed by what you gave me to report to bloody Morgan! Do you all think all foreigners have thick skins? That I will take whatever crap you think will suffice? How can you lose somebody in a lift? It's barely a fucking mobile toilet! Well! Somebody has to make amends and I mean now!"

He peered around. The amount of work to be done by so few in the room depressed him every time he looked.

But he would live through it and by the grace of God so would they, if he had anything to do with it. He dwelt on the immediate problem, which was preferable to looking at the big picture.

He glimpsed a head bobbing over a cubicle screen. That meant somebody was not listening. He had found his victim!

He peered over the top. "What the hell are you doing?"

His officer matched his gaze. "It's a mind puzzle! Perhaps you should try one. Let's start you off at the first level; should test you sufficiently."

"I don't recall you. What's your name?" Rupert ignored the jibe. For now!

"Detective Matt to you!" His officer was offended at the deliberate slight of official recognition.

"Right, Matt! Seeing as you like mind games I want you to tail this suspect further than an elevator. Think you are up to it, son?" Rupert's killer punch. Others winced.

"No problem, old man," came a positive response. Matt clarified. "You just mean tail him, don't you? I don't want any misunderstanding!"

"Here is his file. Tell me what you need, just tail him." Rupert was agreeably surprised. Nevertheless at the same time he felt reservations.

"Nothing at all," Matt smiled at him. "You see, boss, you are old. No offence but you should use technology available to you. Like using plod detective work when now you have DNA. Within half a day I will have a bug on his Valiant and I can follow him right here at my desk! Tail him all over the island, in fact!"

"Good, sounds good to me!" Rupert was already thinking of the next demand.

"I will report back in a couple of days, boss." Ross farewelled him.

❊ ❊ ❊

Morgan sat back in his office, alone on the whole floor, watching the whales' progress on screen as well as through his field glasses. Live was always superior to screen. He was always impressed by the whales' sheer power and beautiful fluid demeanour. He barely heard the timid knock at his door.

"Excuse me! But there is no-one else around."

Their eyes met and smouldered.

Morgan swallowed instinctively at the marvel in his doorway. "Come on in!' he blurted out, all non-composure. He admired her so much more as she hovered into his office.

"I was looking for Bob to thank him for a service he has done for me." Miranda just couldn't believe the magnificent hunk in front of her. She automatically wanted to stay but her gratitude was no excuse to linger. Oh! What to do? "I was told this is his office."

"Not quite! It is my office. Bob works for me, very closely as a matter of fact. He hasn't mentioned you. I am certain I would have remembered." Morgan was puzzled.

Miranda felt her personal space disintegrate. Only this time with genuine blessing. "Are you watching the whales? Just seeing them cavort I see as sensually appealing, what do you think?'

"I think ...," Morgan paused. I cannot believe my good fortune yet he couldn't say so. "I think I am envious of their freedom as appealing. Would you like to view them for a time?"

"Love to!" She moved closer to him. Static energy magnetized them both together. "I would like to whale you!' Morgan was attempting not to breathe hard. His stomach muscles ached at physical reaction plus physical stress.

"I would love to too!" she replied now in his ear.

In a solitary movement Morgan swept work debris clearing his table and elevated her upward effortlessly. "I don't need any coaxing!" she whispered.

He bit her ear gently. "Neither do I!"

He winced. "I haven't fumbled for years. Now is just not the right time!"

"I love fumbling!" she giggled. "Fumbling shows passion. Here, let me guide you."

"Please!" he moaned at her ministrations.

"Yes, it does please me. Just look at the whales nice and slow and graceful. That is what I want!" Miranda loved the touch of his hands over her body. Firm yet gentle, hidden strength kept from view made her feel secure warm and wanted.

He obliged.

Fondly she asked of him, "A little bit more, now?"

"Bitch! No!" Morgan replied. "Nice and slow and graceful! Remember?" He softly bit her lips.

"Bastard!" she managed to squeeze out.

"Miranda!" he added.

The solid table tremored with their mirth and energies.

Finally, "I have to finish!" Morgan conceded. And they lay together embraced bonded by juices and deep animal satisfaction in silence.

"I have to move!" Miranda spoke at last. "It is awkward with an elephant on top."

"I suppose." Morgan peeled himself off. A tearing sound of skin leaving cheap vinyl signalled their separation. Both looked flushed, gorged.

"Look! A small mark on your lovely table. I'll clean it up before it dries." Miranda busied herself.

Morgan held her back, close. "It's like tea leaves! You can read them, you know?"

Miranda held him equally tightly back. "You are the expert! You tell me. Morgan?"

"Well!" Morgan spoke slowly, deliberately. "I can see three E's. Must be Energy, Excitement and Exhilaration. I can also see this must recur soon and often else the magic will be lost!"

"I will bow to your superiority. It's no wonder you deserve this office." She paused by the window. "Some jet skiers are going to tease those whales!"

"Bastards!" Morgan growled. "Well, there is nowhere for them to go to escape. I will deal with them later. That is part of my role and in this case part of my pleasure." He turned away upset by their interruption as well.

❊ ❊ ❊

Eric looked over his shoulder at his hotel and the crowds. Two tourists sidled up to him. "We hear you might cater for us?"

Eric coughed a little. "You are wanting more than a room then. This is a commercial establishment."

"Yep!" the other spoke. "And we can pay whatever you like. Unlike the room we have here we are looking for something a little more exotic."

"You mean room service? After all that is what I am employed to cater for."

"Yep!" The visitor's relief was plain to hear. "I like to be a refuse man and collect and tidy and take out the garbage. My pal prefers to rummage through it afterwards before the trail goes cold."

Eric shook his head. "I cannot help you." He stood emphatic as their heads bowed.

"However I will talk to a Hong Kong national who I am told can do anything. Perhaps he can fulfil your dreams. He is expensive!" he warned.

"Yes! Yes, that is no problem," the tourists satisfied at last. "Though, I am surprised we have not heard of him!"

Eric considered them closely. "This man Chop is bad luck. Nobody likes to mention him, let alone refer to him directly. I have heard he caters for anything. The story goes a tourist tried to test him and asked for a giraffe. But Chop had one and he charged the tourist extra for the use of a stepladder. Plus he took pictures on the side. Are you sure you want me to see this Chop, now?"

"Yes, oh yes. We are not into sick animals as such. Disgusting! But he sounds promising."

Eric shook their hands. "I will see what I can do!"

❋ ❋ ❋

Bob stood on the wharf swallowing. He had just seen outside visitors to a comfortable launch and was waiting for latecomers.

Dr Gregory emerged from a nearby crowd with a companion in his shadow. "Sorry about this. We felt we needed to have paid a short visit upstate."

Bob swallowed. "You mean Cedric, our resident wizard?"

"Wizard he may be, but he has paranoia coming out his ears plus he is a lying toerag. If you want my advice, watch him. It won't take much to set him off!"

"Yes! Yes! I know." Bob's mind was on other things. "I will. Now be careful how you hop into this boat!"

8.
Troubled Waters

Rupert propped against his office door and surveyed his staff with real pride. Loudly he announced, "Tonight is the last chance for the lotto. Someone buy a ticket 'cause we all need your support, right?"

"Right, of course," came politely usual acknowledgements.

"Matt! You have had a good few days now. Come yonder to my office and explain your science to an old plodder!" Rupert's didn't even resemble a request.

"Coming," Matt saluted.

"Don't you need a folder or papers or something?" Rupert enquired. He did not enjoy such reporting.

"Nope!" Matt confirmed all his suspicions from his doorway. "All I need is my screen." He patted his laptop.

"Sit yourself down and prepare to overwhelm me. I am an advocate of new technology!" Superior sarcasm raised the stakes.

"OK. But you won't be too over the moon, boss!" Matt prepared Rupert. "Now if you look at my computer screen here with the map of the roads, I have traced the suspect, Snapper, each day with a different-coloured line. He has done the same thing, same time, every day. I have put a bleeper in his car, tracer, by way of explanation."

"Does sound value for money to me," Rupert observed. "Are you going to tell me more?"

"Better value than other resources," came Matt's dry reply. He smiled up. "Checkmate! I think. However to business. There are two interpretations if you like. Which explanation would suit you first?"

Rupert chose, "Try the shorter. I can tell it will be less productive."

"Quite right, boss! You impress me," Matt started up. "The route our suspect took is taken by most of the working population at the same time every day. Everything is quite innocent. Or at least not criminal and there is nothing to identify him from other commuters. His routine starts with a café breakfast, crosses town to a local Indian dairy, buys a newspaper, goes to the park in the gardens, reads the news, maybe plays with kids for a while, chats with ground staff, and eventually returns by the same route."

"Let's get productive now!" Rupert tired easily. The burden of his workload was not shrinking.

Matt had rehearsed his dialogue. "To start with if he has illegal intentions then he is one smart cookie. I presume so. His route through town makes a tail virtually impossible not to spot. From his breakfast at Gillespie Corner he tracks through the five main traffic lights. Now it's common knowledge all traffic lights are synchronized so by driving to his pattern he can virtually choose which light he wants to turn up at amber. Thus he is the last car to leave unless his tail breaks cover.

"Next he turns off Downs Avenue, which just happens to run at the back of the main police station, and returns, coinciding with a change of shifts. Because the officer's car park is publicly open he views both unmarked and officers' cars. Any questions?"

"What might he be doing then?" As if Rupert didn't know. Confirmation reassured.

"Apart from lulling us into a braindead routine I would guess he is stalking! I cannot say who yet though." Matt lost an edge to his confidence. "I tried a few stunts but he didn't bite."

"An innocent man wouldn't, of course," Rupert noted. "But such as?"

"I created a few incidents for his police scanner," Matt summed up.

"That is just great!" Rupert had heard enough. "Just some small points though. How do you know all about the dairy and the park?"

"Checked him physically myself!" Matt was back to full confidence. "Just noted the times where he was most stationary for and snuck in the background. All I have to do is wait and watch. If he breaks his routine it is time to panic!"

"Fine," Rupert yawned. "Keep a physical eye on his start and finish. Any other pie you have a finger in that I should know about?" he invited deciding to reward this underling.

"Boss! As if!" Matt happily pretended indignation. "Seriously, though, I would like to contribute to bringing down Chop. He's a mean bastard! And Asian to boot. Met him, instantly never trusted the prick. Same as you and this Snapper, I suspect."

Rupert raised an eyebrow. "What do you want then?" Chop was mean alright but smarter than people gave him credit for. It would be good to be rid of him.

Matt was all business. "I want surveillance cameras set over the Black Hole. Most think Chop gets rid of problems there. As do a great many others. I would just like to monitor the place for a while. See just what bait is being thrown to the fishes and who the anglers are. No manpower at all, boss. Um! The cameras are just between you and me, right?"

One good turn deserves another. "So, what can I get you in return?"

"As a matter of fact there has been a funding difficulty at Citadel Investments. No complaint has been made officially so find out what happened, unofficially?" Rupert challenged. He decided to encourage this officer, things looked promising!

"Fine!" Matt accepted easily. Too easily for his employer's liking. "Can I ask how you know such things?"

Rupert's turn to be smug. "No! Later you can take me for a drive just to physically make your demonstration, though it has been tried before with only two cameras in your sole charge. I have some jet skiers to locate as a priority."

❊ ❊ ❊

Snapper finished his breakfast in leisurely manner. This time he had a passenger and he just felt she would be late. She was paying so Snapper felt indifferent. He had allowed for such.

He watched Miranda ghost past the window outside and through the doorway.

"Sorry I am a bit late. Things to do and all that," she purred apology.

"You have time for a coffee, if you like," Snapper putting her at ease. She looked very flushed he thought, more than just a quick sprint to make up a few seconds. "You look a bit piqued. You OK?"

"Fine! Just great!" she positively beamed at him. "A coffee would be just right. Thanks, hot sweet and strong."

"Let me get it. Then we can be on our way." Snapper raised himself from food remnants. He was suspicious. "Wouldn't like a smoke, I suppose?"

Miranda downed her coffee with relish. "No! So this is the big rehearsal. I have been waiting for this for a long time now!"

Snapper was unimpressed. "Well! When you have finished we can go for a drive and I will show you what I expect. All very ordinary I am afraid."

They both got up. "You drive and I drink. It is the only legal safe way." Miranda swirled her way out with the remains of her drink.

Snapper leisurely swung into the traffic. "Alright! After the next two sets of lights there is a larger block. A red Mini with fat wheels will cut us off from the left. Now he is our target. In the next couple of days he is going to crash."

"Nice old car. Yours are what used to be so hot. Not what I would call inconspicuous now though. Cyril has an oldish Nissan. He doesn't drive a Mini so why for?"

"I do know these things! The Mini will drive erratically and between him and us will be Cyril. We will, of course, be going to his assistance. Now shut up!" Snapper's answer explained little, chastised.

They drove on in silence.

❄ ❄ ❄

Cedric looked glum.

Being in charge and having money means you do not make concessions. He sat alone in his inner sanctum. He looked at rows of TV screens. He hated how much they had cost not to mention his efforts required to cover their purposes. Well, he had them now and that completed his security arrangements so it was a most satisfactory accomplishment. Despite his security and comfort he paused unhappily at the gleaming clean apparatus and dust-free opulence.

Perhaps his brother could help. His brother always liked the contradictions here. His expensive electron microscope placed on a cheap simple long stainless steel table, his brother's favourite comparison; sophistication on one hand, ages old on the other. Cyril was always good to lean on in such times. Cedric smiled and ventured out into his world.

"Hello, boss!" Tim greeted him gingerly. Who knows what to expect these days?

"Hi, there. Look! I am sorry about my outburst the other day. I don't know what I am thinking half the time any more. I know they are simple servants but they crawl right under my skin." Suddenly Cedric felt better cruising his equilibrium. "It must be the in-law's death has got to me in some way. I just can't explain it."

Tim was all concern for one of the few he admired. "Yes, well you may be right but if you feel any more bouts coming on, take a couple of reality pills. Let me deal with the bureaucrats. They do not need to see you. They are a pain in the arse you just do not need right now."

"How are you getting on?" Cedric's thoughts turned back on the job.

Tim smiled success. "I am on the right path. I have isolated what I think are the cells causing the havoc but I need living specimens. Let me show you so far. Being right as I am all the time it is a venereal disease. Nothing I have ever seen before nor do the cells have any background to the usual clap. But I am sure I have seen the family tree somewhere in my readings. I will recall it sooner or later or run it through my computer." He paused. "What I really need is a live subject to see how the little bastards operate."

Cedric beamed. Sympathy took Tim by the shoulder. "Sounds great. Sounds right! Show me what you have. I can then maybe rest the others and perhaps the two of us can concentrate. Forget what I said about live subjects. That was just idle fantasy." He could feel a rush coming on! And he had not dismissed his thoughts as easily as he spoke.

❊ ❊ ❊

Adam stood behind the car looking over the reserve down to the distant bay. He admired the view in this light. He looked back to the car. Tommy's wide eyes peered out from the back seat. Moist orbs probing from the gloom. Adam's impatience with Simon melted as he smiled, "Come on out, Tommy! You look like you are about to make a mess in the car, either end."

Others sniggered as Tommy scrambled out. Simon felt for him though he laughed with the others. Perhaps Adam was right. Tommy looked fucking pale!

"Yeah! What's the matter, little one?" Simon demanded as Tommy extricated himself awkwardly.

"Christ!" Adam thought he did everything difficult. Why was that? "You want to sit in the front?"

"I think my guts are going to spill out my mouth!" Tommy spoke plaintively. "I don't think I should sit in front. I eat enough bloody insects in the back. Do we always have to go down the bike trail? It gives me the shits every time."

Simon shook his head. Why do we tolerate him? "Nah! You stay huddled in the back if you like. Christ! You look like your mother!"

Simon decided to concede. It made good diplomatic sense if things turned to crap later. "I have other things to do."

"Thanks." Tommy sounded grateful indeed. "What has happened to Eugene? I haven't seen him for ages." He ignored the laughter following him.

Adam still smiled. "Forget about him. His dad won't let him out of the house. Especially if we are near. What do you think, Simon?"

Simon agreed. "That is right. The whole family wanks."

Adam shook Tommy's head. "Look, I have to be with relations while they are here for the bloody football. You can have my scarf if you like. That should save you a few bugs anyway. Just don't sick in it or you will be cleaning it," he warned jokingly.

Tommy took it in silence.

Adam tried Simon again, better perhaps in public. "Look! Just how much did you take from the bank? I need to know whether we will be chased — and how hard!"

Simon scowled at him. "Never mind about that now. Nobody is pursuing us. Have you seen anyone? I tell you nobody has even missed it at all." He knew Adam was right though. He had withdrawn nearly $60,000 and somebody should miss it.

Interrupting, Ross complained loudly. "Get back in here. Just one more time. I think I have it licked after this last hurdle! Stop that little shit from whining and complaining," he added after checking Tommy was not sitting behind him.

❀ ❀ ❀

In the quiet of the hotel's expansive dining room Chop smiled his 'How can I help you?' professional smile at his host, Eric. "That sportsman's death is most unfortunate. You will have had to move your girls before any investigation asks other questions. If I can help temporarily, just say so."

Eric looked over his counterpart. It was an uneasy made alliance. Chop with his Hong Kong background only traded his girls one way and treated them like crap. At least Eric provided good living standards and medical assistance freely and readily. He prized his assets. "I have already done that. Thanks, I'll send you a couple with what I would call more exotic requests. They should pay a good premium after my refusal."

"Good," Chop nodded. "You will tell them where to find me!" He ambled towards the door scooping up a couple of mints on his way out.

9.
Purple Patch Sunset

Snapper peered into the main residence. The occupants settled from the night save an unexpected phone call. He couldn't ask for better. And the shed-cum-garage he was heading for was self-contained.

He grunted in dismay at the owners. Not even locked! Snapper resisted an impulse to leave them a note, never mind. No wonder crime was rampant.

The Mini was even more grimed close up than it looked before. Some people didn't deserve to own a car. None of his business. A quick check of blackened spark plugs. Christ! How did the poor car run? He tidied them up and with other minor tinkering closed the bonnet satisfied the car would not break down, for the next couple of days anyway.

He checked again that the house was quiet and cautiously opened the driver's door. It was bound to be noisy. To his surprise it wasn't. He took the three discs reading the taste in music. Not bad, he thought, maybe the kid was not that bad. Just a victim of his environment.

Out of his bag he copied one of the driver's choices from his machine. Maybe the third disc; Snapper examined them to see whether he could see any replayed favourite, but there was not. He substituted his altered disc. Timing was everything now and he wasn't ever confident about timing, to take into account too many unknowns. Still he had to be content. He replaced them and snuck away through the early-morning blanket.

❊ ❊ ❊

Simon wondered about Adam. The glue was beginning to loosen, too many questions he didn't want asked, nor to answer. Not that he didn't, he just could not see why he should. Perhaps it was time for another casualty. Yes! That would cement his leadership. He would think about it some more. Perhaps during the coming day.

❊ ❊ ❊

Cedric peered at the screen. Nestled in the cleft were a cluster of little deep purple rectangular grapes. Spiked grapes! Everything Tim had said. Eureka! He needed a closer look, his heart, his brain racing each other. All his life and this was it. Cedric would thank Tim and give him the flick. Nicely of course and not immediately. That would be too crass. Besides, his contribution was still valuable.

Tim transgressed Cedric's thoughts at distance. "You will note that the number of antibodies is not abnormal. Obviously this issue can disguise itself admirably and indeed must do much more. I must see it in action."

"Yes!" Cedric wholeheartedly agreed. "We must see them in action. You have tried, of course?"

"Of course. Nothing seems to work!" Tim added. "Yet!"

❊ ❊ ❊

Morgan watched his fingers drum horse-beats on the shiny surface of his desk. Finally he looked up at the clock laboriously ticking over. He stretched his frame in satisfaction. "You know who the offenders are?" he asked his police representative.

"Yes, boss!" came his acknowledgement.

The drumming recommenced, softly at first. "They all live in the same neighbourhood?"

"Yes, boss."

"Affluent?"

"Yes, boss! Very."

"Three cars, you have cars for each suspect?"

"Yes, boss."

"You might need lights!"

"Yes, boss."

"You can do without sirens?"

"Yes, boss."

"Still, the Lucas family live near?"

"Yes, boss."

"Old man Lucas is still dead blind?"

"Yes, boss."

"Well, if there has been no miracle you had better make a noise. I can deal with a lot less fuss with old man Owens being blind rather than dead."

"Yes, boss."

The drumming silenced.

"Yes, boss?"

"The cells are full from last night?"

"Yes, boss. Completely."

"Have my court chambers set up in the east wing anteroom."

"Yes, boss!"

"Should it be ready for the afternoon?"

"Yes, boss."

Morgan looked up. "OK. Then off you go!"

Watching the chief's diminishing form Morgan called out, "Liz, get your bum in here!"

As her head appeared sheepishly at the door, he continued. "What the hell are you doing here this time of the morning?"

"I didn't win lotto, damn it! So I thought I may as well come back to work," she explained.

"Too bad! How many winners?" Morgan asked. How could he have dismissed it so? Perhaps he is getting old.

"Just the one lucky person," she tutted. "Set for life," she sighed.

"Better not be any complaints, or I will be so pissed off," Morgan mumbled. "Thanks." He dismissed her.

✳ ✳ ✳

Eugene sneaked a look from behind his bedroom curtain. He shuddered with a deep breathy sigh. Tentatively closing his stinging tortured eyes. His nightmare returned instantly cruelly replaying. He heard again the roar of powerful machines. Low-rumbling purrs calling his senses to look, to appreciate, to belong, louder snarls and grunts demanded his attention, roars calling his name outside of his window teasing him to just sneak a look.

He wilted.

Piercing headlights, decorative cars, speed all added to magic. A brief interlude as they turned at the bottom to call upon him again when he saw the shadow of a large car. Not loud but quiet, slowing snaking along the curb till it found his house. Eugene swallowed involuntarily but he couldn't move, no matter how much he willed himself. God knows he tried. Even a small damp patch down his trouser leg went unnoticed otherwise he would have been mortified.

A black bulk emerged out of the gloom, no lights to say it was a car, no form to say it was human. While indistinguishable Eugene felt the anger, the evil, the cruel as physical matter. But it was its sense of sadistic pleasure that made him feel physically sick. The dark grim shadow reached up for him and he cowered back to his bed. Still it pursued him.

Frantically he raced for his father's doorway. His father slept wrapped in the same threatening shadows. He slunk back to bed and pulled the covers up to his big round eyes. Perhaps the shadows were reaching for his girlfriend. The idea a huge lump in his throat.

He wept.

Cursing himself for his weakness. Others were above all this, his friends, adults, even the guy they had stolen from. Yes! That was the start of it all. In the morning he would summon up his courage and tell his parents all. He lay back on his dampened pillow and dreamt his nightmare again.

❊ ❊ ❊

Chop surveyed the now non-elegant bedroom in nonchalant disdain. Blood smeared and gore just part of the décor. The cleaning up a price already paid by others. He turned to his equally casual lieutenant. "Another chapter closed, ah Rooster!"

Rooster never bothered to look at the speaker. "I don't know what got into her head. She must have gone right off the deep end. Demanding rights like that. It's a real shame; she was one of our best earners."

"As she was in death," agreed Chop. "You will give a proper send-off, won't you?"

"Of course, boss! The Black Hole has a voracious appetite. Do you want to see her off?"

"What do you think?" Chop was immediately wary. "Have their cameras been neutralized?"

"Well! No!" Rooster conceded. "But we do dictate what goes into their focus. We are still in debate with that American who should charge what. They seem to think they own our cameras!"

"It is the American tradition not to accept a realistic solution," Chop explained painfully. "A whole society based on complete greed. No wonder they are universally loathed."

Rooster nodded in full agreement. "Yes! If any equipment goes missing I do know where to look. And they are not going to rob us of our share."

"OK then. She was a very good girl. One of my favourites. Perhaps I could stay in the background," Chop decided, still coy. "And we should send her family something too. She could have taught the others so much more." He shook his head. He hated waste.

Rooster looked for acceptance and smarts. "Should have this room cleaned up and ready to use tonight. The girls and customers are squeamish about these things. Never could understand it myself. Perhaps I could put her body in the icebox for a while. If one Westerner likes 'em cold there must be others. We can charge more and this time it is all profit!"

Chop acknowledged. "You are a good boy, Rooster. You should go far."

Rooster flushed with accolades. "Perhaps I should put her in one of our freezers."

They both smiled to themselves and each other as they closed the door and left.

❀ ❀ ❀

Rupert looked at his watch yet again. Now later than he wanted his staff dispatched he did not want to be contactable. He had his perfect excuse.

He smiled. The cafe was beginning to fill now and boisterous banter between the regulars created a positive atmosphere. He wondered at how much they knew about their neighbours, probably didn't even know names.

He looked again at his watch. Matt emerged from through the throng. "Hi, chief! Ready to go? My car."

"Yes!" impatience spoke, and they both left.

From the passenger's side Rupert felt uncomfortable. He always preferred to be driver. He tried to put that aside. He sat back and listened.

"Right!" Matt smiled at him. "First we will go through his manoeuvres. Watch how to get an amber light."

"Not bad," the older conceded. "But be careful on the motorway."

"This is the bit I like," Matt leaned over. "I don't know what I am looking for."

"You are looking for a crash!" said the other.

Suddenly, "Watch out for that Mini! He is mad weaving in and out like that. Bloody kids!" But the car had already veered in and out and was already nearly out of sight.

Matt perked up. "That's what I am looking for. Well done, boss! Did you get his plate?"

"Piss off!" came the terse rebuttal. "Concentrate on your bloody driving!"

Matt was not finished. "Do you think we could catch him up? I am sure I could!"

"I am sure I am an opportunist!" Rupert mimicked him. "Look, I know you get excited now and then but really. Nothing personal but you can see as much into that as I can foretell the future from the folds of my foreskin!"

"I guess," Matt capitulated. "My best results are from intuition."

Rupert reached down as Matt glanced over. "What are you doing? Trying to hide?"

"No! As a matter of fact I am giving you the benefit of the doubt. I will just radio ahead and get a cruiser to pick him up."

"Sorry, boss! Can't let you do that!" Matt exclaimed in alarm slapping the gear from Rupert's hand.

"Sorry. Who did you say was in charge here?" There was anger in the voice at his overture being rebutted.

"What I meant to say was that you have met this Snapper, haven't you?"

"Just the once!"

"Well! Nothing personal but you are the one with the unique accent here and he will pick you up in an instant! We don't want to scare him at this stage."

"Fair enough. Unique ah?" Rupert didn't like or accept defeat.

Matt smiled. "Sounds better than whining."

❆ ❆ ❆

Adam peered into the still waters of the bay. Shoals of fish momentarily designed patterns. Just as fast they scrubbed everything, instantly forming a new one. He saw parallels in his community. Those strayed outside thoughtlessly suffered misfortune while the others swirled about without concern or thought. What was tragically wrong to him was none ever learnt. He knew he would.

He decided to visit Gus. Sit under the tree and talk to him. In the silence and amongst the dead he sought and sometimes found inspiration. Gus talked to him in the only way he knew how.

10.
Like Flies

THE MINI SIDLED UP to other cars, intruding into their space. If tooting of horns meant success the driver was winning. But he had already moved to other interests. Cars were meant not to drive but to be driven, not cosseted from A to B. And drive in the manner meant to be. He liked the song 'On the Road to Nowhere'. That summed up so many of today's motorists, plus he could not get the tune out of his head, so he hummed it repeatedly.

The young driver's days were tedious, repetitive. The cars always the same, same lanes, same speed, same unnecessary braking, same over-indicating. He used these days to edge a few more seconds off his record. The practice was safe enough to one of his ability, not for those lesser.

Miranda closed her mind and screwed up her nose. This was not panning out as she had pictured. "What are we doing in this crap of a car? Do you realize how far away we are? I want to whisper goodbye to him, not scream it over the street for all to hear. You know, something like 'discreet'?"

"This green Toyota is virtually unidentifiable." Snapper tried to explain. "I am certainly not going to use up my Valiant. Things are looking good. The Mini is doing his usual Saint Vitus's waltz and Cyril is only just ahead. All we have to do is wait for the right song. The right moment."

❊ ❊ ❊

Matt sat fused to his desk and doodled on his pad waiting, looking at his laptop screen. Time was up. Perhaps today or tomorrow. Pity it wasn't yesterday when he had his boss captive. He reluctantly pulled the radio mike towards him. "OK, big fella! Come on in. The suspect has finished his run."

"That is a negative, boss! He only left a short time ago. Unless he can teleport he will still be in traffic!" His tail contradicted him.

Matt screamed at his staff. "Jesus!" as he arced over his desk. Fused no longer. He screamed to all of his staff. "Arrest him! Arrest him for having a shadow. I don't care! Get the cars out there now! Oh shit! Better get a bloody ambulance, you never know."

His staff stared back in disbelief. "Not enough to go on" was the chorus as they shook their heads collectively. His world has gone mad. Perhaps he won lotto!

The Mini oodled back indicating towards a curb lane. An instant mindnumbing sound to disorientate pitched full straight at the driver. His car clipped the mudguard of the vehicle he had wedged and dove for the gutter.

The power of the physics was greater than the overpowered driver could cope with and it too wedged, baulked and rolled. The following car drove straight into him. Brake lights swung on up the street all in an insane choreography.

"Bugger!" Snapper smarted. "That bitch in front has responded too well. Hold on, I will have to nudge her into Cyril. Trust her to be too good. I should reward her for that later!"

He shoved the Toyota hard up adding to the other nose-to-tails. "Miranda, get out and stand in front of Cyril's Nissan while I sort this out." They both got out. While Snapper stomped, Miranda wobbled.

The woman's look burned through her window at Snapper.

"I am so very sorry!" Snapper was genuinely contrite. "My fault entirely. Nothing else I can say. I was watching the Mini skipping about when I should have been looking closer to home." He surveyed her damage. "Look! It is not bad. I mean your car is not a write-off! In fact you can still drive it away. More than I can say for some others. And I am in a position to help."

She lowered her window marginally. She swore at him, "You are just a fucking idiot!"

"So are most of the drivers here." He waved his arms expansively to emphasize his point. Again Mr Contrite spoke. "If you lower your window a bit we may be able to settle this fast, and to your satisfaction."

Suspiciously she lowered her window a fraction. There had to be some safety in public. "How do you know what satisfaction is to me?"

Snapper's pleasant smile lingered. "I have shares in a car yard. And I have private income. Look, take my card. Read it and just let me count the stuff out." He shuffled some notes. "Ten thousand should cover it and if you like take my licence as well. You seem to think I shouldn't have one." He offered it all through the window.

She took the money if only to stop it spilling. "That is a lot of money," she began. Money, a lot of money, on offer was so unexpected. The sight and feel and possession of actual funds held an irresistible temptation.

"The car trade is booming thanks to the festivities." Snapper paused in explanation. "Look, you just take it now. We can't go anywhere at the moment and I want to check on that poor fellow in front. He looks a little sickened too. Then I will do what I can when I return."

She afforded an appreciative smile. He moved on.

Cyril leaned back with the window down. "How did that piece of garbage land on the front of my car?" he asked himself out loud.

"I put it there!" Snapper obliged him, his arm resting above the driver's door. "She wants to wave goodbye!"

"What? Where the hell did you come from? As if I don't have enough problems right now!" Cyril bitched at him.

"Say your goodbyes then," Snapper implored.

"Drop dead and rattle her chain before you fuck off!" Cyril snarled. "Do you know who I am?" raising his window to cut off the encounter. "Look at her supercilious smile. I can't believe I used to so look forward to that!"

His window caught on a tube from under Snapper's arm. A hiss and a mist quickly dispersed. Cyril slumped down to be held by his seatbelt.

"It's always good to leave on a high note," Snapper said to himself. "Come on you, back to the car!" he called out to Miranda. "Nothing more we can do here!" as he retired himself.

The woman driver tugged at his passing sleeve. She had had time to reflect. "This is too much here!" she held out to Snapper. Temptation won.

"Let's work it out when you are all in one piece then." Snapper seemed generous. "You have my card," he concluded. "And we seem to be moving a bit. Must dash. Get in touch!" And he was gone.

❀ ❀ ❀

"Well! Congratulate me, chief! The target is/was Cyril. By chance some Mini crashed. Driver's still not conscious. So much for your foresight!" Matt tried to keep sarcasm back.

Rupert shrugged. "Resources. My parents had me docked before I could walk," he smiled, though inwardly fuming. "I have to have a business case for resources and you spent yours wisely on cameras, remember. Such cuts were the vogue at the time. I have something else for your talents. Here are two pictures of kids from the security footage. I want you to bring them in, no questions. I have to report upstairs. You have done well!"

❀ ❀ ❀

Morgan rescanned the leaves of paper laid in front of him. He looked resigned dignity. "Not one redeeming feature, chief. How much do they pay for this crap?"

"Victims of circumstances. Spending time with their peers below made not one iota of difference." The chief appraised. "Other victims have surfaced and are more problematical."

"Go on!" Morgan prompted him.

"Firstly you are right on the button with the bank. It seems this albacore as it was told to me …" He elaborated. "This albacore came in deposited just over two hundred grand. Then before the system was up and running this kid came in and took out seventy grand of it. Different denominations. Well thought out for a kid. No wonder the banker was shitting himself."

"If it's Snapper's money that kid should be shitting himself as well. Do you think the thief knows?" Morgan asked.

"Don't see any reason why he should. Snapper is a stranger to all but his generation. And the bank was quick to make good the loss. Does Conrad need a guard?"

"No," Morgan decided. "Not till we see what happens to the kid anyway. Snapper was always one for keeping things and doing things in order. You had better make finding him a high priority."

"Perhaps someone to keep a passing interest in the banker?"

Morgan had dispensed with this issue. "You are the policeman! It is up to you. Go on! If that is the icing what is the cake?"

"There was an enormous traffic snafu this morning. One victim, Cyril of our richest, died. First checks indicate by heart attack. We have reason to consider other possibilities."

Morgan fumed. "Just let me know the facts as they come in. Cedric has lost his right arm right at the armpit. He will be remorseless in retribution. Where is he now?"

* * *

Tim kept his boss very close to him. His stone features showing no mourning disturbed Tim. He knew they were close. Tim looked deep into his eyes trying to make contact.

"We have this woman coming out who may have been a witness," Tim tried to communicate. With no sign of recognition he carried on. "We just want to establish what she knows and if worthwhile we can probe more. You understand?"

Cedric hissed. "That bitch did it!"

Tim leaned over. "Sorry, boss! What did you say?"

Cedric's expression did not change. "I said the bitch did it. I told Cyril to quit her but he insisted on hosing her down. A seed receptacle is so important, you see. And now the bitch did it!"

The door chimes interrupted them. "Fuck me!" Tim worried.

"Better let me do the questions!"

Tim was very uncomfortable. "Come on in, miss," he invited.

"Wow! What a palace!" She gazed around with wide eyes.

"Have a seat, miss." Cedric as civil as possible. "Come in. Sit yourself down."

"Emily Tye," she nodded to him as the luxury swallowed her up.

"Tell us about your unfortunate experience then," Cedric oozed sympathy.

"I saw this Mini crap out spectacularly and managed to stop in time. The car behind me couldn't stop and shunted me into this car in front. The driver got out, made peace with me and checked the driver. They had words and he got back into his own car and everyone went their separate ways. Say! Is this place your idea?"

"Nope," Cedric soothed her. "I indulge my wife, Olive. All this is her idea. Was there a woman in the other car?"

"I think so. But I only dealt with the guy. He was so big he completely filled the window if you know what I mean."

"Would you know him if you saw him again?" Tim chimed in.

"Damned right!" Emily confirmed. "He was loaded! Rich!"

Cedric butted in. "Did the woman get out of the car? Did you see her around the car in front?"

"Well! She must have got out but what she did I don't know." Emily thought about it. "All my attention was on the guy. But she did get back in their car with him so she must have got out. I honestly don't know her actions though."

"About the other driver?" Tim started.

Cedric showed her a photo cutting him off. "Could this be her?" he asked sweetly. "You see we know her and we are concerned she might be hurting somewhere."

"I don't know," Emily looked hard. She shrugged her shoulders. "Could be. I really can't see for sure. Her body is the same proportions. She was moving OK. I do not think she was hurt," she reassured them.

"The other driver?" Tim tried again.

"Never mind that!" Cedric stifled him again. "Well, my dear, you have been a great help. Let us help you out for your inconvenience." He was gracious as he stood up knowing Emily would follow. "By the way, have the authorities asked at all?" A casual afterthought.

"No. And thank you very much. A really wonderful place you have here," came her parting remarks.

Cedric turned to Tim. "See! I told you the bitch was behind it all! She will pay dearly for this! In fact," he smiled to himself, "you have just found yourself a volunteer."

Tim looked disgusted. "This is all very fine but what about the driver?" Meanwhile hidden back there his hopes ignited.

Cedric smiled again. Tim didn't like this smile at all. Cedric sighed. "I imagine the driver has a particularly venomous history. It does not need to further concern us, if you want to stay healthy. But we will need to secrete our volunteer away with no fuss. It will not be easy!"

Tim was not overly concerned at the suggestion. "I wonder where they are right now?"

❈ ❈ ❈

Morgan sat back in his large official chair. Though he wore a suit he attempted to be casual. He looked at the three youths. Riches bought confidence. They were here because of their money and because a ruling meant no conviction unless they appealed. Morgan turned his prepared screened speech off. They would not appeal and therefore they thought their sentences would be only a minor inconvenience.

"This is a court," he began to explain. "I am in sole charge. I tend to keep procedures informal. Both sides have prepared their accounts. The chief on one side and your lawyers the other. The priest sometimes acts as an independent arbitrator. I do not always take his advice nor should you consider his support a kiss of death. In this case he has included his second in charge as well, who may act in his absence on other occasions."

The three boys lounged back already impatient and as is their custom seeing no need to hide it.

"You, boy!" Morgan pointed to one. "Doesn't your family own the hotel complex on the shore?"

"Two, in fact!" the boy answered curtly. He had other places to be, other things to do.

The chief smiled. The law did not.

"Your family's hotel complexes are only filled by the coming of the whales. Forget the other nonsense presently here. The whales have in only recent times had the confidence to bring themselves in abundance. And you in one act of jet skiing want to ruin all that has been achieved." Morgan finished his reprimand. The offender had not lost any confidence.

Rev Long started to speak. "It is an isolated case of youthful exuberance spiced by amounts of mild alcohol. Hardly an act of maliciousness." Lou nodded in agreement.

"Hardly!" Morgan disagreed. "It is wanton arrogance despite the warnings and the media and the history."

Morgan wanted to carry on but he needed effect. Better to count to ten, twenty would be better.

"This is my decision for the three of you. Six months in total. Two months on The Marks; four months each personally attending to Ramon. By then you should have learnt something of yourselves."

The three had his attention now. Too late!

This was not how it had been evidently promised. Morgan was satisfied. "The paperwork will be completed by tomorrow. You have fourteen days from the receipt of the papers to appeal."

He thanked them all as they left. Raised voices could be heard outside getting less and less as they departed. Usual story, Morgan felt.

"You have the wisdom of Solomon, you know." The chief was pleased. "What do you think, minister?"

"Adequate under the circumstances. Ramon is a nice touch of irony." Long felt pleased it had gone further socially than he thought. Morgan could still unexpectedly surprise him.

"That will do for today. Any other business while you are here, Reverend?"

Long shook his head. He wasn't ready for either.

The chief coughed. "How is your parish? Your nocturnal prowler has been quiet, officially anyway?"

"No, nothing," Louie replied. "Perhaps our prayers have been answered."

"Perhaps!" Morgan thought aloud. He asked, "Long, think about asking your wife? She is likely to hear woman talk."

"No! We do confide in each other. She has been poorly for the last couple of days. I don't want to disturb her at this point," Long explained.

"Fair enough!" Morgan conceded.

"Well! Ah! Maybe we should let sleeping dogs lie," observed Louie. "Don't want to do anything to encourage him. Perhaps the chief knows more?"

"No! The chief does not know more nor does he know who the hell Ramon is either." The chief sounded a little bitter.

Morgan sighed. "Sorry, chief. Ten years or more when the whales came in greater numbers, this Ramon took a surf ski out. The bull sideswiped him. Broke all of his bones, arms, legs, ribs, spine, you name it! Left him face up, lucky for him, totally paralyzed and he still is. Should be a salutatory lesson to the others."

The chief looked downcast. "Yeah, lucky! Thanks."

❊ ❊ ❊

Snapper and Miranda sat quietly in his car at one of the beaches watching the waves, children and families pursued and surrounded by sea birds. "Well, I hope you are satisfied, Miranda. Everything you asked for. You are the last thing he saw so he knows, knew why and he died a most uncomfortable death. Just what you paid for," Snapper concluded his contract. Successfully he felt.

"Yes, I couldn't ask for more. And you did come highly recommended. In fact I am going to ask for detail just to complete the picture, you understand?" Miranda still had an appetite.

"Yes?" Snapper prompted her, curious.

"How did he die?" she asked. "I only saw him slump over!"

"I have this plastic tubing down my sleeve. When he closed his car window I release a gas which takes out all the oxygen and he suffocates very quickly." He fidgeted a bit and held his arm up.

Miranda couldn't believe it. Suddenly she could not breathe. In or out. Alarmingly outside nobody noticed her plight. Right in the middle here she was dying. Being killed and so many people in plain sight all over the place. Her eyes bulged desperately seeking rescue. Already too late for the window.

Panic was suddenly averted by Snapper. He snapped a mask over her nose and mouth with a plunge of a fist into her side. Suddenly she was breathing again.

"Action speaks louder than words. You will be alright in a few minutes so just sit back and relax." Snapper chuckled to himself. He leaned towards her. "There are never any more questions, you know," he whispered to her.

Miranda whistled. "Poor old Cyril. Excellent! What a way to go!" She was smug at last.

"Actually, he was worse. He was administered a dose of poison with it. Well, not poison exactly, more of a muscle relaxant so he gets to enjoy everything," Snapper confessed.

"I could get to like this, Snapper. Are you sure you don't need an assistant? One would be very helpful I would have thought." Miranda's heart raced at the prospect, and she was determined not to let it go easily.

"No! You get not to trust anyone and you seldom relax." Snapper began to deliberately paint it black.

"Not so!" Miranda contradicted him. "You have Morgan and a seemingly endless supply of lady friends."

"What do you know about Morgan? He is a dangerous man. More so than me." Snapper paused. "For Christ's sake, you are laying him, aren't you?" he accused.

"Not on a permanent basis. I prefer married men. No commitments you know," she confessed.

"Well! Stay away from him. He is devoted to Holly and crushes everything that jeopardizes his relationship. Most do not see it coming until too late. You stay away from him! Understand?" Snapper worried. As he had suspected.

"Alright then, I hear what you say," she tutted at him. "But surely you can give me something to test my mettle, so to speak?"

Snapper had reservations. "I don't think you are hearing what I am telling you."

"Oh! I am finely tuned, you know!" Miranda tried to reassure.

"I suppose there is always something in my line of work." Snapper dwelt on it for a few minutes. "Do you play golf?" he decided. "There is a matter of etiquette if you like?"

11.
The Bite

Simon stood so proud on the summit of the reserve. "We have driven everyone away! This is our domain." He looked close to affection to the others. "We were not given this," he proclaimed. "We have taken it! It is ours. From our safety here we can now forage in the city. Ross's driving is the best around!" Boasting is so good for the soul!

The others all saw the truth. Thanks to Ross's driving everybody else deserted the reserve and the others were all gone.

"Same as the wild animals!" Little Tom who watched all the TV documentaries suggested what the others had been thinking. "If this is ours I think I should piss up against that tree. I have seen it on TV. Mark out our territory."

They nodded agreement. Antisocial behaviour held a special appeal. They all walked deliberately over to the oldest largest tree of the island for watering. Tom getting assertive. This was new, and positive. Ross placed his shoe deliberately into weeded steps. It looked like tyres had grooved out miniature cattle tracks through the bank. He didn't say anything. It caused him to wonder.

Simon dissented as well. "Look!" he pointed out. "See those grooves up those embankments. They are not made by animals. They are made by cars. Powerful cars with powerful drivers. V8 I would think. Not VWs, that is for sure. They have marked out their territory and only time has tarnished their images. Those would have been the days. I would have liked to measure myself against them, or perhaps I would be afraid to!"

Ross and Adam only winced. "Those days are gone. Thank God! And so have their drivers. They would only drive wheelchairs now, and dream, or are a long time swimming in the Black Hole.

How much money do we have left now, Simon?" Adam asked.

Simon furious inside replied calmly. "Plenty! Nag! Nag! Nag! Let's go to town!" They all stormed in their now customary seats and sped down the motorway. Town was opening up just for them.

Simon had had enough!

He gazed fixedly out his window, fed up. That bloody Adam has to go! And soon! It was just so hard to plan it out and he didn't want to just seize any moment. In the meantime it would be a good idea to start salting some, no, make that most of it, away. As with the documentaries he would be king only for a limited time. Sooner rather than later someone else would surely take over. He planned to be gone from this land long before another's reign.

❊ ❊ ❊

Past solitary mangrove clumps fishermen's snorkels spread out, fat paddle steamers plus a trailing stick, ships of the line entering the bay. The inhabitant bugs seemingly oblivious to the blood product banquet poised below. Add to the distant couple of four-wheel-drives all shapes were nearly indistinguishable.

But the small fire, the heated vehicle engines and opaque moving forms on the beach represented alluring, tempting nourishing feasts, teasing so close, yet too far away.

The insects toyed at the edge of their comfort zones, collectively swarming enough haze to form shadows on the ground before a reassemble. Soon one would lead off towards meals with an accompanying buzz.

Holly presumed lunch was on the flipper. "Look at that! Poor Bob is left back. Protection from the sharks. Wouldn't delay those eaters for long. I bet he is back there cause he is better and this is his penance."

Morgan navigated towards the sands until he was sure of his footing. These clear waters made depth indeterminable. He made a quick count of the others before standing and waving to his fans.

❊ ❊ ❊

"Right!" Simon dictated. "Hit the mall!" Cruising down the mall parks, Matt stage whispered to the others. "Watch that old mama! I bet I can make her wet herself!" He accelerated gently before cutting the motor.

When he got as close as he dared to the large skirt carrying volumous shopping bags, he leapt on the horn.

Lisa spun round dropping nothing. "Stupid little pricks! Even your fathers did that! Why not ask them? If you even know who they are?"

"Fuck you!" Matt retorted as he restarted the car. "Oldest virgin on the island, aren't you? He jeered with vocal support from the others helping. "Still! If you really want to change we know what it is all about and will help for a small fee!"

"Make that a large fee!" Simon took over. "And we know where you live so we won't worry about cab fare." They laughed generously as one together. Not the start they had wanted but they had still come out on top. That was what was important!

❋ ❋ ❋

The Island's club's noon noise level increased by speculation and rumour. Then the president announced over the address system what every member knew anyway. The sole winning lotto ticket had been sold at the club. Yet to be claimed!

Most were totally unsurprised as most tickets by far had been sold there.

The ground swell increased permeated by excitement, hope, desperation, greed and suspicion, even the walls. Old friends looked suspiciously at all, especially friends. New shirts or even ironed shirts fuelled heated speculation.

Gestures members had known for years construed hidden guilt until yet another suspect emerged, not that new removed old, just added to a lengthening list until at the end of the night most members were potential winners.

Intrigue, greed and conspiracy gouged at the fabric of the club. Open and veiled threats of legal action as a lever to get information fruitless.

Equally the modesty and discretion of the bar staff, doormen and cleaners infuriated those who had profited by them in the past. Court action seemed inevitable once the target emerged despite the warnings of the consequences by the authorities. Especially Morgan!

❊ ❊ ❊

The BMW cruised sedately past the school luring temporary female company. "Look at him!" Matt exclaimed swinging the car over to the familiar bent-over suit. "Stupid old prick!" he screamed out.

The original headmaster looked at his shoes. Gone were the successes of which he was so proud. The dark side has shown itself. He should have beaten the little shits more when he had the chance. Yes! He should have taken all of them opportunities.

Simon called out beside him. "Been smelling your own farts again? It's a lesson we all had to take."

They all heard the reply. "Arseholes!" They laughed out loud and they revved on.

Adam, still smirking, pointed out, "The police will probably be here soon. I don't want to meet them yet. Let's move on."

"Right!" Simon agreed. "Let's go and see if we can find Eugene." They disappeared into the traffic. "Poor Eugene."

❊ ❊ ❊

Snapper stood half in surf. "Bob! If you don't give me some of your catch I will remember."

"My God! We can't have that," Bob fiddled with his bounty and swished a few under water out of sight of the shore to Snapper. He made sure he kept the most edible and the largest.

Morgan swirled shoreward with the swell. "Serves you right for catching the most. I am surprised the sharks are not hungry."

Bob swallowed. "It's because you cannot swim. But I can teach you to dive and hold your breath!"

They all laughed their way up the beach targeting an old half-submerged log in the sand. Still giggling they sat removing flippers and tucking away goggles.

Bob snapped at an insect anchored to his knee. When Snapper slapped his arm they got up as one, a signal for them to move on. Besides all this effort made them hungry.

"Lord, bless this bounty just for our meal." Morgan saw no reason to resist impulses. Lord knows he was unable to in his office.

His brother smiled taking the bait as good-naturedly as it was intended. "Just so long as you don't cook. I have enough iron from your last attempt."

"Louie, Louie, why is it all religious zealots forget nothing?" Morgan laughed.

Louie replied, "Only from long experience because nobody knows when it may be used against us or by us. Just let Holly cook and my prayers will surely be answered."

Holly raised her eyebrows dramatically, idly scratching her leg as she watched the opaque flesh bubble and whiten.

"Boys will be boys!" she muttered to herself. "Go on, Bob," she ordered. "Make yourself useful. Keep the hungry hordes at bay and that includes you. Go on if you want to eat, prepare the beach."

Snapper selected an area of the beach that was just sand and they began smoothing it out. Louie smacked his lips "Good food means good drink and harvesting God's bounty makes gives a man a righteous thirst, eh?"

Morgan jeered at him. "Brother, you are pathetic, but your heart is in the right place so we had better come to your salvation."

Bob rankled; he was the only one doing work.

The insect zeroed in on the scratch. Holly's whole body was illuminated now, a monster of a meal! Her skinned surface lit up fluorescent veins crossing her surface, a pulsating strobe, irresistible invitation. Now was the moment of greatest danger and as he probed the surface as gently as a surgeon he plunged in dual scalpels, his feet dancing a success jig to dine. Immediately his wafer-thin abdomen ballooned out and he secreted the wound as he prepared his departure. Now until he reached sanctuary, his sac bloated, he was at his most venerable.

As he launched himself his swollen body caught every whiff of breeze and tossed him about along with his sea anchor.

He struggled to cover a safe distance before he was forced to rest on the sand exhausted by his load. How many times would this have to be repeated? But he had survived!

Back on the leg the most ferocious of microscopic heated battles engaged. Antibodies poured into the foreign invaders neither giving way. The senses triggered more reinforcements demanded from all organs and produced warnings to the brain. Holly's body shook in involuntary acknowledgement and unable to maintain her faculties the beach raced up to grasp her.

❀ ❀ ❀

"Give us a look at those pictures again!" Rupert examined them in detail. "Alright, these little bastards have to turn up somewhere else.

"Widen your search and take it back to the beginning of the month at least. If you are feeling lazy use the computer. It seems to do all your legwork for you, anyway."

He turned to Matt. "We have taken too long to find them already and they are on somebody's hit list. Let me know as soon as you can."

Matt shrugged. He didn't care for kids at all. He wanted larger game. "Who? How am I supposed to protect them then, boss?"

"Do I have to do every bloody thing?" Rupert snapped at him. "I don't know! Arrest them perhaps. Let the law protect them and remember they have stolen a considerable amount so they shouldn't be too hard to find. I know I wouldn't be!"

"OK! I don't know about that necessarily, boss!"

Matt started his searching by delegating downwards. He had a few ideas to discuss. Plus he was not going to be shown up by a bunch of kids.

His colleagues shook their heads. How did he get away with that? Nobody else dared such lack of respect.

❀ ❀ ❀

In choreograph, as one the men frantically bundled Holly into the most powerful of wagons. Morgan had his lights flashing, Bob was beside her dousing her with blankets, Snapper looked to the fire. It would just have to burn itself out safe enough. He ran after the roaring metal. If their things were there later somebody would pick them up.

Sea birds glanced their departure while swooping on the food. Juggling, squawking, pivoting in the air reluctant to let go or to bully and fight for morsels too hot to swallow.

12.
The Quirt

"MORGAN! WAKE UP! IT is time to go." Snapper cheerfully kicked out at his chair. The chair seemed not overly comfortable to him. Now was his turn to find out.

Morgan sought out his balance and stature. "Shit!" covered it all. "Christ! What is the time?" He looked longingly at the pristine hospital linen. Whitened glare reflected his sense of guilt.

"No change then, I take it?" Snapper took his opportunity to make Morgan feel worse. "I see her sheets are still starched, which tells it own story."

"Yeah!" Morgan came to grips with his surroundings. "It has been like this all night. Coffees can keep a man going for only so long. Bob was here first," he noted.

"Thought it was supposed to be Louie!" Snapper was surprised.

"Lou said he had God's work to do. And Bob never slept, was his only excuse," Morgan explained. "Maybe Bob had God's work to do as well. He looked pretty green, you know."

They both watched Holly motionless. "Whatever," Snapper decided at last. "Bob will be pretty harmless. And what about our patient? She is looking a little jaded as well."

Morgan easily managed a smile. "Nothing fatal I am told. A reaction of some kind. Definitely not our mysterious bug, anyway. That was the first thing I made sure about or I would have had no sleep at all. Not as jaded as Louie, mind you. I have tried to get that bastard Green to influence him, you know?"

Both sat listening to the rhythmic beat of the monitoring machines.

"I guess," Snapper conceded finally. "You and Green go back a long way and as far apart as ever. I don't know why you try."

Morgan shrugged reassured. "Louie is family. I have tried the usual subtle approaches of course."

"And?" Snapper annoyed he had to prompt him.

"A complete waste of time and concern. He forgets family ties and conveniently wraps everything up in religious zeal," Morgan had capitulated. "Poor stupid bastard!" his afterthought ventured.

Snapper took over. "I will have to exert what influence I can then, but I am reluctant to get too involved in family matters, you understand?"

Morgan agreed under a stooped head. "Yes. I know that. You said you would."

Even then Snapper could see tears forming in Morgan's eyes and his whole heart reached out to his friend. Family eh? Nothing but agony and heartache.

"Look," Snapper tried to perk him up. "I'm here now and my time is yours, of course. Why don't you go and have a long shower? Spruce yourself up a bit. Holly probably cannot wake to your stink! Go on! Things are under control here! If something happens I know how to get hold of you. To you I always keep my word."

"Stable enough, I guess, and now that you're here I do have things to attend to while she is in good hands." Morgan raised himself so tired.

Snapper waved him away generously and sat to wait time to pass and amuse himself with sparse magazines.

❄ ❄ ❄

In the police officers' room Rupert examined Matt's efforts. "You have done well. The security footage certainly produced good suspects. It's your case, if you like; who did you have in mind?"

"Well! Bearing in mind we are dealing with juveniles the team consensus is the factory photos and the street photos show the same little bastards. I would like to pick up the two of them at least and see what breaks." Matt spoke for the team. "We don't know who they are but they are local kids so there must be school records for us to start with."

"Right!" Rupert approved. "Go for it. But keep me informed."

❈ ❈ ❈

The kids swirled around their reserve performing circular peaks in their car. They were all more familiar with nuances of the car and driver.

With confidence came a sense of belonging, of reassurance. The ground was theirs.

They had chased off interlopers who knew better than to return. A feeling of belonging to the land and to each other grew each day. Now what had been sufficient was somehow cramped. They looked to the rest of the reserve as rightfully theirs too. They each acknowledged battles were yet to be won, and some maybe not easily, however confidence was more than enough.

Simon stood above the others, as generals do. "This is our sanctuary. We own it. We keep it." He spoke with conviction. "We are the law up here and we don't tolerate trespassers. All the reserve is now ours for the taking and we will. You have your own insignia individual to yourselves."

This was so right to his crew. Each had indeed brought what they wanted: a watch, a mobster hat to be worn backwards, a chrome steering wheel.

Each selection looked good to the others and each secretly wished they had thought of one first. Only little Tom had an implied exemption. He had to give everything to his poor old mum.

Adam stated his reservations. "What we have done is good! Bloody good and we have to give it all to Simon. If we are not happy here we have some huge scraps ahead. So far parents have warned their precious ones to go somewhere else. Much more from us will give attention to the police. I do not need them."

Silence blanketed them as he carried on. "And what about the money? However much it is someone should have missed it? I haven't heard jack shit! It worries me. We will have to listen to Simon and stick together really close from now on. Well! That's what I think anyway."

The idea of the police sobered them all up.

Simon loved his praise. It was so rightful! "I agree with Adam. We will have to stick together alright. And we cannot do anything to involve the law. If any of us think we might do so, they should say. As for the money it is huge to us but squat to the owner. He is so rich the bank must have sucked up to him. I think we are in the clear there."

He hoped he sounded convincing. If rich people were like his father, the more they owned, the more possessive they were. He knew his father would never tolerate any such a loss.

"In the meantime look down there. Somebody is driving on our grounds. We had better see them piss off."

They all turned to see a little blue Beetle trailed by a ribbon of dust weave its way through the reserve entrance. This was too much and something they could address themselves right now! As a team they fought back to the BMW.

❋ ❋ ❋

The rapist inspected everything from the foot of her bed. Satisfied he had planned everything he could progress then. After all the advertising she had forced on him. You just cannot blow hot and cold, you know, at least not with me. The writhing, squirming furious figure now just part of the suite.

He posed in front of the huge mirror admiring his mask. Made it himself! All the best had masks, he knew. Batman, the Lone Ranger, the Phantom, all had special masks and like him they administered justice and retribution in their own form. Yet the press labelled him 'Monster', 'Serial', it was all so unjust. He yearned to explain and defend but he knew of mob mentality.

He had grown up with them, shared childhood secrets, supported them, surely such a monster they described could not walk amongst them. He felt their tacit approval by their very inactions.

Ever so gently he probed her. Perhaps some gel would minimize any discomfort. He smiled as he thought how best to apply some and casually lumbered over her, letting her struggles form the energy. He loved this part, and so did she, he could just tell these things, and by conversations overheard.

For a short interval, time had no meaning to him. He closed his eyes and bit his lip for such moments. In the end though the picture of her pose compelled him to finish his business quickly and efficiently. So clean he knew deep down she would come to appreciate that. No pregnancy, no disease, no forced trauma. Well, not physical anyway. That knowledge made him feel better somehow.

He stood to look and see that no evidence slipped by him. The tears and shaking he dismissed as inconsequential. In fact he was already contemplating a return visit. A sequel if you like. Yes, she would enjoy that!

He left her tied as she was. He picked up her cellphone and dialled emergency. Compassion was an essential part of his makeup.

He knew from past experience he had time to gather his departure and the authorities would check out the call soon enough. Finally, he looked round for his memento. So important! Leisurely he chose personal and closed the door quietly on the way out, wondering how or if the press would write up another success. He deserved at least that much.

❄ ❄ ❄

One weary eye looked at another from across the hospital room, neither registering. "Snapper, oh Snapper!" Holly whispered, daring to wake him. "About bloody time too!" she accused as he stirred.

"Lovely to hear your voice too!" Snapper did not try to keep relief out of his voice. He raised himself to full height. "Morgan wants to know as soon as possible. He has taken all this really badly!"

"No wait, please." Holly settled herself, now more relaxed. "You can stay a while, can't you?"

"Whatever you want," Snapper answered, still standing.

"Come and sit with me. That is a royal order, you know." Holly gazed around setting her bearings. She patted the side of her bed guiding his arm.

He sat down as gestured, waiting.

"Poor old Snapper. How is it you always get the crap shift, eh?" Holly flagged his response away before he could answer.

She took his hand in both of hers. "You know I love you just as much as Morgan. You are both big dumb oafs. I don't understand such a lapse in my judgment and I still have done nothing about it. What do you think?"

Snapper shrugged. "I love you so just as much and I am happy enough you are satisfied with Morgan. I have always felt such a debt, a heavy debt to you both. Things should have been different."

"It is your fault, you know!" Holly accused him. "If you had not been so besotted and made up a proper relationship instead of treating modest women as a piece of meat, things may have been different alright."

"That is so unfair!" Snapper reacted. "The small time I spent with you was real enough, or at least I thought so."

Holly tutted unsympathetically. "Yes, we had a short but marvellous fling. And I always still see that attractive young boy charm in you. Well, young man. But it was never enough, was it? You just had to practise whatever you had been taught on others. Sue started the ball rolling all that time ago when you nailed her in the back of that monster car of yours. She couldn't stop talking about it. Oh yes, we girls do chat about such things, you know. It is not just a man's prerogative. That is when we realized you treated each and every one differently. Industrious little bastard, weren't you?"

"I suppose," Snapper meekly conceded. "Apart from a few genuine cases I did learn a lot. It was not all fun though. The more I found out, the less appeal anybody had. Mostly it wasn't sex. More like a benign torture. But not with you. In fact you could say you were the catalyst. Up till then I always felt guilt. I always received far more than I gave and I determined to address that."

Holly was without sympathy. "You are a lying shit, Snapper! Don't you lay your guilt onto me, you bastard. Address that indeed! What crap! You had most of the starved female population queuing up but because of Lisa you just could not see them. We tried to talk Lisa your way but she was then what she is now. A stubborn obstinate bitch. God knows how we tried."

"Sorry!" was all Snapper could think to say. "I had better be off now and get your lord and master." He paused. "Do you want me to give Bob an explanation?"

"I can deal with it, myself. Poor boy! Good taste though. The last thing that poor boy needs is your heavy hand," she explained. "Besides, I have the perfect partner lined up for him, because he deserved something special. In the meantime I am prepared to indulge myself. It is not often a woman of my vintage can appeal to someone half my age. Having him spill his seed is a big a compliment as I can get."

Snapper shook his head. "You are as pure as the driven snow."

Holly smiled her smile. 'Tell you what. When I get out of here I am going to cook you all the damnedest meal at home."

❅ ❅ ❅

Morgan sat at his desk reviewing papers repeatedly. "Damned nothing is sinking in. Chief, tell me what is going on?"

Emphasis on his title put the chief suitably passive as he replied. "News on a few fronts, boss! We have sufficient evidence now as to who waltzed into the bank. We are picking them up now and I expect them not to be able to withhold questioning. I will not, myself, but I will oversee the operation."

"Good! Good!" Morgan seemed as pleased as Rupert had hoped. "I want a speedy trial on this if you can manage it. I want this out of the way as quickly and as quietly as possible."

"You mean your court?" the chief confirmed.

"Very astute of you," Morgan answered. "What else?"

Rupert started to warm up just a little. He wanted his worst news last. "A check of the hotels has not brought anything for Snapper. But at least we know where he hasn't been. We knew Eric Hood had a few girls on the side. He appears to have a few more than we anticipated. If the source proved conclusive we will move on him as well."

"Right now if he is not hurting anybody, and by that I mean visitors, with diseases you can defer him." Morgan had enough already and the chief was always bleating about resources. "Next?"

"There have been no unexplained deaths that would likely be attributed to Snapper. Perhaps he is on holiday."

"No, chief, he has been with me and I make an ideal alibi. But he never sleeps. I want you to keep an emphasis on him." Morgan began to worry.

"Finally, some good news," the chief concluded. "The doorman at the club apparently won lotto all by himself. So neither of us can contemplate retirement."

"Why is it that lotto always goes to the useless? He is too old to enjoy a fortune like that," Morgan observed.

"True enough, boss," the chief agreed. "There is a dark lining on the silver cloud as well. A few. No, better make that some have contemplated legal challenges."

"Bugger them!" Morgan snapped. "Sort out the biggest losers for me and I will deal with them in my court as well!"

"Rough justice," the chief observed. It had all gone down very well, considering.

❅ ❅ ❅

Chop smiled. "We have planted enough seeds for them to harvest Eric for the next decade and still they do nothing! I will never understand these people."

"I know! And our contacts cannot even confirm the Black Hole cameras, unless yours have?" Rooster agreed. "I cannot wait too long now for space in the freezer. Even though she has been in some demand. Mostly curiosity I think but a couple of genuine requests."

"Yes! Hopeless alright! I would have thought having to separate informants would have us avoid just this situation. Not only that but that American is trying to exert his influence too. I would love to know his sources and what he pays." Chop oozed exasperation.

"You don't think our informants are giving us an exclusive service?" Rooster observed. "Could explain a few things."

"Maybe," Chop conceded. "I think our penalty clauses are clear enough. Perhaps it is time to check them out anyway. You are a good boy, Rooster. No, if anything he will be in cahoots with Eric. Those types always stick together when it suits them."

❀ ❀ ❀

Bob wondered if the time was right for him to check on Holly. He definitely did not want to appear too keen. Plus he had left under such a cloud, discreet of course. For as long as he had felt this way about Holly, which was such long, long, brief times, he had coped well since he had met his new friend by chance at one of the local bars he always haunted.

Eric, his drinking buddy, noted his change in demeanour and before he could help himself Bob had outlined his dilemma. Eric, being the good friend, had coughed up the ideal solution. He had a lady friend who was willing to compromise as a more than suitable substitute. Eric's stocks skyrocketed in Bob's estimation. And he had met and slept with the woman numerous times.

Eric had been right! She turned out to be ideal. A mirror image! Not as refined, of course, and prone to asking endless questions and without the exquisite touches Holly had but nevertheless she knew how to be forceful, gentle and guiding. He grew to love being in her arms, being close, really close so that she smelt good and Bob could hear and see the end of her flowery curls catch and scrap against the enormous pillows. Best of all she seemed available and keen at any hour. Eric was indeed a true friend.

❀ ❀ ❀

Tim smiled to himself, a small self-congratulation. He pressed the increase size frame on his computer. There it was, his antidote. A volunteer would have been priceless, but not essential any more. This did not mean he did not need her for trials, more he needed her to complete his study. He leaned over and pressed Cedric's pager.

Cedric was in a foul mood. He wasn't making progress as

he anticipated, having made the breakthrough. Now some other beckoned him away from his work. He cursed and stomped towards Tim. "What is it now?"

Tim clapped his hands. "I have cracked it! Still some work to go, of course. But let me show you the antidote at work. Moreover, I am sure as there is only one host. So there will never be an epidemic as such. That is why it is so difficult. Now watch the screen."

Cedric sat sullenly. He was glad all attention was on the screen. While he watched, Tim's words demolished his hopes, his dreams. Cedric wanted worldwide attention for his work. He wanted international recognition, articles in the most renowned medical journals, interviews, who knows. At this rate he would have to pay to advertise his own success in the personal columns. What to do about it?

At the end of the screening an ecstatic Tim turned to him. "Well! What do you think?

Cedric put on his bravest face. "Wonderful! Still a lot of work to do. But you are right. You have cracked it. I realize the contagion is limited. I feel we should cultivate a few samples in case of mutations."

Tim stared at him. "Are you mad? We should knock it on the head as soon as we can. It is just a matter of locating the host. Just donkey work."

He thought for a few minutes. "Is there something you are not telling me? Your agenda has changed. What is going on in your head?"

Cedric waved his head in denial. "No! I am just so pleased at our success. I just don't want any screw-ups at this stage to ruin what we have achieved!"

❋ ❋ ❋

At the hospital Holly had seemed lifeless. Bob wasn't confident about his friends' ability to read her pulse nor their medical knowledge. He remained as close as he dared trying to give comfort and trying not to panic.

When after an eternity two surgeons announced that Holly was to be placed in an induced coma but she was in no real life-threatening danger.

Bob manoeuvred himself to stay first.

As soon as the others had left him to his lonely vigil he scurried into the men's toilets. After checking he was alone he secured himself from other visitors, sat in a cubicle and he cried and cried and cried. He cried at his relief, he cried at Holly's present state, he cried over his anguish he felt and he cried over the pain of his tension and trauma withdrawal and the effort that he had overextended during the whole interval.

By the time Bob returned to the room all evidence had dissipated. He waited out his replacement. In the long idle hours his thoughts turned to Holly's still body. The rhythm of the monitoring machines, the regularity of the different beats all reassured him. In the quiet and relief he shocked himself at an impulse to sneak into her bed, to lie beside her, maybe put her arm around him, explore, hear familiar scratchings of the pillow.

He was mortified by his thoughts and the more he suppressed them the more they pressed. Bob felt absolutely disgusted!

Worse was the scenario had he been caught; the resulting vilification, humiliation, the public knowledge, his total loss of community acceptance repeatedly haunted him.

By the time Morgan arrived Bob couldn't remove himself fast enough with any sense of propriety. He could afford to smile now though, pleased nobody suspected.

13.
Swingers

Clarence hated Horace with a passion!

He closed his wettened eyes and pushed down hard into the starched pillow seeking solace in oblivion. He determined to stay dead until it worked no matter what the discomfort.

Clarence loved golf and had done all his life. Unlike many others he was suited to the sport he loved. Like many others he had neither the final self-confidence nor support to the last big step up to professional status.

His vocation for life was therefore to the club as professional coach, tutor, mentor. His mandate all the things he never had. As with others in whatever profession they love and pursue he had built up ample successes and respect of the members.

Set for life!

The course, the club and clubhouse was designed exclusive, smelt exclusive, looked exclusive, felt exclusive, oozed exclusive. The club codes of conduct, dress and so on became so easy to police.

The tainted icing of the cake was Horace.

Horace was hated by most as the worst the English could tolerate. He looked down his nose at everybody and mostly talked down to all the same way. He loudly invoked Victorian morals, his anecdotes pointless and his laughter a full-out donkey bray, totally ignoring others' sensitivities and on every type of occasion.

"Just a new member for your swing, chappie!" Horace introduced the latest member to Clarence, whose now automatic reflex winced inside himself.

Horace was nothing if not predictable. But now instead Clarence smiled.

He knew well the underbelly of this elite. In fact he modestly considered himself a prime mover.

Clarence swivelled from refining the weight of a putter gripped steady in the vice.

He appraised the female form in the doorway rapidly and expertly. She had a full figure, tall but not yet running to age. He knew, as she advanced towards him, she would grow in beauty and stature, but his mind was elsewhere.

"Won't be a minute." He turned back to his work as he heard the familiar solid crunch of Horace's shoes leaving.

The throb of Horace's gnarled fingers over the individual and sets of woods and irons on sale beside the door: Horace always had this instinct to irritate Clarence to perfection. He had never even had to practise.

"Just a new member for your swing, chappie!" Clarence remembered always his first introduction of his very first pupil.

"Just a new member for your swing, chappie!" was the way Clarence later met Rubynn.

Back then he was just Clark but Rubynn convinced him he needed a title more in keeping with the club. It was all so harmless.

Rubynn had her usual share of faults but the one stubborn fault not to be remedied was her feet, or more correctly her posture. Despite a measure of companionship Clarence wasn't to be disturbed by Rubynn intruding in his personal space. And so he persevered.

Finally, during a tirade of frustration, he found brilliance.

He set to work immediately measuring a wooden contraption, adjusting the instep, realigning; he cancelled all lessons and other appointments. At the end of his labours he had constructed a wooden stock for her feet with pegs and cogs to anchor her feet securely in the precisely correct position. A sheer sleek polished burn ran its timber length. Wonderful!

Although it was now getting late in the day, Clarence rang Rubynn.

"I have the answer to your feet," he paused. "Got a cold?" Clarence was all concern.

"Too much to drink, if you must know," she replied. "I'll come right now. I am in the mood for anything."

"I promise you this will shorten your strokes!" Clarence boasted.

And drinking she had been.

"It looks like a set of old-fashioned stocks on the ground." She amused herself fitting her feet in with difficulty despite Horace's expectant attentions.

She stood there, breathing laboured by now flowing like seaweed anchored to the seafloor. It could never last and she fell back giggling.

"Look!" she cried. "No panties! And I promise you this will shorten your strokes!"

Clarence needed no second invitation.

And so began a series of physical gratifications, sometimes each together but not often. Not an affair. No romance. Love was never in their vocabularies. Their catchword 'shorten your strokes!'

Their mischief ended when Rubynn's husband was transferred. Theirs was one last graceful coupling but no tears, no real farewells.

Clarence then went back to his customary duties. He had always assumed this was their little secret and although he had used his contraption with success on other members he had not considered its use for other than legitimate purposes. He shelved the Rubynn experience into one of life's little compartments to bring out and dust off at his whim.

A blonde Amazon, Mrs Fitzpatrick, dusted it off for him one evening when she offered to 'shorten his stroke' and clambered into his contraption before he could reply.

Clarence truly admired the snow-white erotic mound. But he had his work cut out by a total lack of response. He laboured to finish desperately recalling everything that Rubynn had preferred. He closed his eyes and thought of many people. His final image was of a tepid white milk pudding congealed in a motionless container.

"You are not very good, are you?" Mrs Fitzpatrick was less than satisfied.

Clarence had always made it a point to always find something positive to say to his customers. He decided this was more of a statement than question. He said nothing.

"You men are all the same, you know. Find a real body and don't worry about the person." She was putting on her shoes.

If it was consolation it failed completely. "I guess it's a cross we have to bear!"

Clarence doubted he would be dusting this encounter at all.

Ever so cautiously other women requested his special lessons and equally cautiously Clarence obliged. He accrued a goodly number of members, some of whom he would not have otherwise considered at all.

At one point he pictured himself as the sleazy pro caricature he held in utter contempt. He saw no reason to stop.

Another time he was contemplating how to curtail the stroke play Horace's wife invited into his parish. Clarence simply could not resist. What was worse, or better, was that Horace's wife clearly expected to deviate, dominant, submissive, discipline, touring an imaginable spectrum. Clarence willed himself not a hint to Horace, else to bring an end his tutoring, and he was learning as well.

Not much of a secret, he realized. Even worse when a woman member asked if he was interested in selling or making a duplicate. When she confessed to running a house of ill repute, Clarence wondered if the whole world knew.

If the situation was obvious to him then surely other members would also make the connection. Some were pretty bloody sharp.

Still, if they knew, nothing had been said directly to him.

Clarence recalled conversations looking for the innuendos. But nothing and if members knew they at the very least tolerated him and still came to him for genuine lessons. Maybe they had a quiet admiration or envy of him. Perhaps they didn't care.

No, now he was getting paranoid but he would have to watch his step.

Some secret!

Horace introduced Toni. "Just a new member for your swing, chappie!"

For Clarence it was pure unadulterated animal lust at first

sight. Each fibre positively glowed. Yet to Clarence she was no ideal beauty. She had no flesh on her bones, which beautifully accentuated her breasts. Two balloons on a broom handle, he would have described anyone else. Bowlegged instead of designed to take a man, blonde and big-eyed; he adored wisps of facial hair at each corner of her mouth, which produced a quick pixie smile. Such was so unattractive in others.

When she smiled nothing of the world existed; his mind cheerfully overflowed. He never thought who cared, who knew and why he'd no attempts to hide his feelings. What was worst of all was Toni seemed completely oblivious to her natural charms. Most people he got to know but he met Toni for the first time repeatedly.

Clarence had found a perpetual virgin. He tried little deft touches and strokes he had learned or experienced from his harem without response. This lack limitlessly multiplied his passion.

Clarence laboured on her producing faults and in by remedying them installed another. He gleaned few personal trivia to hoard.

Occasionally he met her benefactor. He could not see what hold such a person could possess. A loud Yank, old, treated her not poorly but without sufficient due regard. Fortunately he had no interest in golf nor anything else from his conversations. Perhaps he was too old for anything.

He leaned forward to read the instructions left to him of the amended weight and balance.

Clarence thought of lessons and goals for the day coming and how to fit the woman standing there. He wondered what flaws she would have, guessing at a few from first sight. He wondered about Toni.

As Clarence arched his back in a relieving stretch from bending over his clamp he felt more a blur than an arm snake around his throat. He felt the elbow point lock under his jaw, the arm muscles gently squeeze and he slumped down.

When he revived the place was in shadows. His back pinched a little on the hard wooden floor from the angles his legs were locked by his own device. He peered around trying to make sense of it all.

"She-she," he heard, a low husky whisper. "Who's been naughty then?"

"What the hell's going on?" Clarence demanded.

"You bite hard on this!" She pulled out a wood from his rack and shoved the cover hard into his mouth. Examining the head she peered down at him. "Well! A number one. Well for number one you should have stuck to real golf lessons. Now I will be giving golf lessons."

She took a step back arcing the club behind her head. Clarence's eyes widened in disbelief and denial. He muffled loudly into his gag as she swung down.

The impact surreal!

Clarence's heartbeats shook the floor, his body one enormous deafening pulse. He lost against the force not to look up. He viewed carnage with complete dispassion, not recognizing flimsy cellophane tear-tab flesh as body, let alone his. A thinnest needle of agony gouged his soul, then another. He may have just tolerated a few but they multiplied so very fast. He may not have been able to count them any more but he could identify each single one.

"I am not sure if that was a cut or a slice." He heard her voice somewhere in the background.

Why was this happening to him? Every sex was consensual! He never made first contact! Some he had not really wanted! His gag was taking the force of his voice. He concentrated on his tormentor. She ignored him completely.

"Let's try this number two," she suggested conversationally. Wiping the first wood and substituting a number two. "This gives me no pleasure, you know?" She was coming back over to him.

Clarence screamed and pleaded at her, squirming at the immediate prospect. She shook her head at him and swung again. This time he knew unadulterated agony instantly. He was sure one would have had to die before you could feel such pain.

He fainted away. He never knew the third wood caused the real damage.

Such a nightmare bore no resemblance to reality as he slowly came round. He could sense and feel long before he could see.

He moved his body ever so slightly and the agony spoke loudly to him of injuries. Yet he could not breathe. At least his legs were now free, if reluctant to move.

She waited patiently, pressing her foot on the iron placed across his throat.

When she felt she had his attention she leaned over and hissed at him. "Well, now, better to stick to golf lessons from now on or I will be back to have a session with the irons. I hope you better understand me?" and she jerked the sodden material from his mouth.

He just lay there prostrate taking large sighing gasps of breath. She threw down the iron and stalked out.

Clarence stared at his wooden stock. Revulsion so substituted pride! In the same vigour that he had made it he was now utterly determined to destroy it!

He groaned as he rolled over. He reached for the gag and reinserted it more gently this time and gritting his teeth he bit as he moved. He remembered pulling up his Rios as best he could though they sagged down like an over-full nappy. He treated himself to a little rest.

He fainted how many times on his trip to his invention and finding no physical strength to destroy it, seized upon multiple inflammable materials at hand to bandage it enough destroy its existence.

He gave himself as much strips as he dared for a lengthy fuse and lit it. He dragged his body ever so slowly towards the door. But his body could only survive a limited time on nerves and willpower and he collapsed at the opening of the door and the silhouette.

"In God's name put that bloody fire out! Help me with this poor chap!"

The rest was a welcome darkness.

Clarence leaned back gingerly on the hospital bed waiting for the deputation from the club; the nursing staff had told him they had been asking about him for a couple of days.

He put on his best expression as Horace's face appeared at the door. He drummed his knuckles on the door as if strict etiquette still needed to be observed. Others hovered into his room behind him.

"We haven't been able to piece together what happened or why, I am afraid. The police are pretty keen to speak to you, but first we ought to make this little presentation."

Horace patted him on his shoulder. "We managed to save some of your contraption. We have made quite a trophy out of it, for all of your efforts, you know. Would you like to read the plaque?"

Clarence said nothing.

His already reddened eyes glazed. The dark patches matured to full circles while his complexion waxed. A solitary tear rolled slowly down the side of his nose blending with small pools of mucus.

"Well, I suppose we may have been a bit presumptuous. We will monitor your progress of course, dear boy. But stiff upper lip. Remember, take it like a man!" Horace left hastily with the others. Immediately they had gone Clarence's face contorted in spasms. His groin ached despite his memories. Tears ran freely.

Clarence hated Horace with a real passion!

14.
And Again

"Good morning, chief! In all the excitement I sheer forgot my manners. I apologize. Get me up to speed, won't you?" Morgan had slept well indeed.

"Right!" answered a taken-aback chief. "Firstly we have the little bastards. Two of them anyway. One poor little fellow who didn't wait for questioning. When we approached him his father insisted on a full statement without a solicitor. Sometimes the poor but proud make life easier. Anyway it quickly became obvious he is the dupe.

"The other is a natural ringleader and the centre of some minor complaints. He could go places if we don't watch him! They are both free at the moment but if you want to 'court' them first that will be no trouble. I have also sorted out a good lotto case. Why are the stupid the most greedy?

"Anyway, I have scheduled them in for ten a.m. today and the kid's tomorrow same time. That way you can spend more time with your patient. It should be all very straightforward for you."

"Thanks, chief. I prefer the kids first thing after lunch. Give me the morning to read your summary and papers and I will knock them off. You can handle everything else OK? Good."

Chief shook his head leaving. Today he didn't like to be overturned.

❀ ❀ ❀

Adam looked around in disgust and growing apprehension. Simon was never late like this. His day was always planned. Just maybe he was beginning to hide away the most of his booty. He was never one to share more than necessary. A family trait, he supposed.

Others horsed around and in the car. Occasionally peering into the streets to see what interruptions if any might be on the horizon. Adam spoke at last, impatiently. He couldn't wait any more. "Look, you guys, wait here a bit longer. I am going to see what I can find out."

He was summarily dismissed. "Yeah! Fine! Alright! Whatever." None of the others had concerns.

Adam hurried off searching the main streets while heading for his favourite alley. Nothing was out of the ordinary. He spun into his alley looking back and was hit by a floral-shirted wall.

"Please, mister," he whined, "I am diseased throughout!" How big was this guy? He felt dwarfed.

From somewhere above a quiet voice spoke to him. "I don't give a shit! No! Don't look around, in fact turn and face the street." Adam found himself spun on the spot. A single heavy hand placed on his shoulder, he was immobile.

"Please, mister," he started again.

"Shut up!" came the interjection. "We have already been there. What is with your health anyway?"

"Don't you know anything?" Adam surprised himself as he began. "This is Flintstone Alley. Nobody comes up here without cause."

"Just a tourist," came the explanation from above. "Keep your eyes front now. What is this alley then?"

"Only used for gay purposes," Adam replied. He noticed a constant pressure on his shoulder. All he experienced with tight grips was you hung on for grim death until exhausted. Now part of the wall had morphed out and anchored him.

"Nobody has approached me," the stranger observed.

"I don't know what to say." Adam began to feel the threat perhaps subside. "Maybe your dress sense."

"All this from a boy who hangs around cemeteries, means you should sit in judgment?"

Adam just stood there shocked. How did anybody know this?

Especially the guy behind him! "How did you know that? Never mind. I go there to sit and talk to my friend Gus."

Adam wondered how many knew of his habits. He felt the grip loosen just a little. He was still stuck fast.

"The cemetery is full. How do you know who is talking to you? There must be some mean spirits buried there."

Adam replied simply, "Gus is the only one I know."

"OK, then. Suppose you tell me what you are up to and don't lie. I already know about the cemetery, remember? The whole truth now."

The tight grip returned emphasized danger. "I use this alley because I know I won't be followed. A friend stole a wad of money. Now he is trying to cheat me of my share by hiding bits around the city. I think I know mostly where so I am off to help myself."

Adam felt that was a fair summary.

"Where?" A single-word question.

Adam thought. "Parts of the old school, down by the Black Hole, under the container, and in the ruins." Though he did not list everything. That would just be plain foolish.

The stranger was thoughtful for a moment. "Tell me about the container."

"At the back of the North's freight yard there is an old container on its side. If you can raise the lid and crawl underneath there is a space where a machine for the container used to be. If you are going there you are too big and the lid needs to be propped up safely."

Adam left nothing out.

"Cemetery boy. You stay away from that container. Instead you can go to the car yard where you bought your car with stolen money. At the very back is a wreck of a bus. The rear seats are well padded. Seems a fair exchange." The visitor suddenly knew a hell of a lot. Adam worried even more.

"Thanks!" he said. "What about my cut?"

"Well! I have a small knife, and a large knife. What cut do you want, cemetery boy?"

"I can give it a miss," Adam answered. He had somehow easily gone from relative safety into danger, again.

"Walk back to the main street and don't look back. You may want to think about taking a different road to your friends." Snapper dismissed the youth.

Adam walked ahead puzzled wanting to look back but he had something new to concentrate on. The stranger knew some things surprisingly but was oblivious to others. He made a mental note to check him out later. Then he scrapped it.

❊ ❊ ❊

Bob flitted around Holly, helping her get ready to leave. Preening, caring, tutting, until Holly was completely sick of the attention.

"Go and wait in the car." She finally exhausted herself.

Home comfort was her only priority, diminishing her sensitivity to others by the second. She knew Morgan would be working while she longed for solitude.

Bob walked her bags out with an upbeat jaunt swallowing and chewing away absentmindedly.

❊ ❊ ❊

Snapper sat there too chewing his brunch remorselessly mechanical motions repeatedly over the each same mouthful, looking at nothing. Even though the eating house was full with diners and noise he could feel her eyes, her impatience bearing down on him.

He reminded himself of the objectivity of the lesson and how it had saved him on many occasions.

The first to move, to breathe, to step in or up, always gave the advantage to the adversary mostly fatally. Would she learn the essentials? So much to take in. He was lucky to have had a communicative tutor. What about her?

Miranda sat impassively opposite him seething inward. Having tried to imitate Snapper's eating habits she had long ago given up. She sat keen to hear his words. "Well?" she surrendered. "How was your meal?"

Snapper thought back. She had done better than he had at the same time. But had she learnt?

"Here." He passed her an envelope. "Our client is very pleased with your efforts. And I think you have done well. Not too much, not too little, listened to the client's request, listened to me. Very good indeed."

Miranda wallowed in the unexpected praise. Her anticipation of how to improve comments was groundless. From now on she would try not to anticipate. Snapper had been right. It filled life with red herrings and unnecessary anguish. She felt deep fulfilment that had been missing all her life.

Snapper leaned forward. "You still have to take the last final step, and it is a big one. Anyone can beat anybody up. This doesn't differentiate you from the masses. I have decided to give you something completely different this time. Being typecast has been the downfall of many."

Miranda felt her heart race. She was still so keen to be seen to do a good job. "Tell me more?" She smiled at him.

"I want you to go to a disco, boogie the night away." Snapper read her disappointment. "I will tell you more as we walk. I have a court sitting to attend to shortly, and I don't want to be late."

❋ ❋ ❋

He sat by himself outside the big hall, a lonely sculpture. Some things just didn't seem right. He surveyed around without moving. Adults everywhere, some he knew, others he knew of. Should he just wait?

Simon nursed his ear. The smack his father delivered surpassed previous blows of which there had been many.

When he looked after his father in his old age Simon would remind him of this moment then he would rip his ear off and make him eat it, slowly. There was justice, surely.

The priest's sidekick had come up to him. When Simon looked up Louie didn't even look down. "You are a dumb little shit! On security as plain as day!" and with that he just walked away.

His father was laughing with his legal rep and shaking hands. Surely his rep should be speaking to him. Perhaps his father had sold him out. That's what it looked like. And now he thought about it, where were the bankers?

No! This stunk somehow!

The door at the far end of the hall creaked open. The ghost of Eugene wafted in family company. Simon had never seen anybody so pale. If Eugene was going to be a witness against him then this witness was dead meat. And so was he.

Neither individuals nor families acknowledged any other presence.

A shorter old grey fellow finally came up to him, shaking his head. "Simon?" he asked.

"That's right."

"Well! You are going to be in a tribunal in a minute or two. It is not a real court as such and it is done this way to avoid giving you a conviction." He reached into his pocket. In his palm he showed a small purple flower, hardly more than a bud. "You know what this is?"

"Yes," said Simon. "It is a sacred flower for the most part but where did you get it? And who the hell are you anyway?"

"I am a chief of the police assigned to the minister who will be presiding over your case. If you want the flower take it and wear it with pride. It may help you. God knows you need it. I would recommend it myself, but it is up to you."

Simon took it hesitantly. "I don't know what is going on."

"OK," Rupert explained to him. "Your legal rep has already given the minister or judge your version of events in writing and I have given the legal side in writing so he has had plenty of time to read all arguments. But before he makes a decision he likes to hear what you have to say, and anybody else. That is where we are at now."

A tall thin usher swallowing hard came out of the room gesturing all to enter.

This is great, Simon thought to himself. No conviction, they can't take back the money if he doesn't have it. Nobody would find where he salted most of it.

His legal counsel came over. "Thank you, chief. Come on, you boy. Now just do as you are told, if you can." He looked appraising Simon over.

He demanded, "Where did you get that flower? Never mind that now but the justice will ask you about it. Just don't be smart."

He paused, as if he didn't know where to start. "Just talk as if normal conversation. Don't rush things and don't garble. Your ear looks agony. Show the court as much as you can of that side. You need to do as much as you can to work in your favour."

Inside the presiding figure sat by himself with papers open in front of him. No other records, no microphone Simon could see. To one side sat the chief and the local churchman. Aside sat a big man alone with no interest displayed in proceedings. Now Simon had seen him up close he realized this was his victim and he worried. He looked to the churchman and saw a family resemblance with the court.

He was doomed!

He tried to avoid eye contact until he realized the stranger already dismissed eye contact with everyone present. Briefly Simon thought of him as a caged animal but he had more pressing issues and he discarded the thought.

Two other tables had been set aside. One for his family of which there were a few and Eugene's of which there were many. Simon wondered which was better.

Everybody sat down.

Morgan started. "This is what I know. The bank was entered before noon and a large withdrawal made illegally. Earlier that morning a factory was trespassed resulting in a fatality. Both youths have been caught on security tapes, at the factory and on the street. Simon here was taped entering the Citadel bank and withdrawing funds before returning to the street where the rest of the group waited."

He nodded to the counsels. "There is no disagreement here," one replied. "Same!" said the other.

"What we need to know is the method by which the information was gathered." Morgan hoped his tone was neutral as he felt he was bleating through the motions.

He continued, "We have retained a recording device containing information necessary to make the withdrawal and the device belongs to Eugene."

Simon's heart beat. Eugene would have spoken but was obviously not permitted. This all looked good.

"Eugene! You have something to say?" Morgan invited him.

"Yes! It was, is, mine." A small squeaking voice trembled acknowledgement. "But I loaned it out. I didn't use it. Surely your security confirms that."

"No!" Morgan dashed his hopes. "Simon, you were present, in fact taking an active role. Do you wish to speak?"

Simon stood up, his mind racing. "Yes, sir, I was as you say where you have said. No doubt about it. And I handled Eugene's camera. But I don't know how it works. Maybe if I had more time I could. You will have to ask the owner if you need to know more. I cannot help you. I am so sorry!' He paused, guessing at unspoken messages from his lawyer.

"And it was only me who went into the bank. I had to take the risk or suffer from the others. It was not easy for me and it hasn't been easy since. I am so glad it is now all out in the open."

"Thank you, Simon!" Morgan had heard all. "I notice you have the national bloom. Almost impossible to get, I understand. You know what it means?"

Simon nodded. "Yes, the wearer has a long prosperous life or a short violent one." He sat down without waiting. His lawyer winced!

"Sit back down." Morgan sighed impatiently quiet. "Yes, father, I see you wish to comment."

"I do indeed. Stop playing with the boy. I know you earned such a stem yourself the hard way. You seem happy to ignore what doesn't suit you." Rev Long grew agitated.

Papers from the two files spilled out. Morgan hastily gathered them up. The chief looked on in quiet amusement. His boss never dropped anything. He would just have to be patient and see how things would unfold.

Long waited. He continued, "Eugene is cast as the villain here but I know him as a quiet boy. Never been in trouble before, comes from a good family with strong values. I know it is a poorer part of the island, nevertheless he has made real efforts to improve himself."

Simon choked back a strong urge to not only giggle but more to roar with mirth. He looked down daring not to give himself away. This was all just beyond belief.

He listened attentively now as the church minister droned on. "The lad has recently found himself a good solid stable girlfriend, which may develop into something permanent and wholesome. A sentence would jeopardize all this and should be taken into account."

Simon bowed down lower than ever. A stifled sneeze the only sign betraying his tremendous effort struggling with his self-control.

Morgan spoke at last. "Alright! I have heard enough. Eugene, you have been in the centre of everything wrong. You have had the most to lose and gain. It is your equipment that demonstrates your intent and your arrogance by your lack of respect in that you have not even deleted the most basic of incriminating evidence."

He spoke accusingly: "You have sought to blame others and your refusal to co-operate in providing any information asked of you demonstrates to me the contempt that you hold this society.

"I have taken into account the minister's testimony and your youth. You are therefore to spend the next two months in The Marks offshore. There you should consider your actions and your future."

Every word struck Eugene physically!

The chief looked a little bemused but satisfied.

"Is the boy's father in court?" Morgan demanded.

A man stood unsteadily using the table for support.

"Your name?" Morgan demanded.

"Boyd!" he answered, an upset single word.

His tone lost to the process. "Well, how can you be proud of what you have permitted? Your son out all hours, stubborn refusal to respect authority. Did you not wonder about his new-found wealth? It would have given me cause for concern!"

The preacher stood up; little purple veins on his nose and neck ballooned out against a mottled complexion. "How dare you? How dare you? Everybody knows the wealth came from the girl! Didn't I just tell you he was poor?"

Morgan breathed out hard. "What do you say, Boyd?"

Boyd stood silently for a moment. "In our generation we would not have accepted from the girl. But now it has all changed. I don't know what else to say. We accept your ruling and at the end of sentence I will just have to try harder!"

"Simon." Morgan turned to the other. "You have been caught up in bad company. I understand your desire to appease others and the hardship in opposing their combined willpower. I appreciate all you have said in court. You therefore have been given an equal sentence of time but you will spend it on probation."

Long leapt to his feet. Others cowered before his temper. He struggled to get his words out.

Spittle shot from an over-pressured body. "This is preposterous! Your ruling equates exactly to the numbers of votes you receive from each community. I have never been so appalled in my life!"

Morgan snarled back at him. "You forget yourself! This is a court of law, not some personal grandstand! I will not tolerate such contempt from anybody!

"If you do not like the proceedings you do not have to be a part of them. The papers are always here for you to sign! Now if you like! I can find a replacement easy enough.

"If you feel so strongly then use your substantial church funds in support of the boy's appeal. I will listen to them whenever is convenient for you!"

The minister sat. "I have no such funds available!"

Morgan stood. "Well! That concludes this sitting. I thank you all!" and he stalked out.

Simon looked up at his father. Tears covered his cheeks still overflowing from his eyes, his lips quivered.

His father gave him a thumbs-up victory sign and he looked pleased. This was unusual in itself. Silas congratulated the legal counsel. "Wonderful job! Wonderful result!"

"Well, this was not all my doing, you know. I don't know if I have done all I could for Simon." The lawyer was concerned.

"Relax! It's all over now and we can move on." Silas was elated. He took his son by the shoulder. He had won again.

"There may be more," the solicitor warned.

Silas turned on him so rudely severing this moment of triumph. "What? You want more fees. I suppose you have earned it. Name your price?"

"No! Only you will know the price!" his counsel capitulated.

Simon held his father. Perhaps he was not so bad. "Wanker," he whispered in the elder's ear.

"That's right," Silas agreed. "The world is full of them!"

"Amen." Simon had the last word.

As they all filed out Morgan leaned over to the chief. "What do you think? The boy will survive?"

The chief looked back at him. "I am beginning to suspect you have just made sure he will be the only one to survive."

15.
Yields Dividends

MORGAN PRESIDED OVER HIS next court official-ishly. Intense public interest demanded respectability. He looked over at the three in court nestled up to their lawyers and then gave Cad the same scrutiny sitting humbly by himself.

Morgan had made a special effort to ensure Snapper had a seat close to him. They were as close as anybody had seen with Cad. He even accepted Long having a prime seat dressed in his regalia.

Morgan clapped his hands for quiet. "The summary is not contested by either party?" He held up the winning ticket in its cellophane wrapping. Unconsciously he rubbed it between finger and thumb for luck. Just a little slip of paper worth the effort and triumph for the victor. He caught himself and sheepishly placed it open in the middle of the table. "The ticket was bought by Cad at the club and is the sole winning ticket?"

"That is so," one of the men's counsel agreed. "The background is in question!" The others gave their support.

"The background being that all four men have been in a syndicate for some time. The same numbers and each having a turn. And on this occasion Cad had his turn."

Morgan looked for confirmation from the group and received a strong endorsement from each except for one who spent the entire proceedings head down facing the floor.

"Like most syndicates at the club there are no formal records, nor informal records at all." Morgan finished. "And there is the rub. Do I believe the four of you for what is common practice or do I believe Cad who bought it by himself?"

He shook his head. "This is difficult, indeed. The three of you have almost identical stories, times, dates, winnings all of which checks out."

They all waited for the murmur of the public gallery to cease. "Do any of the law representatives have anything to add?"

Their spokesman stood up. "I am instructed to say the evidence is overwhelming. The records date back a substantial period and all verifiable by public record. It is all conclusive."

Morgan's demeanour turned serious. "That's right. To my mind, all the details being remembered by all of your clients is extraordinary. I, myself, could tell you, for instance, how to get to the town centre from here but I could not be certain of the names of all the streets and the twists and turns required."

The spokesman shot up again, upset. "What is it you are implying? There is a suggestion here you already have a decision!" The group looked uncomfortable, their legal representatives disturbed at the unexpected direction this session was taking.

"Not at all!" Morgan reassured them. "I merely wish to emphasize the seriousness of these proceedings. One party or the other will be found wrong and will face real court time and sentences to match the gravity of the claims made. I point out to you that this is the last opportunity to revise your claim before we reach the point of no return.

"I will recess for sufficient time for you to consult your clients and receive what will be your final instructions. I hope I am making myself very clear about this. There will be no room for misunderstandings."

"Understood completely," the three representatives acknowledged.

"Good! Good! You have twenty minutes by which time I will return. The public gallery may well wish to take advantage of the break as well," Morgan granted them as he raised himself for his brief absence.

When he returned nothing had changed noticeably. Certainly the public gallery was not about to budge. Cad and Snapper sat back calmly without showing overly concern.

"Well! Do you all wish to proceed?" Morgan invited them.

The counsels all nodded.

"No! I want to hear your decisions by each of the group!" Morgan demanded angrily.

Two stood immediately. "Yes! We demand our right to justice!" they announced.

"What about you with your head down? You don't look too elated to be set for life! Will you look up?" Morgan instructed the third.

He raised his head and looked around. "I have agreed to continue," he spoke quietly.

Morgan gave him a long scrutiny. "I know you! You look familiar indeed," he virtually accused.

"Boyd!" he responded. "You have dealt with my son!"

"Right! Of course!" Morgan confirmed. "Well, you had better sit with your compatriots."

He beckoned to Bob ever hovering in the background. "There is one simple test for you to pass. Over in a matter of minutes really!" Morgan tried to pacify his complainants.

"Right!" Morgan instructed. "My colleague will give you pen and paper and you write down answers to my simple questions."

The spokesman stood up. "This is most irregular! This is a judicial court and we expect court procedures to be followed." The others murmured agreement.

"Too bad!" Morgan shouted them down. "This is my court and I decide what will happen. If your clients fail you will have plenty of opportunity for court procedures. I can promise you that!"

They sat reluctantly watching their clients painfully.

"Now to carry on." Morgan was back to pleasantries. "Each of you is to write your full name and telephone number. My assistant will check when you have finished so take all the time you need." He ignored a rise in tempo from the public gallery.

"All correct!" proclaimed Bob with a minimum of checks.

"See?" reassured Morgan cheerfully. "Nothing difficult about these proceedings."

The lawyers struggled in their seats but said nothing.

"Second question," Morgan continued. "I want you each to

write a family birth date. Any member you can remember. It is important you get it correct so take your time, please."

The spokesman stood in alarm. "This is highly irregular. What you ask for has nothing to do with the case. It is improper as we have not covered this dubious aspect in briefings and we have not received instructions from our clients."

"All correct!" Bob cut in.

The gallery leaned forward as one. Morgan picked up the winning ticket and held it to read in front of him.

"Lastly, I have the winning ticket here," he waved it to the gallery. "There are ten lines purchased of which nine are not prize winners. All you need to do is write any three sets of numbers of those nine lines. I will even let you confer with each other, if you see the need. Now it is still important you are accurate so take your time, as before."

All three lawyers leapt to their feet. They all had the same aghast, frantic, defeated expressions. "This is preposterous! What sort of mockery is this? My client will have nothing to do with this charade!"

Morgan turned to the gallery. "By way of explanation, if the syndicate have bought the same numbers for as long as alleged, if the syndicate chose the numbers, if the syndicate had knowledge of the others' selections, they would most likely be from something they know personally. Birthdays, for example. Perhaps telephone numbers? The answers should be as easy as the first questions."

Boyd sat heavily and screwed his paper up. The others looked bewildered. This had not been part of their rehearsals.

Cad sat impervious to the chaos around him. Snapper sat beside him wearing a slight smile.

'Enough!" Morgan growled on his feet. "It is clear to me now what actually eventuated. Your three clients face serious criminal charges and your individual conducts will come under scrutiny. This judgment is the owner of the lotto winnings is the legal and clear and only recipient. I hope he is set for life. Are there any other matters in these proceedings before this case is closed?"

Snapper raised himself and the gallery went quiet. "I wish to speak on behalf of the defendant 'Boyd'."

Morgan sat back down. "I thought you were in support of the winner, not the complainants."

Snapper gestured with his hands. "That is so. But I feel strongly enough to comment and commit to this citizen." He began: "Boyd has lost all. I don't mean money although he has lost that as well. He has lost all his values, entirely. All his life he has followed others as he has been brought up and been taught to depend on for his own wellbeing. All the institutions he has depended on, relied on, supported are destroyed, completely.

"All his good works of which there are many he realizes now are not for the greater good, not for the community, not for his church, not for his society, not for institutions but a facade for decisions of individuals. And they stripped him destitute! Left him to find his own feet at the moment he needs support to re-find his own goals. He will no longer be a servant of others."

Quite right! Long agreed in his mind. He has so lost a very valuable member for his church. He will no doubt still volunteer but his wholehearted contribution is gone, and what to do about it? Because it could spread!

Morgan frowned. "Rubbish! He is his own man and he has family, sort of. He has been given every opportunity to stop at any time. He knew the consequences but has not seen fit to act on them." Mentally he tossed a coin. "What I will do is sentence him to The Marks for the same time as his son, so he may contemplate on his own situation. The others may consider themselves to be on bail until official proceedings commence."

He turned to Bob. "Now! Clear the rooms!" And he walked out.

❋ ❋ ❋

The banker had been content in his past and in the midst of this noisy hall he reflected back. After all this was where it all began.

Conrad had outstanding organizational skills which only he did not appreciate. But others including the church did, including many dances and concerts.

He had met Molly here right on this very spot.

He was chatting to her about, well, he could not recall, when she asked if something was amiss. "I need to scratch my balls," he had said without thinking. So she did for him there and then right in public. "Be gentle?" He was bemused at such a public transgression nobody else even noticed.

"No!" she simply replied.

Conrad smiled at the memory. It was the start of a solid relationship. Both held no secrets from each other and supported any ideas regardless of how they thought privately.

Conrad's climbing up the banks rungs was largely Molly's drive. He, alone, probably would not have mostly applied. The couple had no children but not from lack of trying.

It all came to a tragic end when Molly one day just fell over. She had an undiagnosed heart condition all her life and this day it caught up with her.

Conrad carried on as before, organizing, helping customers with money matters gaining greater respect and public stature still only he did not realize. His life was complete.

Then one dark day long ago the Minister of Justice and bank officials requested him to freeze an account without explanation or justification. Conrad protested mightily not only at the legality but he had read the papers, heard the gossip and knew this was a danger to himself personally.

Morgan gave such solid reassurances Conrad had tentatively believed, added to which he had no real option anyway. Now it had come back to haunt him, seriously.

He mused as to how he would be remembered. So many prestigious people who had done so much were remembered by a solitary senseless act. Was this to be his act? Not tonight, he knew, glancing at his protection, laughing, clapping, enjoying themselves at the dance along with the others.

All in all Conrad was satisfied. Soon enough the night would finish and, as mostly, he helped clean up and lock up afterwards. Despite his popularity, his blinkered vision meant he mostly left alone.

Out of the midst a new, very attractive woman emerged to thank him for his efforts. She was no longer a juvenile by any means but still very, very impressive.

Conrad liked her body. Her perfume or scent or whatever was intoxicating, added to her appeal. She had come with a party but had cast them aside during the evening. Her offer to help clean up was readily accepted.

Conrad looked over to his protection. The knowing wink confirmed all his hopes. He felt safe in the knowledge she was not Snapper.

In comfort on top of his bed she was as light as on her feet. Conrad liked that and now inside they were clumsy and giggly.

She subtly helped guide him through pretence of foreplay. He rediscovered repressed appetites and enthusiasm. He tried to recall how Molly had been pleased and went through a moment of guilt even though his period of mourning had been generous.

She encouraged him with deft moves and soft praise while he responded. He couldn't remember how time went. He savoured every second. Suppressed urges overwhelmed him completely and he gave into them completely.

Finally he lay there totally exhausted fighting off incessant demands for sleep. Conrad's confidence grew in that short interval. With her by his side he knew he could be a definite place on the board instead of present temporary status. He held her tight and felt strong hands stroke his head, guided into her bosom. How he loved her smells, her comfort. He would have to say so much in the morning but for now he was so very, very tired.

How lucky was he to have such a second chance? Hell! He still didn't even know her name!

The perfume was indeed heavy stuff. Conrad coughed a little to get his breath. His mind fuelled of crazy ideas of bank services. Things he would never have thought of before. Right now they seemed so logical as they flashed past. He hoped he could remember them later. Breathing was getting difficult for some reason he did not understand as he nestled deep into his comfort.

He tried hard to stay awake but he felt so overcome by sleep as he happily rested his eyes.

She looked down. How could death be so arbitrary? Here was such a good man! Somebody she should have met long ago. She gently caressed him and held him rocking slowly from side to side. He had done so much good even she was proud of him and his achievements.

She allowed tears to flow freely.

As he slowly chilled so did her demeanour. She knew even had she known him their relationship would never have lasted.

She gently wiped his body with a hand towel she had carefully placed in her bag with other personal items. Finally she put him to bed and slipped out without a single glance back.

16.
The Lid

RUPERT SHOOK HIS HEAD. Surely this morning could not surpass yesterday's. He sighed loudly and gratefully accepted the implied temporary sanctuary his office door offered.

"Matt! Get in here!" He had begun his day on a loud note. Then he paused. At least be objective.

"Morning, staff!" he challenged overly cheerful but not pausing for response and shut his door closely behind his staff.

"Morning, boss!" Matt began. "There are some issues to report."

"Go on!" he was prompted.

Matt tried the obvious first. "The kids have been decided. Not the way I would handle it but well? The kids can be considered a success and nothing more to pursue. Another serial rape. Nothing different from the others but we must get a break. This is an open sore we need to lance as soon as. It is my continuing highest priority. I have not heard from the banker lately. The closing of the games has raised our staff resources pretty much as we anticipated," Matt reported.

"Forget banking! You are wrong about the kids! I want whatever protection you can afford until I say otherwise," Rupert instructed. "I know resources. And you can tell me why there are still expensive cameras sitting on your desk? The closing of the games doesn't mean we can wind down for some time yet so keep the pressure on."

Matt smiled meanly. "I need you to trust me on this one, boss. I know what I am doing. And by the way you have reminded me. I have a couple of shyster lawyers on my back. We don't have a couple of lotto claimants in custody, do we? I have made the usual checks. It seems they have disappeared."

"Not to my knowledge. Given their unpopularity they have probably gone to ground. I know I would have." Rupert appeared unconcerned. "Ask their agents if they have been paid yet. Our staff are not someone else's collection agency."

❀ ❀ ❀

Tim peered into his research. He was worried. Now he wanted out but how to do it gracefully? Cedric was no fool but he was changing. Deteriorating badly. Not always immaculate, now he whined over his departed brother. His conclusions and hypotheses not always complete, not by his standards. He decided on the Petri dishes already in his hands. If they did not successfully cultivate should be sufficient.

Cedric looked sideways at his assistant. Tim had lost enthusiasm just when Cedric needed it. He would have to go but how to do it without being obvious?

Other staff were easier. Their contribution relatively small and insignificant.

Tim's concentration on other projects in the past were acceptable but not now when Cedric wanted so much plus he was convinced Tim was smarming round those inspectors. No! It was time for him to go, and not necessarily with grace.

What was the biggest problem at the moment? It was growing the bug! They had it for small periods but life proved elusive. Yes! Cedric decided. That was it. If Tim's Petri dishes continued to fail would provide adequate grounds. Especially now he thought the solution was in one of his options.

Cedric looked over at Tim. Tim acknowledged him with a nod. Both smiled.

Turning his back Tim held his thumb over the thin glass phial, a thumb vacuum holding inside clear liquid. Checking Cedric was not watching he lifted his digit. Two, maybe three, drops fell into the small clear oval below. Immediately fluid clouded milky circles widening from the centre. Like egg whites his potion almost at once settled and blurred into the surroundings. Tim was happy.

His part was now complete except to wait and mentally rehearse his already refined anguish. Time to throw in his easier deflection. "What about your brother? He has been dead a while now. People are beginning to speculate!"

Cedric nodded without looking up. What a nag! He always brings this up! That settles it — he has got to go!

"Well, I still have to make peace with Cyril. I know it seems odd but it is a very personal thing. Then he can share his life with his wife forever. Thanks for reminding me." Cedric sounded sickening pathetic. He felt he could throw up. Instead he smiled a brief acknowledgement to Tim and they happily turned back to work.

❊ ❊ ❊

Simon looked around, guilt and greed searching for any sign out of the ordinary. Satisfied! Casually now he threw his bulging duffel bag over his shoulder. "I'm out of here, Dad. Thanks very much for the ride."

His father's car pulled neatly to the kerb. "Just relax now. And don't get into any more trouble. Your mother loves you so. She has taken all these mischiefs of yours very badly."

"OK, Dad!" Simon waved goodbye. What was happening? His father was now not the imposing figure he once was. Still a very small shaky bridge over a massive gulf. And if his son had done the same to him, his son would have got the same as well, perhaps more, Simon conceded. His own plans were not changed.

As he strolled towards one of his hideouts he wondered about such things as he waited, scanning the surroundings. Looking for the smallest of changes. He even felt he could part with some of his own money, not salt the lot.

No! Stop, he wondered why this would be. His father was loaded. Yet his father had never expressed concern for his mother before, nor anyone or thing.

Simon had plenty of time to think, he knew. Waiting, watching hidden, maybe up to two hours or more in the shadows of overhung machinery. Simon did not want to jeopardize his money. He was sure his gang was watching him and Adam was a real curse. Nobody could guess how much Adam actually knew. He hated secretive people, he decided. Still no movement at all at the old derelict container. Perhaps he should wait just a little longer. Simon stretched himself out for comfort. For the moment everything was as good as it gets. Perhaps, after all, nobody else knew of his sanctuaries.

❈ ❈ ❈

Snapper wore his serious face as he leaned forward in his seat. Miranda leaned towards him in unconscious response. "Well done. Did you have any misgivings? At all? Going all the way is a major step, you know?"

Miranda exercised her shoulders. "I had my moments, I admit. It is still one big learning curve and I have had a good professional approach. A good teacher. Do you have another assignment for your star pupil?"

"Yes! But this is personal. No money in this for you. Are you still interested?" Snapper viewed her for signs.

She gazed back at him, stirring in the white of her coffee. Just like him, she thought. Mild looking on top, tasty and sweet, but underneath cruel hard crystals swirled so strong of flavour. She loved to sip hard. "Money is not yet a prime motivator. Plenty of time when I freelance. I have so much yet to learn. The world is far from what I knew just a few days ago. What will I know next month?"

Snapper nodded his head. "If you don't keep your wits about you, you may well be dead. I take that as a 'yes'. What I want is not his death but a good hard lesson on how to treat others as he would like to be treated himself. Others want him dead but I want him to realize the enormity of what he is doing, I just want him stopped emphatically! He must know what his victims feel. I have to tell you it is something I would not want to get personally involved in, because I am."

Miranda's interest was piqued. "Fine! I can do it, of course. Not for money but for lessons. For years I have known about men's bodies. Now I know not near enough. Fair enough?" She took a good final drink. "Tell more!" At last she had some credit and therefore leverage.

"Fine then, later." Snapper looked at the time. "Well, I have to go now. I have an appointment shortly with another who also has to be taught the facts of life, apparently." And with that afterthought he took his leave.

She admired his departure. A big man in a small tight café. Yet he moved without touching other customers. Perhaps a boxer, she wondered. Exceptional peripheral vision. She amused herself wondering how to find out. She took one last slurp from her cup, the inviting topping now gone.

❊ ❊ ❊

Rooster smiled politely up at his boss. "Now would seem to be a good time for garbage disposal. I am told the two cameras at our tip are inoperative. We have made all the money we can reasonably expect, plus I need room."

"I agree," Chop nodded. "My own sources say the replacements are still sitting on his senior's desk. We can only patch her up for so long, you know. I cannot understand how Europeans in particular can afford resources but not use them. Just not economic."

Still, Rooster smiled politely. "She and her now plastic remains were one of your favourites. If that is still so, do you want to see her off? Discreetly, of course. After all, both our sources cannot each give wrong messages."

"Of course they can!" Chop disagreed. "Remember just one undisciplined moment can undo lives, but not in our case because we are dealing with worthless caste populations. Even the American poses no threat. One who does is Eric, who unfortunately has his own lawful problems."

Rooster took that as a yes and a compliment. He felt fine. Chop had no family and no heir apparent. Others curried favour in such sickening disgusting fawning tones. Surely, only he was to take over.

Here an opportunity invited itself. He felt concern though he only had one chance. Chop was pure shark and others lost limbs and worse because they lapsed only momentarily. Rooster did so admire such a trait.

Careful planning was now essential with total discretion combined with a foolproof escape option if he was to survive Chop.

"Pity!" he despaired. "She amongst the locals had a real knack of making everybody love her. Me included."

Chop agreed. "Yes! My heart went out to her also. But one cannot mix business with pleasure and sometimes love just is not enough."

"Right!" Rooster observed. "Even when business is pleasure." They both laughed.

❀ ❀ ❀

Snapper scanned the deserted yard. This was to be a game of patience and one he enjoyed. The first to move inevitably lost. Slowly he stretched his legs out. Like his opponent he kept them well out of the sun. He took out his glasses and scanned the corner slowly, methodically. The container sat there rusting slowly, a mute witness to the passing of life. Its broken door wavered above the ground. To get under, one would have to prise it up and prop it with a piece of timber. He knew he was in time and began to respect his young opponent, not that that would affect the results, he felt. He leaned back confident.

Snapper lurched forward, more insight than movement. He took his glasses and peered intently. Yes! He had won. Now the lid was propped up by lumber and two legs writhed like snakes into shelter. He yawned. He had time to move now.

Far below, Simon felt vulnerable and he did not like it.

He had waited an eternity before moving, denying his instincts not to move. He pushed the bag of money ahead of him. Out of sight he would feel secure and confidence would better his temperament. Past routines taught him that. At last he reached the shelf for machinery in the container, refrigeration, he thought. All stripped away, the space was ideal for storage.

Simon could not recall how he had found it while thoughts of his trial plagued his head. His memories of Eugene's expressions and verdict both left him invulnerable, with a fit of giggles. He stomached backwards to the entrance in tears and laughter.

Alarm wrought his whole body as he kicked back an obstacle when there should have been air. If he swiped his prop he would surely die under here with two broken legs and agony for company. Being lying backward he could not see; twisting his body around, his prop was not in his sight, multiplying his frustration.

His legs were still intact. He racked his brain as to what it could be. He wiped his eyes for a better view but there was nothing for it but to reverse back under and turn to head from the outside.

The unexpected struggles left him sticky and moist and concerned about time. He arced his head back for a straightforward view. Still no obstacle! Time to get the hell out of here and he reached his arms out for best leverage.

Two legs appeared. Huge arms dragged his lower torso to freedom, at the same time trapping him so he could barely see out. Simon could only make out a large bulk. The sun and upside-down view conspired against him to make out particulars. He sighed, wiped his eyes clear again. His wooden prop had been moved to a corner. No wonder he could not find it.

Snapper looked down at the helpless figure. "You have stolen from me a considerable amount. I want whatever remains back including what you have just stashed."

"I can't see a bloody thing here. I don't know you from shit!" Simon wondered just who this madman was and where he had escaped from. Now was no time to panic.

"You should know me!" Snapper countered. "After all you masqueraded as me at the Citadel and withdrew my savings. Ring a bell?"

In the heat and grime Simon went an unhealthy pale. He said nothing. He heard distant sirens and the wails were getting louder. The stranger seemed undisturbed. Perhaps only Simon was listening to his exit!

"Understand this." Snapper demanded breaking his thoughts.

"I know where to find you. I know your family, I know how much remains after your buying your car with my money and what you shared out to your friends, you little miser. I want it back within twenty-four hours or you and your family will be the consequences. Talk to your father, if you dare."

Snapper paused. "Oh, and this ambulance is coming for you."

Simon demanded, "How am I supposed to do that?"

Snapper reflected. "If you can rob a bank, you can find a way." He kicked the support away.

"Arsehole!" Simon was screaming even before the lid cruelly struck to pinion his legs.

17.
Mr Inbetween

MATT AND RUPERT SAT there, smug twins in front of the enormous desk of their master, big men but dwarfed physically. Bob hovered in the backdrop like an extra curtain.

"Good news indeed!" Rupert's sheer gloat. "By Matt's camera, stealth and cunning we have Mr Chop Pun presiding over a most unceremonious burial at the Black Hole. I do not know what made him so careless but I will take what I can against him every time. He is being apprehended as we speak."

Bob swallowed in sharing their enjoyment. Morgan too nodded and smiled. "Good! A good day for law and order and a good day for the community. His power base corrupted. I wonder what will now come out of the woodwork."

"We already know!" Rupert gloated. "We pursued your friend Snapper through hotels without success. It seems two pimp masters share a temporary alliance in the estate. Chop managed most of the, shall we say, exotic market but the larger of the two is one Eric Standing who covered mainstream demands."

The spare curtain billowed. Bob coughed. "I know of Eric superficially of course. Met him a number of times, drinks at the same bar et cetera but he is only a single employee at a single hotel. He told me at one of our encounters he is saving hard for an overseas trip. Are you sure?"

Matt leaned forward. "Oh! Yes! Eric has a profile lower than street cleaners. Our investigations into his affairs show he is a multi-millionaire financially, and in property, and in shares. None of which is in his own name. Not only is he good but he has a personal following that would make it difficult to make a complete case against him. But we have enough to bring him in."

Bob thoroughly inspected his shoes.

※ ※ ※

Dr Gregory mused to his company, Dr Wylie, as they ambled up the bleached concrete stone patterns. "This is the most difficult island I have ever come across. But I feel our work here is done."

Wylie nodded in agreement. "I won't be sorry to be going. Even though we have little enough to show there is clearly no evidence of an epidemic, in fact cases have dwindled away dramatically."

Gregory looked up. "A massive place. We are not diplomats. I do not feel we should have to say goodbye to all. Especially this one! He scares me more than any other I have met in this job."

Wylie agreed. "Let's get this over as quick as we can. Neither of us ever needs to return. My belongings are all ready to go as it is." She surveyed the monument of wealth.

A curtain and blind moved above. "The ugly little gnome is spying on us. If his mind matches his appearance I do not want to venture inside."

"Hear, hear!" her companion in full support.

Behind the window Tim was gesturing furiously for them to leave. He knew they had seen him. How could they be so stupid?

A door burst open. In the same instant Cedric filled the frame. "You two can just fuck off!" His venom filled the air.

"We just wish to express our condolences and advise of our departure." Dr Gregory spread his hands open.

Cedric swung a shotgun from behind him wavering the gun between his visitors.

Dr Wylie blanched. "Obviously not good timing. Well! Farewell and all the best for your future."

As one they turned away and walked hurriedly, pointedly to their car.

Cedric stood until they were out of sight and rested his gun against the door. How was it, he wondered, why even the best-educated persons who knew of all poisons and equally lethal cures ignore such potential threats but like laymen instantly recognized old-fashioned weapons?

He shook his head at the lack of logic!

Tim emerged from interior shadows. "Well, boss! That was pretty dramatic! What is your next trick going to be? Any more assistance to help the departed? You know, sometimes I worry about you — and how much attention have you brought upon us. I am nearly complete. I do not need visitors at all!"

Cedric turned on him. It was hard to tell if he had heard or comprehended, his face warped by fury. "Nearly finished? Nearly finished? You cannot even grow a classroom culture. You are no bloody use to me! Get out!"

Tim stood his ground. "Bloody insulting! If you are so bloody good, you try. I have tried to carry you but this is the last straw. I am out. You are on your own and don't worry about cutting any deals. You understand I am gone. I have other matters needing my overdue attention. You are no longer trustworthy!"

Cedric had no acknowledgement. "I said get the hell off my property! Don't worry about visitors! My security supersedes anything on this bloody island and I control it all. Now get out!"

Tim stomped out. "Fine!" he muttered as he brushed passed Cedric. Sometimes he liked to have the last word.

He stumbled his way to the car park and Cedric watched his disappearing back. As he picked up his gun and as Tim started his car, they both paused, thinking it had all gone rather well!

18.
Masticatations

SNAPPER LAY BACK IN the sun with his arms behind his head. A meal with Holly! That was something to look forward to. She would cook a combination of native, Asian and European styles. He didn't know how she did it. He had watched her at work just grabbing a handful of this and that hovering over three or four simmering pots. A dietitian's nightmare. If you believed the experts he would have to work out for a year to be rid of the excess.

No formal training. If a gardener had green fingers, Holly's would be golden dough.

He did the two things she admired — punctuality and gluttony — and he could do both without effort. He reached down with a smile to pat his tum. "You are in for hell!"

❈ ❈ ❈

Louie was preparing for this meal. Holly was something special and afterwards he would have a special dessert with his new lover. He would have to think of an excuse to leave but, hell, there was no time to dwell on that now. He wondered how to dress smart but casual. As for now it was so humid even his shorts clung viciously.

He climbed the ladder to his ceiling for his mementos coiled about the entrance. All halos carefully laid out hanging in their little boxes. He knew them all by name, date and event. Just one smallest peek was all he needed to recall entire encounters. Again and again hung like that he could see all of them at once. He also liked privacy, for his dark spirits.

Louie sometimes saw something wrong within him in that one

day his treasures were just so completely sensual yet the next he could deliberate and shuffle them completely dispassionately.

Christ! The ladder wobbled! One of these days he would have to fix it before he had a nasty accident. Suddenly he slipped backwards, catching his head on the frame.

Things turned black.

"Wakey! Wakey!" he heard a voice for afar. As Louie composed himself he felt so uncomfortably high off the ground, his arms pinned below him. Confused he looked around but he couldn't move his head or talk. His head was tied down to something from his forehead and his mouth forced open bound under the chin. His body stretched out undressed before him.

Louie's head stung. He looked around; he knew at least he was still in his home. He got the impression he was secured to his ironing board. And by Jesus! He was going to be late!

"Been looking at your hobby. Impressive, a real work of art and yet still some vacant places?" The woman approached him from above his head.

❉ ❉ ❉

Snapper stood round with Morgan, both watching Holly in anticipation.

"Are you two going to help?" She looked for volunteers.

"We are!"

"Men are bloody useless, you know. Even Louie has his limitations."

Snapper could not let this pass. "Are you accusing us of not being constructive?"

Morgan smiled, shaking his head slightly. He knew when and when not to take Holly on.

Holly smattered him with a little paste. "Nope! See, I needed to check the consistency here. And it's running down you at just the right rate."

Morgan ushered Snapper to a side room to wipe up, both sniggering like schoolboys.

"Quick! Give us a little taste?"

"Piss off!"

They heard her royal command. "What are you two doing in there? You two have always been trouble!"

Caught again! Morgan wedged his cheeky face in the doorway. "Men's stuff."

"Perhaps the both of you could leave my bowl and clear the table and get it ready?"

"Right! Come on, Snapper, we have been summoned."

Holly shook her head in resignation.

"How many bums on seats?" Snapper tried to weasel his way back.

"Four!" she retorted. "Remember Louie is coming even if he is a bit late. It's not like him, you know. And you can eat on the step with the dog. You both have equal manners."

Snapper tried to look shocked, unsuccessfully.

"Don't worry, old friend." Morgan put a heavy hand on his shoulder. "I will save you yet from this wretched demon cook."

Snapper whined back, "Perhaps there might be a place for me?"

❋ ❋ ❋

"Perhaps there might be a place for me?" The voice came from beyond Lou's head.

A woman! Yes, there might be a place for you if you are my type of lover, he thought.

Suddenly she was standing over him. And a real beauty, a lover indeed!

Slowly, sensually, she removed her clothes flaunting a full body, full rich breasts and finally the closeness of a rich pubic mass with just a tease of succulent flesh.

He attempted speech but with his jaw wide he couldn't articulate a simple single word. His bound forehead and jaw prised his mouth open.

"Let's see the cause of havoc!" A none-too-gentle slap tested his bonds. Strength, not words, was his only salvation.

Staring up he saw over an auburn haze, only large heartless brown eyes and he felt very insecure.

She squatted herself into his mouth rocking gently, firmly.

His mouth filled with pungent soft fluffy marshmallow, pliable nougat, embroidered with soft down that teased his palate, lips and nose. He tasted motherly and it was so, so heavenly. Nothing would be better to make passionate love to. He felt himself stiffen so much it ached.

She peered down contemptuously. Every time they looked up with their stupid bewildering child-innocent eyes, regardless of their history it all made her feel sick.

She eased up and checked for the indentations but not seeing much she pressed back down harder this time.

Lou started to struggle. The comfort factor was ebbing away. He struggled for breath. Her hair lost it softness and clawed at his palate and tongue. He struggled for thoughts to cope.

It was no use! He was totally intoxicated.

If only he could lie back and just treasure the moment but he wasn't in control this time, the accompanying knowledge giving him an edge of panic.

She grimaced to herself. She didn't want to suffocate him, not kill him, not even for justice. On top of all that he was bloody useless. Didn't he know he had a tongue?

She eased up for another inspection. This didn't seem like working. Perhaps she should have given herself a trim. Well! It was too late now and she pressed as hard as she could.

Lou was really struggling now. His mouth was being torn up. Breathing seemed intermittent. He was worried he was going to die here today. He just could not stand it any more and convulsed.

"Jesus!" she thought alarmed. "I've gone too far." Then she felt the scalding dribbles amble down her back coursed by nature. It raised a smile and determination.

She stood up and checked herself. At last she was on the right track. Yes, indeed, his bite left a good impression.

❊ ❊ ❊

"I hope you are going to make a good impression?" Holly accused Snapper.

Snapper had been self-musing around his plate taking extra pleasure in deciding what to start with, what would be the best combination, how much would be polite to wedge onto his fork.

"Don't worry, Holly. You won't even have to wash any of my dishes no matter how many you bring out."

"In fact," Morgan sided with him, "if Lou doesn't make it we will take care of his scraps."

Holly acknowledged the compliment. "Perhaps you could ring him?"

"After we have finished eating!"

Mostly they ate in silence. Holly tried to question Snapper who was evasive. In the end she gave up. He would tell her what he wanted when he wanted. He always had. She rose from the table to tend and bring out the next course.

"May this torture never end?" Snapper conceded defeat. But he knew he would eat on. Home-cooked food was a rarity for him and he was not going to miss anything. "What is your thinking, Morgan?"

"Oh, I don't know," Morgan replied. "All these bloody games and what not. I have real administrative nightmares. Your company and Holly's support plus this marvellous dining have been a welcome distraction."

Snapper winked at Holly. "It is time for us men to take over. But it's more healthy for the gluttony to settle."

Morgan relaxed with a big sigh. Was it his lot in life to clean after others? He loved the challenge and wondered if he could do a better job. He stretched his large frame and just lay back.

❋ ❋ ❋

Lou lay back, his whole body breathed for him. This would be an unforgettable experience. Already he was wondering how to replicate it.

"You poor fool!" the voice came from the top of his head. He still couldn't concentrate. Now where the hell was she? He just knew he could have fun here! He tried to look around.

She moved into his sight standing over his still-heaving chest. She had her undies in her hands squeezing them into a ball. What heaven was he in to deserve this?

Abruptly she shoved them into his mouth and pasted tape down hard from ear to ear.

A kaleidoscope of emotions flooded into Lou. Elastic snagged between his lip and gum. Panic that it was not all over, panic for the unknown. Once more his breathing laboured, his body fought against his restrictions, his temperature lifted, he felt uncomfortable from top to bottom.

She reached forward lifting his head. "You don't want to miss a moment of this," he heard her say.

But she was wrong; he didn't want any part of it at all. Yet she was right too. Lou wanted all alright! He wanted it all his own way! The irony completely escaped him!

She returned back to his body straddling his midriff. Reaching down she clamped his asset. Lou was really desperate now. He could feel the pressure trapped yet still increasing. He tasted, smelt nearly fresh lawn. He thought 'limp' but his body denied him.

She stroked him against her radiant triangle plunging down to start again. Acute sensations forced a muffled grunt counting each movement.

Discomfort multiplied rapidly! His gag acrid in his senses moving down with each breath, inching ever so slowly that he was sure to suffocate any time now. His eyes were trapped as he forced himself to look away, failing. He squirmed, hated anticipation of the next movement, he wanted any variation, he hated any variation. He wanted it all to stop. Would it ever stop? He finally recognized the taste as slight soiling. He felt revolted yet tolerable.

It was all agony. It was all excruciating. It was exhilarating!

With expertise she traced his completing juices into her cleavage.

Instantly his body pushed to reject his gag, his breath unable to function, whole body repelling.

His member still in an unmovable grip was a glowing rainbow

of pink and purple. He could barely identify it as his body part sensitive to air and space.

She leaned forward temporarily permitting him badly needed oxygen. But it was no respite.

Lou screamed at her as he watched in utter horror as the crown of her head receded toe-ward. He felt sudden pressure in his bladder. He did not need this right now!

All she could hear though was a slight mew to which she was totally indifferent. She blew gently onto the candle rigid in her hands causing consternation on the torso below him. She licked moisture onto her lips.

❈ ❈ ❈

Holly licked taste from her lips, sweet and indulgent. She sashayed around behind her two men poking, prodding them into cleaning up and although they were doing a satisfactory job it was her responsibility to stay on their backs. This was one of life's moments.

Pity about Lou! She hoped he was OK. He was just bloody useless on occasions. Perhaps she should nag Morgan into using his official capacity to get someone to go and check on him. After all there had been a lot of funny goings on lately.

It was very pleasing the way Snapper fitted back in. Morgan was happier than she had seen him for a long time. That may be what he needed — a friend to confide in and trust.

He confided in her all the time but it seemed he could be very distant and difficult on some domestic issues. Maybe he was getting on; maybe he was feeling the pressure!

❈ ❈ ❈

Lou had never felt such pressure, unrelenting torment in his life. His body writhed against its structure. He tried to shrink away to nothing, then to the other extreme. Perhaps this would make things finish the faster. If he could relieve himself just maybe he could drown her.

He pleaded to God to stop this nightmare.

Another part of him recognized the self same tactics by some of his lovers. But this just couldn't be right. They had all flirted with him one way or another, the casual teasing friendship, the sly look, the beckoning smile, the alluring stance. They had done it all. And he had loved them all. Secretly, unknown, holding their confidences.

But they had all enjoyed his attentions. Which of them had cried "Please!" so he had loved her twice. It was all there in his mementos. Necklaces of so precious moments, personal moments. He was furious she had trespassed into his domain!

Other lovers had, after, in the light of day leaned on his shoulder for support so he had visited them again even though he had not planned to.

He now faced the reality others had called him a monster. Even though he had not wanted to be, stinging tears rolled down his eyes, a part of him stood aside for his physical body.

How was he to make amends? *Well!* He could start with her!

Perhaps she had read his thoughts. She lifted her head up. Perhaps now it was to be all over. Why had it taken this much to see the light?

A twist of hair brushed him each an anchor that individually scoured and gouged a pitted surface. Lou writhed in fresh paroxysms.

She looked into his reddened eyes and smiled. Christ! How could a smile instil such fear!

With no effort she gave him a couple of paint strokes and then went back to work.

Lou was fuelled with black rage!

Not because of the suffering he was enduring though he did hate her for that. Not because she had violated his home though he hated her for that too. But because he now had to relive, to re-endure what her respite had granted him. It had been deliberate and he cursed her with everything he could. Physically the gag negated all.

He unreservedly hated them all. So he may have used force, now he could see his justification. They deserved everything anybody had ever done to them. If he survived this there was no way he was going to stop now and he screamed that to her with his every being. The agony got the better of him.

Finally she stood up; moving over him she smacked him in the ear. "This is what you get, padre! Your DNA's all over my body. Understand that? Then understand this! I will make a complaint against you! I will win! I will give you to each of your victims before you face justice! Understand? You are so pathetic! Guys seek and pay for much more than this. I'm off to find some football teams for real sex."

Lou was thankful it was all over. He had survived this; he would somehow face the future. He closed his eyes to think. Lack of pain was a physical reaction. He felt his legs flop down and his feet hit the floor. He did not have the energy to react. So he rested.

When he opened his eyes she was gone. He was free! What a bloody nightmare! He embraced himself with relief. What could he do now? First he should ring his brother and say something about being late. But first he needed to see what the bitch had done with his precious collection.

Slowly he kicked aside his low table. His body shook against the ladder. Shock, he supposed. He mounted each step gingerly; things were really sensitive, and probably would be for some time. He peered over the manhole. He twisted his head taking in all the changes, furious still that anyone dared touch them.

There he slipped.

One of his boxes caught him under his chin, lodged onto his throat, held there by ribbon. His panic kicked the ladder away. The ribbon tightened by his weight.

He was feeling faint. Life passed him, frame by frame.

From far away somewhere he felt himself go to the toilet. What a special feeling that was! He didn't know such simple pleasure.

If only he could lift his hands to support himself but determination lost to lack of energy and his body rotated slowly knotting the rope. The last noise he heard above was the edge of the manhole and the rope scraping.

❈ ❈ ❈

Morgan lifted his head when he heard the scrape on the drive. Perhaps Lou had walked. He hadn't heard Lou's car. At least now he wouldn't have to find him, not even to answer the knock.

Panic stood Holly up. "Something's wrong! It can't be Lou! Oh God! See who's knocking, Morgan!" She looked around in desperation. Even Snapper looked concerned.

Morgan got up to answer the door.

Rupert stood in the doorway. His expression silenced all of them.

19.
Flight of Fancy

Liz knocked on Morgan's door passively before opening it just a smidgen. "Boss, I have someone here to see you. He has no appointment but he seems an agitated and determined sort of professional."

Morgan sat at his desk with his hands propping a fallen head. Liz was startled and full of concern. She had never seen him in a slumped state. Morgan peered out and smiled wanly at her. "Better invite him in then."

He propped himself up as the figure filled the doorway. He recognized him from somewhere but was yet to place him.

"Tim McLear!" the stranger announced himself. "Dr McLear, actually."

Morgan waved him in. "Of course! Now, you are one of Cedric's rising stars, aren't you? Plus a lucrative private practice, as well. Doctor ah? Modesty indeed."

Tim always tried to dismiss speculation. "That is by the bye," he added. "I have success at the Island Seat Practice, which is financially rewarding and medically gratifying. I find myself in an unfortunate circumstance and I need independent advice."

"No!" Morgan cut in. How many audiences like this sought him out? He always sent them packing, but better not to hear him first. "You need to go to the police for whatever."

"You are the police," Tim countered. "Besides you are best because you are personally involved so by law makes you exempt."

"Go on!" Morgan began a slow slump. Personal involvement always equalled trouble!

"It is like this. Cedric has involved a female party of your acquaintance. Now I feel he has overstepped the mark. Considerably actually! And I need someone to put a stop to it, in all conscience." Tim concluded his summary.

"You are not innocent, then?" Morgan saw Tim's first omission.

"Factually not," Tim agreed. "In relative terms though I am as pure as you can get."

Morgan released building tensions. "Relax, I am not asking as a point of law and I have no interest in what you may have been up to. Seeing as you are here I guess you are at a loose end?"

"Well! I am not idle if that is what you mean, but if there is any work I can do for you it will be made part of my schedule." Tim worried about making concessions.

Morgan growled at him. "You medicals are all the bloody same. There is something you may do for me. Nothing much of a challenge really. My morgue is overflowing from sports and crowds and all. It would assist me immensely and help the families grieve and finalize matters if you can help formally identify some bodies, and so on."

Tim relaxed. "Do you have coroner's records?"

Morgan fluffed around his desk searching while passing them over. "Some, most are computer recorded. I will override security to allow you access!" He pushed over his screen and papers then he waited.

"Looks straightforward to me," Tim spoke as he read. "DNA on the kids will be straightforward. Should not be necessary. Not my area of expertise but nothing I cannot handle."

"There are some questions surrounding the kids hence the extra attention. Where any doubts have been raised it is part of my responsibilities to independently examine the records. In reality I depend on expert opinion meaning the coroner, the police and individuals such as yourself. And I have to say this being a small nation I have personal knowledge of all the deceased. Makes my job so much harder." Morgan set out his position.

Tim nodded. He passed a file back. "This is a bit different."

"I don't know why?" Morgan observed drily. "It is the same scenario. We have one young driver. All the others are just bits of body parts. Drivers are suddenly immune to seatbelts. See what happens."

"That is so," Tim agreed.

"Great! That is good news. Wouldn't have it any other way. Let me know how you get on. I want progress reports. I will personally deal with the issue of Cedric with my force. Your part is deemed not significant." Morgan seemed happy enough boosting positive body language.

"You government officials are all the bloody same." Tim was satisfied as he raised himself to leave.

20.
The Monster Debate

MORGAN LOUNGED BACK ON his deck feeling pride at the scenic beauty spread out before him. "Come and look at all this, Holly," he invited. "You have nothing to do."

Holly came out wringing a cloth in her hands. "Yes, it does look nice up here in the hills." She sat beside him in her twin chair. He put his hand in her arm.

"Paradise!" Together they watched the world go by.

The mansions running up the other side of the valley. The coloured tops of roofs stretching below. The seaside where kids and families played safely. The distant town centre with drinks and dancing and romance with its varying degrees of success. The triple blues of the bay, the deep waters against a sky perforated by occasional soft white clouds. Colours hinting at evening.

"Look at that. Over the valley. Some fool is not controlling his barbecue," Holly growled at the sight.

Morgan even more upset. "Christ! The dickhead will cremate everything. He has really just ruined my mood now," he complained. The moment was stolen from them. "Let's go inside!"

❈ ❈ ❈

Silas had driven for once carelessly into his drive. Thoughtlessly a wheel edged his lawn.

Depression scoured any energy of thought from his mind.

How could life have come to this? All his goals cherished in life evaporated!

Silas just stood outside his home and wondered.

He was early. Unusual but with most staff attending an afternoon funeral he had bowed to the inevitable.

He looked down at his immaculate lawn. Edges laser-sharp trim. Grass green, greener despite the climate, a mat he was so proud to walk on. Now he saw blank, nothing.

He looked up at the windows that sparkled back at him. Unlike the neighbour's panes soiled mottled specks by the sun's rays. So what?

Little acrid black bile men jack-hammered and crowbarred at his tear ducts extracting painful acrid black bile tears. Others pounded his facial muscles, his top lip in anger twitched.

Inside he just knew his polystyrene wife had cooked her tasteless polystyrene meal and he would sit on his polystyrene furniture and listen to his polystyrene music.

What happened to the wife Silas had loved so much? He always looked forward to her affectionate embrace. Now it was all unfeeling and dry and constantly irritating. He had always relished her cooking of which she laboured so proud. Now he chewed everything in robotic polystyrene dejection.

He would then automatically sink into his especially imported chair and listen to music or TV from the finest of systems. Now no such pleasures, just distant drones, no sense of appreciation. Did he still love his precious Sue? Sometimes he wondered.

How did it all start? When did it all begin?

Then there was his boy inside with two legs in plaster. Times had certainly changed, he mused. Hell, he had given and received a few black eyes and maybe an occasional broken limb over a woman. But he was no thief.

Silas summoned all plummeting hollow disappointment. How many hours had he spent on the boy patiently trying to explain things to him? To show him values, give direction. Such wasted, wasted hours!

He used precious credits in society avoiding a conviction let alone a prison term for Simon. But Silas's standing in the community had been irreparably damaged. Surely, staff laughed at him behind his back. He could always do something about that, despite the new owners. At least you could not say Simon was no petty thief.

Silas reflected as a young man when he had started work how he struggled.

But he had taken the cursed machinery home until each challenge became second nature, while he looked after his family. Others smarter than him cheated, and still cheated as bosses. He learnt to tolerate them.

When he was promoted to the production line he always made two extra to critically compare the first product with the last ensuring no drop in quality.

The old owners knew this and praised him accordingly. Silas made steady if unspectacular progress. He knew this result was he had never applied until he felt he was ready and sometimes that took considerable effort. Unlike some others.

When he had got there he insisted his staff worked to his standards. He made sure his staff reaped the rewards.

When he eventually had to let one go he was mindful of the traumas he was inflicting on the individual and family. He had since learnt to toughen himself up.

He soon noticed production improved with dismissals and in time this became an effective tool in evening out the cycles of labour.

Silas studied difficult complex labour laws, not following reason or logic. When he was sure of his understanding of his powers he would dismiss someone as a test. Much the same as others tested holiday and sick leave provisions. There was nothing personal and surely the legislators had granted such responsibilities for him to better the business. The tears and anguish or loathing disturbed him but the game had to be played correctly to the end. He dismissed such feelings about the same time as the employee.

The new owners who supported him publicly, chastised him in private. They simply just refused to understand his explanations but they needed his expertise as he became more covert.

Reluctantly, Silas permitted himself to swing through his door, unable to choke back a sigh.

His wife cowered by the oven.

More so than usual, he noted. He had always liked rough

sex and even his wife gave him a black eye once he recalled with such satisfaction. Where was that woman now? Where was the appeal?

Simon lurched!

"Shut up, boy!" And an afterthought: "Get rid of that bloody flower!"

"We have a visitor!" his wife positively quivered.

"When will it all end?" Silas talked to himself.

"Dad! This is the fuck who broke my legs!" Simon's bleat brought him back to earth like nothing else.

So, at the end of the day the boy still had confidence in his father. Silas felt satisfaction, and a challenge. In his house there was no need to size up anybody so he walked to his chair. It was going to be a long evening so he may as well be comfortable. He still had to decide how it was all going to end, this was living again!

A mirage of sensations whirled around his head emerging from a desert of grey. His pulse massaged his body, his mouth dried, his brain again supremely active. Semiconsciously Silas swaggered to his seat. This was indeed living! Now after a long, long time Silas was elated!

He steadied himself on an ironing board and sat absorbing, extracting, quality within his chair.

What the hell is the ironing board doing here anyway? His strictest rule blatantly ignored. A modest bottle of spirits leaning there jeering at him also. Has the world gone mad? He would lecture his wife later; he just didn't drink crap, the indent of her iron a more subtle lesson than actual burn. Though he toyed with the idea.

"The iron upsets you?" Snapper pierced his euphemism. "I left it there!"

Silas turned to the speaker for the first time. Just what I need. A big fat gay wife! No man ironed. This just got better and better.

Turning slowly, triumphantly, and equally slowly he spoke. "I seem to have missed something here. My boy seems to have acquired a few coins and for that you have seen fit to cripple him, ruin him for life and as if that is not enough you introduce yourself, you're unwelcome values into my house."

"We all have different values. And we each act accordingly. I treasure my possessions and what I have worked hard for. You, on the other hand, have ruined many, many lives just because you can," Snapper countered.

Silas felt his temper rise. "I know of you, and your reputation. You ran like a coward and you are here as a coward! You ruined lives before you fled and from the headlines and death notices you are back." The words spat out.

"Ruined! Ruined, you say. I have never caused hardship, except in recompense," Snapper added as an afterthought. "Never taken a man's livelihood, taken from his simple labours his hard conscientious efforts used to support his family."

"Bah!" Silas dismissed the argument. How many times had he heard this before? Like some noxious weed it always, always popped up! "Hardship builds character! Hardship makes a man! I worked for everything you see before you, bloody hard! Adversity builds character and the strong overcome it! Overcome it with pride. And society is better!"

"Yes! You have worked hard." Snapper's only concession. "But you have worked from a secure base. You have never taken risks! You have never overcome adversity! You have never faced adversity, until now. Your employees worked with pride but still you dispensed with them, for what? Feel like a change of socks? At least three died from your administration, died by pride! Stripped by you!"

"They were weak! I have no blood on my conscience. Can you say that?" Silas carried the conversation.

Snapper raised himself and stretched out. He was getting sick of this. Trying to make headway. What a waste of time with poor old Silas.

Snapper manoeuvred himself behind Silas's chair holding his shoulders down massaging them and his spine.

"So much weight on your shoulders. But I will lift them for you. No, I do have blood on my hands as you would say and even by people in the wrong place at the wrong time. But the innocents die without suffering and where possible without knowing anything. I do other people's bidding because they dream and pay me to make it reality.

"In contrast to you.

"You who personally delight in making them suffer and then when your toy is boring you just turn them loose. See, you have no discipline, take no responsibility. You see no part of the suicides after your participation?"

"No!" Silas knew the answer to that!

Snapper squeezed his grip and Silas felt it down the length of his spine. "They took their own lives by their own hands. My wife …"

His wife sat back silent in tears looking at the carpet.

"Ah yes! Your Sue. I will take her to heaven. You may mention her but you are not even thinking of her. She is just a red herring. Ask her now what she wants."

"I want to be first. Please don't let me see my family suffer!" Sue had a voice at last.

Snapper smiled from behind at him. "No! No more. See, you don't even have her answer. How long have you been married?"

He shuffled to be behind her. "Close your eyes, gently. Think of a highlight, in the past, something only you have treasured, secretly."

"Take me home. Remember? Back to the Valiant just for one last time."

Snapper leaned her forward and placed a cushion gently behind her. "I remember like it was today. Like this?" he whispered in her ear.

"Please!"

He murmured, "A simple request," softly caressed her neck and shoulders quietly humming their old favourite, in ever increasing circles of her back and upper torso.

She closed her eyes a satisfied expression though still hungry for more. Tears fell unashamedly. She hummed away to herself.

Simon looked on bewildered. He swallowed his first instinct to protect his mother. He could do nothing anyway.

How many sides were there to this character? Where was the monster who casually broke his legs? Here was a compassionate, caring, gentle soul, at least until he turned around.

His mother looked to be in real peace.

In fact to him she looked younger and he could now perceive the attractiveness which appealed to his father. Simon had never seen that before either.

He knew parents had sex but he had not realized they could still enjoy it. Not to this extent.

His mind recognized the tune as one his mother used to comfort him so long ago. It still gave him a maternal security he had long forgotten. Oddly, he was so pleased for his mother.

Clearly the stranger knew her sometime before his father. Would things have been any better if his mother had stayed with this man? Perhaps he would have turned out completely different.

Smug now as then, Silas thought confidently. Even before he proposed he had spent a very expensive hour just reading her personal medical records and had marked her religious card including confessions. Apart from the usual childhood symptoms she was as pristine as you could get. And confident she was still intact he had proceeded boldly to the next step.

Silas motioned out of his chair. From somewhere a large concrete slab deep within his chest vacuumed him down. "Disgusting! Just bloody disgusting! A simple hypnotic gesture and you get away with murder!"

Snapper looked up. "Look at her, she is at peace now. Perhaps for the second time in her life and it is twice with me. You could have done this for her. You should have! All I feel are lesions, and tensions and scar tissue. Even her wedding day, probably her only day, would be manipulated by you."

Silas just glared at him. Snapper gently placed her hands in her lap and stood up. She looked in peaceful slumber. Only a slowly widening stain dampened the carpet at her feet.

"Still deluding yourself, I see. Many will attend her funeral and genuinely grieve and be thankful to me. Who will attend your funeral except to see you buried or for the food? There will be no dearth of pallbearers for you. Plenty will rejoice your passing."

Simon swallowed hard. He could read the message. How he had picked the wrong mark and cast doom all around him. "

If he is to die it may as well be by my hand."

Perhaps though it may also be his redemption.

"If you wish, boy. Maybe this is your out." Snapper invited him.

Christ! Who was this who could read his thoughts? You have to grab at every straw. Simon nodded meekly.

"You see even your blood wants your blood." Snapper drew himself up at the iron beside Silas.

"Get fucked!" Silas still fought. Fought the invader, fought to live, fought the family, fought the world. Victory is sweeter the harder the conflict.

Snapper twisted his tools to bare the wires. The pliers sat on the armrest, the screws on the floor. The wires just adhered to his victim's heaving chest.

Silas struggled, struggled to move, to wave his arms, to get out of the chair somehow to fight this invader but he was solidly sunk low as part of the chair. He would deal with his son later, he knew as usual. His immediate and only concern was to extricate himself. The pliers fell to the floor.

Snapper sprinkled the spirits liberally over his seated host then stood back to review his handiwork.

"Well, my little thief, I am going to have to move you to the switch. Once you flick it the house will be very consumed by fire. Perhaps if you can make it to the door you can live again."

Simon had to be content. His eyes spoke volumes, his voice said nothing. He helped his tormentor as much as he could dragging him to the wall where he now sat his hand ready. He just knew he would live! Not what he had dreamed, but the only acceptable option.

"Surviving will not be easy. I have cleared all obstacles and wedged the door so you only have to open it. My advice is not to open it wide until you really have to." Snapper looked from father to son and nodded his consent. "Personally I wouldn't bet on you but I would do more so than your father."

Simon flicked. His father's face turned puce and he sighed and slumped. Instantly a thin aurora of blue surrounded his body.

Immediately Silas's chair engulfed spewing up black stinking smoke enveloping the ceiling. Already the heat was terrific as Simon struggled for the door. Being on the ground had small advantages. The fire leapt incredibly around the room indifferent to the best fire-resistant materials.

The smoke reached down to the squirming youth labouring his breath, forcing the heat down, down, down. The thick carpet turned sand pulling his efforts back, eroding his determination, his agony increasing each second.

Every breath sucked in red-hot grit. His hands and arms rubbed raw searching for purchase against his weight. Rolling over brought temporary relief but cost so much energy.

The room was turning pitch black before his eyes, which grated in powder overwhelming sight, engulfing his tears. Still he struggled along the floor!

Simon felt he must be surely near the door. He turned to look back. Perhaps he could see something familiar in this hell he used to take for granted. The distant plaster on his legs shimmered and steam wafted off.

If he could have ripped them and legs away he would give anything to do so. If this is how meat cooked he would be vegetarian for the rest of his days! Survival instincts dragged his senses back to the present.

Simon's agony was unbearable, and screaming through clenched teeth he snatched the small purple flower and threw it into the inferno. It hissed as it curled up into a ball and disappeared in a blue flash against the black background.

He felt the edge of the door. Perhaps he could save something of himself using it as a ladder. He pulled it towards him.

The fresh oxygen was welcomed by the all-consuming rage. Simon conceded finally and sat up. He hardly felt the pure hell and poisons fuelled his throat.

The monster fire took over, caressed and enveloped all the bodies. The rest of the house was now showing full signs of fire.

❊ ❊ ❊

In the hours before in another faraway part of the island, granite squealed against neighbours under intense pressure, squirming, groaning, before sheering a corner in dust, perhaps a spark. The hearse tyres pressed on slowly with their heavy burden, this single noise lost in the crunch of road noise.

Adjacent to other pallbearers Morgan and Rupert silently sat in the corner, their tears evident from the drama. Morgan leaned towards his lieutenant: "You have removed all connections of your investigations to the deceased?"

"Of course, the trails now steer away to a mystery man but the evidence remains and I cannot erase memories, boss."

"Naturally, but there is one final step to encourage the peace of the family for me to take."

Rupert looked nonplussed. "What do you want of me?"

"I just wish for a quiet word with the clergy in private. I don't want you or anybody else interrupting or even in close earshot." Morgan peered into the distance.

"Yep!" the acknowledgement was little more than a whisper.

Morgan grunted "Good. Now we must get on and over our grieving. Christ! I so hate this process."

The mourners ambled around the open plot waiting for the final rites to start. Morgan ambled over to the minister wearing his positively benign expression.

Morgan started the conversation. "Losing your second in charge must be devastating. Got any thoughts on a replacement?"

"Now is not the time or place!" Long tried to be curt yet sensitive to the occasion. We are here to bury your brother. Isn't that enough?"

"Is that a rebuke?" Nothing! Morgan stood still; sometimes silence is louder than words. The minister was getting upset with himself because … he didn't know why. That man, that bloody man always did this to him!

"Long, I was thinking of offering myself. Temporarily, of course. As I have administered to your, well, our, flock over such a long time now. Surely a simple change of emphasis is all."

"Louie was devoted. Devoted, I say, his life to administering and caring and providing for others in their time of need in God's name. Do not compare yourself to him!" The minister could feel himself going and nothing could stop it. He did not want to anyway.

"No! He was a selfish prick!" Morgan upped the ante. "Your selection was not good. My brother stalked your parish and parishioners. He may have covered it well, but ..."

The denial was immediate. "How can you stand there and say such things? I knew him just as I know you. I have known both of you and your family since your birth. Right now I see that I knew him better than you."

"Better than me, I doubt that!" Snapper jeered at him.

"He was a better man than you and has been for a long, long time. He was calm when all others including me got too involved in many affairs. There is so much to thank him for. Did you not hear the tributes? Little wonder you never spoke yourself."

The tirade was at an end and as he dwelled on what he had said he could tell by Morgan's body language the trap had been sprung. But for now he afforded to ignore his intuition.

"His calmness, yes, and other tributes masked his identity. Fooled you and those who sought comfort or solace or guidance from him."

"Enough of your games, by God! Spit out whatever vile insinuations you have in mind!"

"No insinuations! You know on those occasions when he did lose his calm his lisp became progressively pronounced?"

"Yes! Yes! Poor boy!"

"Well, all I am saying is that he used his mask well outside of the Lord's work not only to hide his features but also his lisp!"

"Dear Lord! Your own brother! You are suggesting your own brother has been the plague in this community?"

"Yep! We are presently one sinner less. One bad sinner less."

"You evil twisted perverted monster! You have done many, many wrongs to the public and it is as if your brother has had to do so much good to compensate."

"Louie — you are talking about my brother Louie? I think you have the roles mixed here, padre!" Morgan just had to add a little bit extra.

"What sort of monster sworn to protect the community who knew, who has known about this for how long failed to address it?"

"I have suspected for some time now but blood is thicker than water. Well, holy water anyway! Besides, you knew him better than me. You must have known about him as well. You said so yourself."

"No! No! You must be wrong. This is some sort of evil sick joke!"

But Long knew already it wasn't. In fact now it had been pointed out to him, so many things fell into place. He stood there silent, a vacant gaze out, his eyes looking inward.

"What am I to do?" he asked nobody or everybody. He was lost by it all.

"You will tend to your flock as you always have. They will need a strong man such as you now more than ever." Morgan brought him back to proceedings.

"That was a rhetorical question!" Long did not thank him.

Morgan tried conciliation. "Nevertheless our community was not at risk as such any more. Your parish was! I had suspicions only. I hoped for the best! It was only at his death, my suspicions were confirmed. For that I am indeed guilty!"

He handed the minister a folded sheet. "He sort of left a list of his victims. Some he visited more than once. There are several names who never came forward. We are counselling them very discreetly already. You must do the same."

Meantime Holly lost patience. Those two were always at loggerheads and this was not the place to continue their feuding.

She casually brushed past Rupert. "Come along, you two. Anyone would think you don't want to bury your brother and colleague."

"Yes!" her husband replied. "It is time we both buried him." He allowed himself to be led away.

"That churchman is a real wanker! Why don't you stay away from him? Leave him alone." Holly was upset.

Morgan easily chastised her. "Long has done considerable service to this community that surpasses all my efforts. His forms the essence of our lives. Fortunately he is too pious to acknowledge it but I can tell you although everybody takes his contribution for granted his values are deeply ingrained, thank heavens.

"Their absence would result in anarchy and people would be

desperately clambering just as if they were denied water or oxygen."

"Good God! I never ever thought I would hear such from your lips. My dear, tell me again!"

"No, Holly, it is time you mingled."

He motioned over Rupert. "All done now. If Long had the courage he would denounce Louie loudly and publicly and move on. He would be so much stronger for it, but all he can see at the moment is all of his work unravelling and permanent shame, as any of it is his fault. No, he will close it down."

"Did you give him the list?" Rupert asked.

"Yes. Did you remove his wife's name?" Morgan suddenly remembered.

"Of course. What will his next move be?"

"He will probably sulk for a while and mope a bit. Searching your soul, they call it. Never did anything for me but then Long is a real wanker."

The Reverend Long stood alone at the edge of the verge. Perhaps waiting for, wanting the ground to rise up and swallow him. The good Lord has really tested him this time and he was not prepared. He found himself wanting. All the advice over the ages he had tended others were now, worse, of no use to himself.

Depression scoured any energy for thought from his mind.

How could life have come to this? All Long's goals cherished in life evaporated.

21.
Guilt Edged

MORGAN SAT HEAVILY WIPING his brow in opposition to his office's personally set air-conditioning. Holidays were times to relax for everybody else it seemed. He had not slept well and he shivered involuntarily. "Sit down and talk me through it all slowly. Very slowly, chief!"

"Well!" Rupert was never comfortable with his title being used with emphasis. Experience taught him it was not a good omen for the day.

"Tell me about the deaths. Then we can work back," Morgan gave him a lead. The distant sirens from last night harboured in his ears. "The banker, Conrad, has been found in his flat. He died in his sleep so we won't have to worry about protection now, will we? How do you know these things so fast, anyway?"

Rupert never ceased to be surprised. He watched and waited for another wipe of the brow. Does this guy never sleep?

Morgan resigned himself. Being in charge meant he had to stay focused and positive. He tried a smile. "Make it a preliminary murder investigation, just to be sure. Let me know what the coroner says in due course. Any others?"

"A couple of tourists, but while it is a tragedy there is no suspicion and plenty of witnesses. Too drunk. Locally a family burnt to death during the night. Still looking into that but it seems initially the father was pissed while mending an electrical appliance. At least I am told that is how the fire started. I will keep you apprised. What is of real concern is that the boy was the one you had in court and he had two broken legs. So I classed it a homicide as such." The chief waited for a response.

"I have other work to do!" Morgan seemed satisfied to him at least. "I have to have breakfast or I will never see out this day. You have done well enough so far. Come back about ten and we will see where everything goes."

"Yes, boss!" Rupert acknowledged. Bugger the omens after all. "Sending that lad to The Marks may have turned out to be his salvation," he observed.

Morgan ignored him. "If you are right, chief, then you will need to bring in Snapper if only to eliminate him. See you at ten, then!" He waved his supervisor away.

The large clock hands hovered on the ten mark. The shadow of the room shimmied along its length. Below, Morgan drummed his fingers, deciding which option was best to pursue. He decided reconfirmation. Perhaps also his own reluctant involvement.

"So you are telling me you lost him!"

"That's right. First he was driving one car and then he wasn't!"

"Well! That's fucking great! How many resources have you put in place, chief?"

The chief sighed. "Three cars and seven undercover at the park. He has been there every day for the last eight days, you know."

Morgan attempted to be sympathetic. "I know what I told you, but you don't seem to understand. I don't know how simple I can put things."

Morgan felt himself failing. He tried another tack. "Your undercovers are good, aren't they? I don't want him alerted. Now look …"

His telephone interrupted him. "What?" he growled. His lips tightened. "Just a minute, I need to put this on the speaker phone. I can hardly hear you." He pointed his finger at his chief meaning silence.

"OK, Snapper. That is better. Um, where are you?"

"Well!' they heard Snapper say. "I was going to the park as is my custom but there were a few extra groundsmen, power guys and newly pregnant women around. The park's obviously preparing for something special. I didn't want to be an interference so I went for a drive instead. Relaxing, driving, you know."

Morgan's expression grew darker at each word. He screwed up a page from an open file in front of him into a tight ball and flung it at his chief. "I will look into it. How many would you say were there?" His tone kept light. The chief let the ball bounce off his forehead but he kept it. He couldn't be sure in the clamour it didn't contain something important enough not to be lost.

"Seven, I guess."

The chief shrugged his shoulders and left the room quietly. "I have some pressing matters!" he mouthed.

"Give me a ring later, would you?" Morgan continued.

"Sure."

Morgan cut a path to his doorway. "Get back in here. We are going to have to work this out." And stomped back to his desk.

The chief returned and sat down uninvited. The two looked at each other in silence.

"Boss, I am going to need your help! You know the guy! Do I need my elite squad?"

Morgan wiped his large hand down his face. "This means I cannot touch the judicial process once I agree, you know. Have your squad on standby and for heaven's sake don't refer to them as elite. I just can't take that at the moment!"

"Yes, I know the limitations," the policeman acknowledged. "But it can't go on."

"No, it can't!" Morgan agreed drumming his fingers. "You can do the paperwork later. I want you to start at the beginning. Get the bloody hotel records and I want an officer with the best general knowledge and can best things like logic puzzles. He or she doesn't have to be the best officer. In fact I doubt if he would be. And get him up here now! Do you have anyone in mind?"

"Yep! Matt sticks out like a sore thumb. Very useful on some things, useless on others. You perhaps met him once to my knowledge. What is the first step we know Snapper took?" Rupert knew who he wanted straight away.

"That would be the Clear View Towers!" Morgan claimed the advantage. "I want to see your Matt with those hotel register records! And you had better have a copy here!"

"Of course." The chief seemed to have left for just a minute when he returned with his officer.

Morgan welcomed them cheerfully, positively into his room. "Come in, chief, and Matt, is it?" He accepted a tower of papers onto his desk, making room on top of other towers.

"Yes!" Matt looked like a shark, Morgan thought. Slanting forehead with a long aquiline nose falling back to a receding chin and teeth and streamlined body. He was even dressed in grey. He thought a fin or two wouldn't look out of place.

"Here, boy, you will be sitting in my seat for this exercise, but don't answer the phone," he joked, as he propelled Matt into his chair with his desk assorted with hotel records.

"What I want you to do is list suspect names. By that I mean double meanings — Ben Dover, for instance. Go back to the start of the month and check them out discreetly. Some parents are not kind to their children. You may have to go back further. A month at a time if necessary."

"Right," Matt acknowledged. "Should not take a day to list and two days for the personal checks. OK?"

"You are the boss!" Morgan stared him. "And remember, don't answer the phone. Contact me by the chief when you feel the need. He and I are going on a little walkabout."

As they left the room Morgan put his hand conciliatory on the chief's shoulder. "Where to next, my friend?"

"We have an older car registered to him. You might like to start there."

Morgan sighed. It was going to be a long day. "A Valiant?"

"Yes, how did you know?"

"Top of the Hill?"

"Yes again." Then an afterthought: "Shit!"

"Your staff have questioned the owner, of course?"

"Of course. And gone into his records but nothing."

"Better to let me try, ah? It's not far away. We can walk. I need time to think." And they obliged to silence.

"Top of the Hill," the salesman greeted them. His check jacket louder than neon and contrast to the already heat of the day.

"You have met the chief?" Morgan dispensed with courtesies.

"Yes, but I haven't made a sale yet."

"You know who I am?"

"Yes, but I haven't made a sale yet." He paused. "I have done nothing wrong, you know!"

"I agree," Morgan replied. "But that won't still won't stop me closing you down. There are plenty with eyes for this piece of soil!"

"Even on his deathbed, Dad said you were a big prick!"

"I hope you listened then." The chief raised an eyebrow. Morgan continued. "You have received instructions?"

"Yes!"

"Full co-operation?"

"Yes!"

"You are only trying to make a dollar?"

"What are you — some sort of fucking duo?"

"Tell me about the deal then."

"Well, I sold this big dude an old Valiant. It was a good sale actually. Anyway, he said he might like to try different cars and he would pay a premium. In fact he paid handsome premiums. You know what it was like when Dad let you kids have the cars. They always came back better than when they left. So it seemed fine with me."

"Go on?" Morgan prompted him.

"Nothing more to tell. He looked destitute but turned out as rich as."

What do you think, chief? Close him down!"

"I agree wholeheartedly after what he neglected to tell us!" The chief was irate. The salesman was now sweating freely.

"What else happened?" Morgan didn't hide his impatience.

"One car came back later with a minor fender bender but the dude paid for it all to be fixed properly."

"A green Toyota?" The chief was getting up to speed.

"For Christ's sake, if you know all this why are you hassling me?" the salesman was pleading. "I have done everything I was told. This has been his script so far!"

"Did he ask about other sales?" Morgan maintained pressure.

"Yes! No, no, I seem to recall he did ask something. It didn't seem important and I don't remember."

"It's important now!" the salesman was prompted by the chief.

"Give me time, for God's sake! Yes! That's right, he asked about a BMW I sold to some kids the same day. Cash! He asked about the kids as much as about the car. Rich little pricks! That's all! I swear that's all now!"

"Relax." Morgan was all reassurances now. "You can search out the records for the BMW and give the papers to the chief, OK?"

"Fine!" concluded the chief cutting out the salesman. "*Now* I have all the information I wanted," he said. "You might make a sale over there if you want us to go."

"Thanks very much!" he called to the disappearing backs. From now on it would be just straight sales. He didn't need all this again.

❋ ❋ ❋

The shark smiled. "I need to talk to the boss first if that's alright, Mr Politician. I can tell you this guy is a piece of work but once you get into his brain it is all so obvious. Saved me hours."

"We are all grown-ups here." The chief wanted to be open.

"OK, then. This is how he operated. He booked in three different rooms in three different names. Each room was about a week apart but he was in a position to observe any goings on in the previous rooms. This means he plays percentages. He moves on when there is a probable link in a probable time. See, most others wait until they have exhausted their asset as such but you will never catch this fellow in this manner. Very, very good really."

Matt stopped for a drink and to gather his thoughts. "Systematic. I would wager he checked in, in three different staff shifts."

He swallowed at his prospects. "The names follow in sequence. Well, they do after the first one. The first alias I discovered was 'Albert Abbey'. See, you can shorten his name to Al hence to 'alibi'. Next week there came Mr Evan Dents, or 'evidence'. And if you work back in the same proportions he first registered as Mr Alby Baukor. It must mean 'I'll be back' or something like that. I will have to work on that a bit more. Not a fish any more."

Morgan beamed at him. "You have done very well indeed! Don't worry about the names any further."

Matt cleared his throat nervously. "Well, thanks! I sent for their passports and they are all the same person. Bloody good quality though. If hadn't seen them together I wouldn't have picked them. And that Baukor room is right next to where that sports guy died."

He swallowed hard. "I also did comparative checks on other guests and found three. They are a Mrs Eve Endswell, a Miss Evelyn Horsewell and a Miss Yvonne Thwaites. They are the same person. He had an accomplice."

"Oh fuck!" the chief moaned. "Could it get any worse? Do we know who she is?"

"Yes, we all do!' The shark bit tentatively. "She has been Morgan's recent companion!"

"Are you sure?" the chief exclaimed. "What about the names?"

Morgan stared out the window. "All's well that ends well! We had better find her." The pieces were fitting together.

The chief looked downcast. "She has disappeared. We have been on the lookout for her for a couple of days now!"

The three sat and pondered their next move. Matt lost patience first. "You are right about some parents. Do you want to know what they call their offspring?" He chuckled to himself. "I wouldn't thank you!"

"Not just now!" the chief sighed. "You can return to your duties now. You really have excelled. Say, boss, do you think he may have used other hotels? I could have them checked out. The major ones anyway!"

"I am not condoning one of your fishing expeditions." Morgan expressed doubts.

"No! It would not. That just wouldn't do, right at this time."

"OK, then, as long as we are clear about that. And I will keep Matt here with me for now."

22.
Boys Will Be

Beers flowed freely from both can and bottle. Ross sat on top of, for the time being now, his car and tried to look cheerful. By default he was leader. The mantle sat uncomfortably heavy on him.

Simon was missing, perhaps even dead, and Ross knew he had no resources to fuel let alone maintain the car beneath. He contemplated driving the last into the Black Hole. He looked down and tutted to himself. Froth spilled from all the mouths hungry for more. He was sure poor little toots Tom was only gargling.

Ross leaned towards him. "You don't have to drink if you don't like it. Nobody will judge you on that!"

Tom spat back. "I am one of us. What you all do, so will I."

Ross shrugged concern off his shoulders. All he wished for was to experience *drive*. Not just twisting the steering wheel like motorists, but throwing the car around, pushing the boundaries, challenging others, feeling squeezed by the force — all increased his heartbeat.

He thought of Adam. He had always respected his quiet friend. Adam never spoke unless he had something to say, always worth listening to. Now here was a potential leader! Plus he was a natural with the girls. They would flock to him and shy away from Simon. Probably influenced by their parents.

Except now since the death of his friend Adam remained troubled, spending time alone at the cemetery, talking to the dead; he was troubled, seriously troubled. But he did know a lot!

Perhaps Adam knew where Simon's treasure stashes were. That would help! Yes! Ross would seek him out tomorrow. Perhaps even be able to talk him into taking the main role.

Ross perked himself up. From the pinnacle of the reserve he looked at the far bay, nearby he watched his passengers knowing he had dominated all and he lazed as he awaited fresh challenges. Who knows, perhaps even the law? He glimpsed at the many trails of the reserve, the criss-crossing he knew intermittently, the slopes and places set aside for walkers, bikes, boarders. He knew them all and how to turn them to his advantage. What was it — ten acres? Sometimes ample, sometimes short.

He watched the ocean pool far below. Boats hovered about the perimeter of the whale sanctuary like ants round a saucer. No, Ross decided seeing as it was the sea, more like a giant jellyfish with mammoths in the centre. Tentacles flashed and submerged pulsing in and out in a slow rhythmic beat. The wakes of tourist boats keeping mathematical precision both from each other and from the pod, daring then fearful.

Stapling them in place were the fishermen, patient yet struggling at their limited resource. One of nature's own clocks.

Idyllic!

Despite a swig from his bottle, Ross felt his mouth dry in anticipation. At the gateway to the reserve a throaty roar of a heavy engine called an animal challenge to a leader. Trails of dust and grit showed the driver was fast and skilled. Ross slid down into the driver's seat. His instincts told him 'not the pretenders he had outdriven totally inside his comfort zone. In fact it was harder to frighten his passengers and Lord knows he tried!

This was to be a real challenge! This would be his day!

He checked on his crew and wondered if they realized as he planted his foot for the entrance. He spun down the slope careering into the gentle arc. So often this manoeuvre had caused the other driver to slide down the camber away from the road and into the tide. Game over!

But the opponent was already there waiting, anchored solid. Ross could see it was just not going to move. A big car! Bigger than anything he had faced so far. And black, just sitting there engine purring. He swung the car sideways towards the higher fork in the road and braced for impact!

The BMW tore great widths out of the road; its engine screamed in response to the driver's insistence and rocked up the grove. Ross fought control, comfort zone all abandoned and then they were gone. The opposition car turned from black to a dark purple.

Had they hit? Ross did not see how they could not have. He snapped a look at the driver opposite and for just a second thought he saw him smile with his arm casually resting along the seat. Surely not! Back to driving though and he had to really concentrate not to over-adjust. He felt he knew where the next encounter would be and he had the advantage. Nobody could drive that fast on the lower ground to beat him to the destination.

Well, we will see soon enough, Ross thought from out of the bush the dust and shingle conditions would highlight just where things stood. He started to slow down. "Now keep a good eye out for the prick!" he commanded. And the others were happy enough to do so, to see for themselves, to reassure themselves, and to be part of it all to make such a contribution to the winning team. It was all to be part of the team.

"Christ almighty!" little Tommy cried out. "Look at that. It's more like a small aircraft. Look at the dust. Nobody can drive like that!"

They all saw. Dust spewed up furiously as if the wake of a boat. How could a car be going so fast it was actually fully clear of the dust? "I think we are dead meat!" A voice from the back echoed their thoughts.

Except for Ross.

He was not one to be overawed. "Look. Nobody can drive like that and live. You have seen for yourselves. You have all heard tales from your mum and dads. How many has the Black Hole become a permanent car park to madmen like that? I am going to the hump track for the dirt bikes. He cannot follow us there. He will want us to come down to his level. How wrong can you get?"

He drove on with intent. His passengers began to feel some comfort. Ross did not bother to look at them. They were making him upset!

"See!" he demanded as he fishtailed dramatically spinning into the starting arena. "Nowhere in sight! Make the most of the moment. I will think this out!"

In his mirror he saw the car already facing round the corner as floating a hovercraft. Ross could not recall even stunt drivers being so good.

"Holy crap! He is bloody good alright!" Ross screamed to his passengers, "Hang on tight! The bastard can't follow us over the offroad traps!"

"Can't you just shove him off? You have done it before. We remember them from here, before." The back sought desperate reassurance.

"You can't fight an iron bar with a skewer, you stupid shits!" he answered back. "Look at our small bomb compared to that mobile backyard." The BMW lurched over the crest squeezing the occupants into a solitary seat. "Here we go! Hold on to the floor now!" The car launched into the air.

At the thud Ross screamed to his passengers, "Can you see him? I need to know where he is!"

"All I can see are feet!" Before any other response the car again tussled with gravity, dropping occupants, stomachs and positives.

Groans followed the three-peats as Ross fought to control the car; he had not gone down the race near this pace before. Finally the BMW succumbed to gravity; the occupants had long ago. At the long end of this short journey he spun the car around a semicircle in the soft dirt trying to find their pursuer himself. When he needed them the others proved useless!

Despite the circumstances Ross had made it to the bottom. Success! The first he knew of who had survived. Christ, he was good!

Part of Ross's brain remained detached from the reality of driving. When had his confidence slowed?

Perhaps when he saw his opponent. Expecting the usual Japanese sedan, seemingly the chosen favourite, he baulked momentarily at the sight of the wide steel-encased American monster Valiant.

Instantly he revised his tactics. Somehow now his decisions were less resolute.

Whereas his driving to this point of success was based on instinct and judgment, now his options were based on hope and desperation. Was this the same for everybody? Despite knowing the reserve like the back of his hand, he was choosing not what he wanted. In fact he was being dictated to! Manipulated! He knew of a half-moon bay short of the road to the Black Hole. He braked forcefully!

"What was it?" the others demanded of him. Clearly they could not read his thoughts. Just as well!

Ross looked around earnestly. Yes! He was right! "Bugger me! Where is the dust cloud? Can anyone see the dust cloud of the other car?" he screamed at them again. For once he did not know what to do next.

He raced the car over the lip of the bay. He saw only the Valiant facing him, filling his world, monstering him! Instantly he knew he was wrong, instantly his world was filled with blinding headlights and car horns. Blindly Ross gunned the BMW into a bank!

Luck ran out. The car rotated sideways to face the bank. The Valiant cruised up behind them, all the time in the world.

Abject fear held the kids in their seats. They all watched as the large driver approached their car. Worse, they now recognized him from the bank. Where was Simon when you needed him? This was all his fault!

Snapper tore open the driver's door. Ross made his move far too late. He was grabbed and thrown forward in a single movement that rocked the whole car. His steering wheel seemed to disappear into his chest. He turned off-cream as his face contorted, his lips a little round circle blowing out little fish bubbles. The others could just stare in terror at pure agony.

The passenger door ripped open and Snapper hauled out the occupant. The back seat noted with alarm he never reappeared. This momentary thaw galvanized them into reaction. But Snapper sat in the front seat and reached back.

The side passenger behind propelled between the seats. He began to say something but was silenced by a cuff across his mouth.

Snapper examined him and shook his head.

"You! Boy! Are stupid? Do you think wearing a ridiculous hat backwards gives you special powers you would otherwise not possess? You should have been proud just to be yourself. You should have bought it with your own money, not mine. Nobody else can help you now.

"Gangsters rely on others and cowardice, even the law, to survive. The only power that counts is intelligence and strength and money and you unfortunately have not enough."

His backhanded sound completely filled the car. From the back the victim slumped back, his head lolled sideways and he didn't move. Watery discharged from this nose and pooled into his lip.

"What about you, son? Nice watch with my money?" Like a roll call, Snapper thought to himself.

A shy nod, the owner's fate accepted. Snapper reached back and the boy slid down symmetrical to the other side asleep. "Guess your time has run out," Snapper observed to nobody. Well, that was all done easily.

A groan in the back startled him. He reached over and fumbled around bodies.

With an effort etched on his face he hauled up Tom. "You must be the runt, right?" He examined the quivering form up and down.

In the end he gave up. "Well, runt? How have you spent my money? Can't see anything. Buy yourself a pair of nappies, jock?" he laughed at Tom.

The runt blew out sheer temper. "Arsehole! Gave it all to Mum. She's fucking dying. Would have spent it for you two to swap places!" Where it came from Tom could not understand. He had nothing to lose.

"Lying little runt?" Snapper challenged him. "I do not think I have your full attention."

"For God's sake, look around! None of my friends are here any more. Why the hell would I lie to the likes of you?" Tom carried on. "If you are so pissed, why does your expression not show it at all? This is no ordinary conversation, pal!" he added. "Couldn't even raise your fucking voice!"

"OK, little runt. Everybody lies to me regardless. I will tell you what I will do," Snapper answered, same tone as always. "If you are lying, you are dead. Understand? Dead! Your mum will be your company as will your family. If you are being truthful, your dear old mum will get whatever I can for her to live to a ripe old age. And you have to follow your dreams. Live to a ripe old age as well. Maybe even tell your grandchildren on your knee about this very day. Even if it means growth shots. Same as your retelling will grow. But to do so you have to take a ride on your car. Understand?"

"No!" Tom just knew he was dead. "This is over the top for a few bucks."

Snapper shook his finger at him. "Money is one thing. Dominating pedestrians is another!" He hauled Tom to the top of the car. "No, you have to sit here for as long as you can. Hold as tight as you can!"

❁ ❁ ❁

"Good, good, come to me. Oh, so innocent!" Cedric watched as Miranda casually stepped into the alley.

The shadows did not intrude into her elation. This whole new world was exciting, dangerous, stealthy, plus relationships she cursed before were now a major weapon. And she was learning fast. Learning to be finely tuned, to understand body language rather than instinct. What a sheltered life she had led!

She hardly noticed a drunk propped supporting the arch. There were so many around thanks to the sports. The blow delivered from nowhere. No sound, no indication, no giveaway, as if a surgical move.

Cedric always impressed himself at his expertise. "Hope you like my volunteer?" Cedric bundled her into the van obscured by the arch. "What I have always wished for!" His enthusiasm glowed. "No complaints, no administration difficulties, for as long as I want. Marvellous!"

❁ ❁ ❁

Matt looked at the small cartons on his desk. He rearranged them into a pyramid shape. That wasn't right so he knocked them over. He tried square, castle, rectangle, but the camera packages just stared back at him. He tumbled them over his desk yet again.

Colleagues knew this behaviour. How he thought things out like this was beyond them. They knew if at the end of the day whatever was in the cardboard shuffle was destined to be broken while he worked out what to do.

Matt looked into space. All these cameras and staff with not one to trust. He would have to work it out somehow alone. He knew pressured instant results were expected.

His cellphone on vibrate mode shuffled a path between small containers. He watched until it moved no more. Now that he had lost his habit he picked it up. "What?" Matt not bothering to disguise he was not happy.

Others watched in open disgust as Matt disappeared out the door. "Cameras have caught a car going over the Black Hole. I have got to get out there!" There are limits as to how much official business can cover voyeurism.

Two others got up slower. "He will need help. If anyone wants to know he asked us to help him." They too left, shaking their heads. Others started to gossip, secretly hoping the pictures showed clear images or better yet video.

Matt politely approached the officer in charge of the scene. He had restored his demeanour on his drive down. "What can you tell us so far?"

"Sorry, boss, not allowed to say. You know the regulations. No speculation — leave it all to the experts."

Matt felt frustration rising in a solid lump in his throat at bureaucracy. "Look, you are in charge. All I am asking is a personal opinion, nothing official! For Christ's sake! Before every man and his dog come and muddle it up."

The officer pointed at an arriving police car. "Like those two?"

"That's right," Matt pushed. "Even though they are with me. They are prone to making errors of judgment. Now just between you and me before they get within earshot."

"OK, then. A group of local boys hooned around in their car too fast for the Hole. It has happened before and it will happen again. This time they crashed it into that outcrop over there instead of it disappearing completely. Driver died at the wheel, impaled into his chest. Would not have felt much, I don't think.

"Couple of others shot through the windscreen, and," he sighed, "only one survivor was this squirt sitting on the roof. He is in shock, as you would expect, and we are about to take him away. Here are your mates."

"Thank you!" Matt was pleased. "Thank you so much!"

"That's OK." The officer was all concessionary. "We were not first on the scene. The gulls are now a bit fatter. In fact the locals always ring us first when they start to gather. But," he shrugged, "I guess they are hungrier than us. Until next time." And he walked away.

Matt turned to his helpers. "There is one survivor. Find out where he has been taken and if he has anything at all to say!"

"Right, boss." The smaller of the two turned to go.

"No!" Matt called him back. "I have other work for you. Send your mate." The other gestured acceptance and left.

"Now you have me curious!" his help asked. "Any of us can do routine tasks. What have you planned for me?"

Matt smarted at him. "Sometimes you can be too clever for your own good! But you are right, of course. You are to check out the movements from the security monitors and once you have them, the cameras are non-functional, understand?"

"Of course, boss," he grinned. "In fact I am lucky to get what I do!" He thought for a minute. "Do you want me to collect them?"

They then smiled. "Very good! Leave them in my car then follow me down to the final moments at the rocks."

Matt followed the wheel treads down to the edge. He could see they had braked but far too late. He tossed up between race or chase. Security should tell. He peered over the edge.

The disaster was now old. The car lay face down; shattered windows and birds have left their telltale signs. Tarpaulins lay in a neat row and because of the size of the occupants nobody would say confidently whether all the bodies were beneath. A tow truck waited in the background.

The assistant leaned forward using Matt to balance. "What a waste! Do you want to see the bodies at all?"

"Nope!" Matt replied. "Do you know if they are easily identified? And do you know if any are missing? You may have to ask the survivor."

"Yes! Identification is not a problem, according to one of the searchers," the assistant advised solemnly. "Don't know how many we should be looking for but I will by the end of the day. Funny how only some cars get those rocks. I guess some drivers are better than others."

"I guess," Matt agreed. "Better drivers does not mean better off though, does it?" He backed up to the road. "Take the cameras off the back seat and see what you can find. I want to linger here a little longer." He added, "By myself."

"Finished, boss?" the other returned. "I have bad news and bad news for you, I'm afraid."

"What?" Matt more or less demanded. "Don't leave me in suspense."

"I have kept a beat policeman with the kid. The doctor tells me he has amnesia. Can't say whether it is genuine yet so we will have to wait. His lawyers are already there and we will have trouble getting anything but basic facts. The beat guy will keep us informed as soon as possible as things develop."

Matt was surprised. "His lawyers are there already. That's crap. Obviously his amnesia is confined to the recent turn of events."

His assistant shook his head. "Do not know, boss. His lawyers are Rich and Co, who live up to their name. I do not think the boy knows anything about them yet," he added.

Matt hesitated. "This is getting queer. Those bastards live up to their name for sure. How can a kid afford them? Only a dozen or so people in the whole island can even afford a look in."

"Well, he must be rich alright," the assistant commented. "The lawyers have taken him to the Island Seat Practice, as poncey as you can get. Plus his mother is now there too and just as well or she would be dead by now."

"This is amazing. The car is funny, the victim is funny, the hospice is funny, the lawyers are funny, his amnesia is funny. Everything is so wrong. You two see if you can find out who is financing him and his family, and if his agents care to enlighten us on anything. They won't in my experience, just out of principle."

They watched from their cars as the scene slowly wound up. Sometimes it's good just to watch others at work without having to worry about motive, yet keeping an interest.

Finally the camp deserted the three leaving a solitary caretaker.

"Right!" Matt said. "I know you both can't do much more tonight but report to me by midday tomorrow with your progress. I just want to look over the scene a few times. Maybe I can see something I missed before."

He watched them leave in the same officious way they arrived and wondered what conversations would be going on as they travelled. Once out of sight he hummed to himself as he opened the boot and discreetly took out some replacement security equipment. He hoped nobody touched the empty boxes on his desk.

23.
Cedric

Spontaneous laughter and chuckles reverberated around the small hall. The small group stood around casually in support of Matt who was doubled over and in an orb of hurt not even aware of his surroundings. Through misty eyes he somehow focused on a shoe tread remnant on the polished floor.

Small imprints had resisted solvents, the ammonias and bleaches which made up the cleaning fluids. Edges had flicked away by buffeting by seasons of polishing machines. Ends of hair prickled out where they had been caught and mostly snapped or harshly torn away.

Matt was sure he would never walk upright ever again. Agony far beyond physiotherapy relief. The same hand that put him in this position roughly grabbed the front of his shirt and snapped him upright. Through gritted teeth Matt moaned out loud. His torso ripped in half, his vertebrae accordioned out and muscled back. Through his haze he heard Rupert's tone of voice give solace.

His sphere splintered in shards of bitterness as he realized the perpetrator was to be the recipient, not him. Matt resurveyed his surroundings.

An elite squad, 'The Titans', seemed cast from a single clone mould. Variations of ingredients meant some were shorter than others but all their builds solid, identical.

Strong, even their wrists were thicker than his neck. They all laughed and had fun and moved as one. In their full armour they had looked to Matt as European knights of past centuries. Heavy and cumbersome and strength-sapping even to move. Their gestures and moves in horseplay appeared ordinary, which brought Matt's self estimate to his downfall.

A blow to his lower back as they made him, and the others, welcome in their camaraderie. And instant concern and regret when Matt fell like a chopped tree.

"Look! I am really sorry!" the trooper was saying. "But I only tapped him. No power in it at all!" The others trying hard to make him feel bad.

Rupert held his shoulder. "Don't worry. I would not give him a moment's thought about it. Valuable lesson there. He should thank you, really."

The other laughed at the idea watching Matt slowly recover. He watched carefully as the group went about playful punches and lunges in good humour. As he gingerly probed and examined himself he wondered how they could tolerate hefty smacks if his had been so gentle. He found new respect and warmed towards them.

"Alright now!" Rupert called for their attention. "You have seen the maps of the place and the alterations. Any questions there?"

A dutiful silence permitted Rupert to continue. "We are not sure what his defences are likely to be. We have not discounted chemicals, after all that is one of his specialties. We have especially kitted you all up individually to additionally monitor adverse reactions. It is good. Take comfort we will know before you even start to sweat. Cedric has shown no inclination towards their use, in fact far from it, but you need to be warned. We do know he waves about a shotgun."

This brought a round of jovial cynicism.

"Look!" Rupert demanded. "I know of your record and understand your confidence but this particular one man in his own lair is something far different for you to handle. He will have in his control weapons, electronics and chemicals. He has an IQ higher than all of us put together. He has more money than the rest of all the island and he has survived so far through his wit and cunning. Do not underestimate your target! He has at least one female prisoner we think is being kept alive."

He changed tactics. "The team will be going in following the Island's second in charge.

Cedric has requested him and we want to make use of any

distraction we can. He has agreed and is heading up there as I speak. I want them and you all back here alive and intact." He pointed to Matt. "You can pick out any half dozen. They only have to beat one man!"

❊ ❊ ❊

Morgan walked purposefully up the centre line of the wide luxurious drive. The pure-white, wide paving stones seemed to follow him though he could not work out why. Now was no time to dwell on it. He continued a laborious march.

There outlined at the entrance to the great structure in the mammoth doorway Cedric waited impatiently. "Morgan!" he called, waving him over.

He held his hand out in greeting. "Morgan, I realize we have not met before but, my friend, I feel I know so much about you."

"Likewise!" Morgan accepted his greeting but looked back. "I can't help feeling I have been followed."

"Dear man," Cedric explained cheerfully. "In a sense you have. It says something about you to even notice. As a matter of fact the stones shine to reflect your presence. A basic sensor device built into each stone activates your presence. Works better, much better, at night, of course." He dismissed it. "Just a simple toy."

"Yes! Well, I was warned you wave a big gun around perhaps recklessly." Morgan felt he was straying from the point.

"Tut, tut. Now that would be uncouth, and totally unnecessary. I have such a gun inside, of course. I know you have come alone because that is what was agreed with your staff and what my security confirms to me." Cedric ushered Morgan inside.

"Perhaps you should frisk me!" Morgan warned.

Cedric chuckled. "Too much TV, I am afraid. I mean you must watch too much. My doorway is as secure as found at any major airport. My machines have already stripped you naked and would have warned me if anything untoward was identified. And at the same time render useless any recording or communications devices you may think to carry."

"What I don't know, I guess." Morgan shrugged off his doubts.

Tim had been spot on. He was glad he had listened. He had seen none of this coming.

They walked in silence through the antechamber. "Your plans in my office show a wall here, where there is nothing?" Morgan questioned him.

"And something where there is nothing," Cedric completed for him. "I have planned for the plans. Didn't Tim tell you all?" he asked.

"Some things of course," Morgan acknowledged. "But mostly scientific stuff I do not understand nor care really." Morgan gazed around in awe. So many machines all in pristine condition. He could only guess their functions. He knew they were all bloody expensive.

Cedric patiently let him gaze and wonder. "Come on!" he invited Morgan. "Let me show you my prize!"

"Can't wait!" Morgan mumbled. There was no denying Cedric his excitement.

Cedric gestured with the shotgun to a further inner chamber.

Morgan was shocked. Miranda was pinioned to a mobile frame on a wall staring, glaring at them, mouthing. Even naked before him without supports, without make-up, without dignity, she cut a magnificent figure.

"It's alright! I just got sick of her noise. I negated her vocals for my peace and quiet," Cedric dismissed her. "She will need another anaesthetic shot soon. But she has not lacked for sustenance. I've looked after her properly, you know?"

"Yes! I see benefits in that." Morgan chastised himself for a momentary lack of compassion. He shrugged. "You could put some clothes on her though? Maybe put that shotgun down, or at least don't wave it around."

"Of course!" Cedric placed it down gently on a bench. "Not the gracious host. I do apologize so. You can give the bitch a spin if you like. She is on a pivot. It dispenses with bedsores and the like. But I digress."

"What is with all these flat TV screens? Do you love yourself so much?" Morgan interrupted him as he began to appreciate the massive extent of Cedric's foresight and planning. He picked up

Cedric's gun admiring it, inspecting it fondly. Like everything else, expensive and lovingly cared for.

"Those, my friend, are body monitors. In particular individual monitors for your specialist unit. I don't recall its title. Something grand, I am sure. Though I am sure they will burst in to save us," Cedric tutted. Small talk while he assessed his circumstance.

"Those are state-of-the-art secure confidential equipment!" Morgan could still be shocked. "We only just have them ourselves."

"I suppose," Cedric agreed. How could such a major figure be so naive? "I follow the principle that what one man can invent, another man can buy." This topic was of no consequence to him. He wanted to move on.

"Now Miranda here is my pride and joy! She is the whole package! A world first! And she is all mine. Who should I name her with after myself? Fuck the Nobel prizes!" Cedric gloated, oblivious of company in his moment. He went over and gave her a playful spin. "What every scientist craves right here, all mine!"

She tried to spit on him.

"You have lost me completely. And you have lost it totally!" Morgan sat passively on a stool watching, waiting, patient.

Cedric sighed. No wonder what they say about government officials. "I will take you through step by step. Layman's terms, of course!" He bent over his panel, his back to the room.

"I can handle patronizing but first I have a few questions to put to her. Don't worry, yes or no answers. She needs only to nod her head." Morgan was all business. "Now, my love?" he started pausing only to make sure he had her attention.

A spark of intimacy! Miranda felt her hopes rise. His look dashed them. In her chaos she tried to remember Snapper's advice. She only recalled his warning and she was furious with herself, confident though if Snapper could extricate himself from this predicament then she could.

"You have been a busy girl, haven't you?" Morgan asked.

"You are bloody right there. She butchered Cyril! I have eyewitnesses," Cedric spat out.

"Is that so?" Morgan asked towards her. "Yes! That would make sense."

Miranda raised her eyes but no confirmation or denial. She wanted to work out just how much Morgan actually knew before committing to anything.

Morgan smiled. Miranda did not like that at all. "Let me put it this way so a child can understand — a nursery rhyme. 'Rub-a-dub-dub, three men in the tub, and who do you think they would be? The brother, the banker and the game breaker, I think you had a hand in all three.' Yes?" he asked. "But were there any others?"

Miranda plummeted in despair.

"What a bitch!" Cedric hissed. "I just knew she was all bad! Any others? There is nobody left in the population now!"

"Your answer?" Morgan demanded, ignoring his outburst.

She nodded. And mouthed a reply.

"What's that?" Morgan asked, reading her lips. Then he worked it out. "Of course, the golfer!" He could sense he knew all from her now relaxed body.

"Here!" Cedric beside himself. "Take my gun! When I am finished, shoot the bitch before I do something much worse." He played at his keyboard.

Morgan instinctively took the offered weapon.

A big screen burst into life. Of the whole screen a small dot held centre. "This is the little bug slightly magnified so you can see something. This is one of my living specimens. I will increase magnification times a thousand. Fascinating! Watch!"

The pudding bowl image enlarged to melon shape. Even Morgan felt sickened by its off-purple streaked colours; sickly little feeler thingies surrounded its body and even at this great range the edges remained obscure, unfocused. "Shit! It moved!" he suddenly realized.

"Of course it did." Cedric hated repetition. "I said it was alive, didn't I? Now look see all those barbs. This is the infection cycle, if you like, and those enzymes it excretes on the perimeter act as a numbing agent while it digests the host. I would show you but it takes too long. Perhaps a speed frame show later. What is it?"

He sensed questions without even looking up.

"Don't tell me we sneeze those in?" Morgan didn't like such an idea. "The UN officials seemed to think it was one of the most likely scenarios."

"No," Cedric chortled as he spoke. "UN are morons. It is a type of VD. That is why Miranda is so important. You see, after you screwed her, it attached to your manhood. But relax, men never know if they have it. But by screwing others you deposit it in your lover. Lovers plural if you are a pig. Sort of like bees and flowers pollinating. OK. Now this one likes women, well some women. I cannot yet give you a definitive list, but I am working on it. In the women he does like, this little fellow commences to eat them from the inside. By the time the body can tell, the internals have ceased to function. Of course by then it is too late. Miles too late. You with me so far?"

"Yes!" Morgan replied. "You have my full attention now!"

"Good. Good." Cedric was pleased. He wondered if he sounded patronizing. He liked patronizing. "Now if it were a simple process you would expect the female population to be decimated. No! Indeed you have to have the right ingredients with the right nutrition and temperatures. You see, he is very selective."

"What is its time frame?" Morgan interrupted him in full flow.

"Not what you think." Cedric conceded a decent query. "I have not actually starved a little blighter. I would think in the natural course of events perhaps two weeks per male but it is the female that is interesting. You see the process can be subverted by menstrual cycles, menopause, pregnancy, maybe even foreplay. It is just so hard to make an informed guess. Say at least a week to germinate, and not a single clue. Admirable!"

Morgan looked up at Miranda. She was mouthing denials, shaking her head, anger written everywhere.

She looked aghast at the transformation of her lover. The more appealing the features had been, the greater they turned gargoyle. Was his expression of a little boy with his newest best present? Were quivering lips meant he was to weep? Perhaps real anger?

Smothering emotions? A child's anticipation? Delight? Not really a smile suppressed, but something positive, she prayed.

"Oh look! Your friends have announced their imminent arrival." Cedric watched the little waves and numbers print on his multiple screens, a single string in row after row of blank screens. "See number four. Well, he may be excited but his graph shows a heart abnormality. See! Only half a dozen bodies. Less than half the corps. I should feel insulted." He smiled to himself.

"Can't see anything!" Morgan looked on vaguely. He looked up at Miranda. "Been helping Snapper?" More an accusation than a question. He knew he knew the answer.

Cedric grunted. Surely the crowning moment of his life. Some liked the night sky but Cedric just loved the little twinkling lights, security he designed and could read, a variation of disease, his brother's killer, an almost complete cycle of infection, real documentation, plus his government official guarantee of safety, wealth. He wanted nothing more. Others in the room barely existed!

"Never mind. I will warn him about it later. Free of charge, of course," Cedric seemed genuinely concerned.

"Too late for that!" Morgan replied.

The shot shucked the back of Cedric's head like soft spread. He died without changing expression as the gunfire reverberated around the room. He fell forward collapsing into his own mess.

Miranda breathed out. Perhaps she could hope.

Morgan took rebound steps back and fired in instinctive reaction. An instant tunnel carved out Miranda's lower abdomen. Gore illuminated her tunnelled interior. Small bits started to mount onto the floor at her feet. Her stomach spasmed, arched down, threatening to spill down.

A second shot blew into her lower chest. Her breast now not supported leaned inward. The wound lightly covered by a wafer-skin portcullis provided a modest wavering screen to dark black tissue contrasting white and yellow carnage behind. Blood sludged down some of the gaps destined for a disinfected floor.

Morgan could not bear to look at either of them. Instead he kept his attention to the screens as he waited for his forces to arrive. He wondered about his security and the screens and how could you read number four and make anything of it.

He sat and waited.

What to say!

24.
Joss

Snapper peered maudlin from the same reserve peak that had thrilled the kids. Clouds ambled out to sea hinting at him to do the same. Gentle puffs of wind nudged him from behind in turn to assist him in the direction. He felt all, but unnecessarily, he knew it was time to go. He looked longingly at his Valiant. In such a short time he had grown to love his car more than at first sight. They just do not make them like that any more. He swivelled around asserting his privacy.

Alone now, tears fell openly, freely. Blurred, he spied the pod in the a faraway deep blue pool below making signs to leave. Seemed to him even they gave broad hints. He took them all on board.

He slowly drudged to his car taking from a small white linened bucket he so gently lifted a wafer strip into his big hands as he directed himself for the enormous old tree with its mass of roots.

He murmured an old island prayer of mourning and burial ritual as he walked. Pausing, he whispered reverently, "Goodbye, warrior! You have played an important role for your country. It is a pity you and everyone else will never know but at least I can give you honour."

A softly gravel voice came from the tree. "Yes! Goodbye, warrior!"

Snapper turned massively red at this invasion of his most private moment; he wiped his hands across his mouth.

"Christ!" he exclaimed. Even looking around now he could not see Cad emerge. This worried him.

Cad held out a small wooden box. "I have brought you a casket. Your lessons are overdue anyway. You are surprised to see me? Why?"

"Yes and no," Snapper conceded. "Help me with these bloody rituals and his burial. I have been away and you know them off by heart."

"What is the essence here?" Cad asked Snapper.

Snapper sighed. "You bury the local good in the roots of the tree. The body breaks down and the tree absorbs them thus the tree holds all the generations of islanders."

Yes! "What else do you need to know?" Cad asked. "You know you yourself have peed up against the tree, have you not? Of course you have! We all have but nobody has told us to or not to, have they? That is because it is in our genes."

Snapper blushed at the thought even though there was no hint of retribution. "And what about those bodies down there?" he accused, pointing to shadows outlined in the earth.

In silence they dug to arm's length under one of the heavy roots and placed the small wooden container. In silence they covered their tracks and stood watching, inspecting leaving no signs.

"They are also part of the island now," Cad concluded. "Now for your lessons so when you return you can teach others."

"Others! Others? What others? You have never told of any others?" Snapper was shocked.

Cad snapped at him. "You think you are special! Nothing special about you. Your arrogance is a sin and you are best rid of it!"

"I am here to serve the island!" Snapper cried angrily.

"Yes! And you have done well but what do you think has happened in your absence?" Cad asked. "Never crossed your mind, did it? Perhaps now you are thinking who?"

Snapper looked crestfallen. "You are right, as always. What to do now? All these non-islanders here."

Cad conceded a little. "There are not that many of concern. Two from Honk Kong will never make trial. The policeman has been given his message. But he has not shown his colours yet. It is time for you to go. I, myself, have been in the same dilemma. There used to be three but in my grandeur made it two. I have the mantle of humility, which has been my burden since. So you have learnt more than I did faster. Time for you to farewell."

Snapper nodded. He looked around one last time. How he loved this place! Absent-mindedly he brushed some bushes. Not even dusty, despite their environment. Perhaps there is something in them that repels the dust and crap, he thought. In different circumstances he could market that.

Then he climbed into his car. He drove, his head against an old dead trunk in place of the headrest, to where the BMW started its final leg.

Satisfied he had planned everything he furtively inspected the hidden cameras set for motion. Sliding down between the seats he started the car rolling clutching his little bucket tight. How fast it gathered momentum! He felt himself tip over and pressure squeeze him till he winced.

Guessing he had ducked further, the trunk still managed to scrape the side of his head before exploding forward through the glass as the car came to rest the same as those before.

He had no time for discomfort now as he kicked himself out before gingerly, religiously, delicately stir his little bucket. Each time he felt tears in his eyes and a lump in his throat demanding he show his grief before his gods.

Snapper cautiously followed the remnants of a path past the cameras and into the surroundings.

❀ ❀ ❀

Matt looked over the scene, all too familiar with him now. He was pleased there were no kids involved. Just a driver and probable suicide. Thank heavens for a bit of normality.

He reversed back along the trail to one of his cameras. Better to check everything first!

❀ ❀ ❀

Matt stared at the tiny screen and replayed it again and again. There was no doubt about it. Morgan's friend Snapper was clearly in the driver's seat. There may have been someone beside him, but the lens had not picked it up, just a blur, and not even much of that. He decided not to involve his principles at this stage. Pity the cameras missed the actual crash.

"You!" he called to another underling at the scene. "Get me my phone!" He decided to ring Bob. Bob always knew what to do discreetly and everybody trusted him.

"OK!" Matt signalled to his staff. "You can take over. I have to see the boss's assistant when he gets here." And he ambled away from the scene.

❀ ❀ ❀

Bob bowed his head after listening to Matt. He swallowed. "The timing sucks! In a few days it is Cedric's funeral. Fortunately it starts around noon. You will need to be at Morgan's office by nine. I will get the bosses there and you can give them a full report."

"Who are you ringing now?" Matt asked Bob.

"The coroner is busy. I will have to try Dr McLear," he replied.

25.
Dovetail

WHILE MORGAN SAT IN his chair, others gathered as if a social occasion, mingling freely, casual.

"Address us, Matt!" Morgan started the ball rolling.

"There is evidence we have found Snapper and he has suffered a misfortune!" Matt began his story.

Rupert interrupted at the sound of that. "That is too bad!" He was mindful Snapper's friends were present. "What precisely have you got?" For once he loved patsy questions.

"I have video evidence Snapper went into the Black Hole. No body but he left body parts behind attached to his car. Sufficient for us to think whoever the driver was must be dead," Matt told them.

"That is so," Tim agreed. "The authority has other DNA to match the youths. There is no such match for this adult."

"Is there a way around it? Seems to be a closed option to me," Morgan seemed resigned.

"Nothing has been made public yet," Rupert added. "With no body and other funerals to come and go I am not satisfied. The public have not missed him and I have kept a lid on it to avoid speculation."

Tim nodded. "Not necessarily. Remember it is not my expertise but precedents have been set in criminal cases where family DNA is sufficient identification for conviction by family association. It may also be so here. I have checked as a matter of priority." He cautioned, "I cannot alter whatever the evidence reveals!"

Rupert wanted more. "I am satisfied Snapper has departed. However as questions remain I will hold his file open until proven otherwise by Rupert and Matt. Now we should make our way to Cedric's funeral. Nobody will want to miss the passing of this dignitary."

❋ ❋ ❋

Cedric's funeral procession wound its way laboriously, snaking painfully around those fresh gravesites to the latest hole in the ground. Most bowed their heads at that poor family burned so horribly.

Everybody recognized the wife's buried marker festooned still with bright huge bouquets. The son saw leftover flowers while the father's was in contrast near barren. Indeed, some drivers lowered their windows and proudly spat. No retribution now!

Bob weaved his department car around the back of the endless block of flats. Nobody could see through the tinted passenger windows.

He wished no-one could see the driver either but he knew to persevere. His instruction had been spelt out specifically both in execution and timing. He swallowed as he pulled to a halt and cursed his own failings.

Confusion spelt out time. Bob thought bewildered at the array of emotions. He felt wonder so powerful it could not be contained.

Holly had stood there even in mourning black, a picture of perfect health. No signs evident of her struggles. To Bob her magnificence strained to choke him. Thank heavens he remained at the edge of the frame.

He instantly wanted her so bad he had no control! No control at all!

Thanks heavens for his thin frame so that his suit baggy hid embarrassing evidence of his state. He stayed circling in the background. He admired her tact with dealing with the widow, respectful yet polite and a personal touch, at least as much as he could hear. To get closer would draw attention and Bob was sure his heart could not take it.

Lightning struck from out of the blue. Bob heard from her own lips. Holly was to be readmitted to hospital. The afternoon of this very funeral. What a brave soul! Still at death's door and not a shred of a hint that all was not well. Bob could not stand to hear more.

His love tore him mercilessly. He staggered away stripped, looking for ground to open up and consume him. He swallowed so hard again and again. Dare he cry out his agony and fill the churchyard. No! Of course not. He could not stand to stay but how to get out?

Through tear-filled eyes he saw Morgan emerge. "I want you to do me a favour. Take the official car and follow my instructions."

Bob accepted gratefully. Perhaps there is a God after all and if not in a churchyard then where else?

❋ ❋ ❋

Now! How would Morgan have handled this? Well! With authority for a start! And so Bob stomped up the indoor spiral staircase. Movement and shadows under the flat door halted him. He swallowed again, cursed himself again and timidly tapped on the door.

Snapper stood in the doorway and they looked at each other.

"You are remarkably healthy for a dead man," Bob broke the silence. "And a new suitcase to boot."

"Well! You know how it is. A collection of a few home keepsakes, a few mementos, souvenirs, maybe a little money," Snapper mused. "Anyway, what makes you think I am deceased?"

Bob swallowed. "Just little things really. Your little death notice in the paper, your DNA found in the wreckage of your car, and so on."

"Ah! Yes! Science. Where would we be without it?" Snapper picked up his bag effortlessly and ushered Bob down the stairs, closing the door behind him with a final-sounding snap. "Family is so precious to me, you know?"

❋ ❋ ❋

"Olive!" Olive heard her name being called yet again. She was so, so sick of it. Sick of putting on a face even at the burial of her husband.

Surely it would be over soon. She turned. Rev Long's eulogy made her want to throw up. Only she knew more than his public face.

Holly wrapped a heavy arm around her shoulders and spoke quietly. "Burying the bastard then!"

Olive smiled hesitantly, privately. "Yes! A terrible public affair. Look at all those cameras — they don't give me a moment's peace!"

"Well! He was a complicated man, ambitious and ruthless. Nevertheless he did a lot of good for the public and you should acknowledge that. Plus you are now the richest woman on the island. Everybody wants to shag you, you know?" Holly always knew how to put it in a nutshell.

Olive grinned back. "Right. That is right, isn't it? Well, his will is complicated like a bird's nest so much so I doubt it will be finalized by the next generation of lawyers. Still, I will want for nothing for the rest of my days. I must thank Morgan for his public service and I don't mean his words yet to come. Doesn't he look somber?"

Holly sniggered with the widow. "You mean sober!"

The reverend started calling his flock together to attention. He hadn't finished all his words. Perspiration came not from the heat, though there was plenty. More his recollection of his last visit and that cursed Morgan. As he looked over his congregation he wept inside as to how he had so let them down. But he didn't know. How could he have known?

He prayed constantly for forgiveness, unsuccessfully.

Even his wife had been cold in her support. How had she known? Had Morgan spoken to her? He doubted it, not his style. Yet there was no other explanation. He spent hours finding a way to introduce the subject but gave up defeated. Just so monstrous!

Now Morgan was back! Would he say something now in public to bring it to everybody's attention and rightfully point the finger right at him? He mopped his brow and coughed to start.

❈ ❈ ❈

Snapper didn't bother to look out the window. There was nothing he wanted to see any more. "If you drive erratically like that people will say you are suicidal. Bob! What the hell is the matter?"

Bob drove melancholy. "Why can't I be like you? You don't have any worries, or at least don't show any."

"Jesus!" Snapper growled at him. "You are just the same as me. Just different times is all. Worried about Holly, are we? How long, Bob? Tell me how long?"

"I don't know," Bob said, as more tears welled up in his eyes. "I do know you work miracles. Work one for Holly. She just has to live!" he pleaded.

Snapper tried blunt sympathy. "I don't work miracles at all. Only time will tell. I can't tell at all, but we should be optimistic."

Bob's grip on the steering wheel tensed. The car wavered and shimmied in response. "You bastard!" he wept physically, emotionally. "You bastard! Don't give a shit about anything now, do you?"

"Yes! I do! As a matter of fact Holly and I go way back. I should stay and comfort her. Physically. If you know what I mean!" Snapper suggested.

Bob pulled the car to the side. He did not dare drive in this state. His grip tightened on the wheel. His veins bulged. How he wanted to kill in the back!

Snapper sat back to see the effect. "That's right now, isn't it? You don't care about yourself any more. Broken glass, nails, electricity, acid, nothing would cause you a moment's hesitation. See, you have always thought your own preservation would get in the way but all you needed was focus. Now you have it. I have given you a gift all people have but choose not to. It doesn't have to be negative. So, capture and recall this moment of yours. Make it a positive force."

Bob glared at him. Unspoken he thought if this is his life he would be welcome to it. Energy-sapping, fretful, lonely. His realizations could not douse the embers of elation burning deep inside.

Unmoved, Snapper carried on. "You have lost your swallow habit. Now you are just like me, or at least you could be. If you want!" he emphasized. "To me Holly is history. There is no going back for me so you may as well take me to the airport."

❋ ❋ ❋

Morgan moved up in support of both Olive and Holly. He was all business though.

"Thank you, Morgan, for turning up after all the turmoil and hell you have been through. I don't know how you do it," Olive thanked him.

"It's OK. Personally I haven't done much for you, I am afraid. Otherwise it is all part of the job. Not a frequent occurrence though, thank heavens. I know it is really not diplomatic but have you made any decisions about your newly acquired assets?"

"Some," Olive said. "I know nothing about Cedric's work. As far as I am concerned the state can have them. Cedric did want his employees to have first options at buying them and even financed them at very generous terms for him. Obviously, Tim was one if his favourites, but they haven't been consulted yet, so who knows. He agreed here at the funeral to give Holly her final check and clearance, so we are all in good hands."

"Sounds very sensible to me," Holly observed. "Who is that young man sitting under the trees?"

Adam vaguely watched from the only shade in the grounds. "Well, Gus, what do you make of it all? Most people we know seem to have ended up here. Only The Marks may have saved a couple. I am sure we can do better though; from all the mounds of fresh dirt we will have to be really cautious. Else I may join you before I want! I so wish you were here just to hear my thoughts and fears."

"That young man," answered Morgan, "was a good friend of the lad who fell through that skylight and impaled himself. I am told he is a frequent visitor."

Olive sneaked a look. "Well, he must miss him." A sense of her loss came from nowhere. "God knows I sometimes miss that ugly little gnome. More than he would miss me." She hoped this feeling would not recur too often.

26.
New Episode

Occasionally, Adam threw pebbles into the black waters making ripples, which teased and mesmerized him beneath his toes over his perch. He reflected on what might have been. He just knew Simon's plan was substantial, but somehow disastrously flawed had ended in the deaths of most of his friends. He would have liked to be able to ask the others, except their leader got burnt to death with his family. That was most unusual of all. It still disturbed him.

Where had it started to go wrong? It was just so hard to pick a point.

But with patience he knew he would find it. A tear trickled down at the thought of Gus. The silly big oaf! He was confident once he had it sorted out he could revise his operation and start again. This time smarter and better.

Adam considered the peripheral players. The banker had gone though he was of no consequence. Adam didn't consider him. In addition he knew the bank security had not worked out its weakness. And he would exploit the breach for his own ends. Perhaps he was wrong. Perhaps that was the mistake Simon had made, but logically not so.

He thought of the island authorities. Cumbersome, slow, but it seemed once they had you in their sights they would eventually track you down. The lotto was a good example.

Better to remain invisible even if it meant lowering your living standards despite your wealth and the desire to spend it. Definitely one of Simon's weaknesses. But again on reflection the law was mostly decent people and not mass killers who he could not see.

Adam wished he had somebody to confide in.

He thought some more of the locals. Perhaps he could ask the American, but even that was fraught with danger with a reputation of being a hungry mouth to feed. Still, apparently his girlfriend was stunning and the old prick couldn't satisfy her.

He stretched up, standing to watch a plane shrink in the distance. There would be no quick answers alright.

He revisited the locals.

He thought about the tourist. This one had not behaved as a victim should and he had not moved in the circles would have drawn his attention to Adam. No, the element he was searching had very good detailed local knowledge beyond what a stranger to the islands could possibly know or gather in a matter of weeks. Discarded initially with reluctance despite what he had demonstrated at their meeting.

❈ ❈ ❈

Eating up the distance on the aircraft, Snapper sagged back. He knew Lisa was safe. He allowed tears in his eyes when he thought back long ago.

He had tried all his newfound wiles on Lisa whom he had always found precious and although he had spent the night with her, she reminded him Ben was to be her man. She had permitted only so much manipulation. The desperate man in Snapper ignored all her rebuttals, concentrating on the scraps of positive physical contact, twisting the rods of despair until he cried in anguish. Each rebuttal shrank the tortured man inside but desperation increased toppling waves of avalanche until it disappeared leaving Snapper physically and emotionally exhausted. While Snapper cried unashamedly in her arms most of the night she comforted him throughout, telling him he would weep for many others yet.

By morning Snapper had no tears left. Curiously he harboured no offensive thoughts etching the electricity of every moment, drowning in a selfless passion. He had never felt anything like this before, instantly elated, grateful for this and each moment.

Her departing kiss consumed his universe. He could feel such power in his surroundings in his efforts just to move one leg after the other.

Only then did he determine to cry for nobody else and indeed he had not but he stilled loved his Lisa as the only person on the earth.

He had promised to stay in touch but knew he had to leave that day as the community pressures built up. Morgan had taken him to the airport and he had never returned since despite efforts directly and more subtly of others.

The hostess nudged him. "Still on for that drink?"

Snapper smiled. He would have no trouble substituting Lisa from the depths and the hostess seemed willing. In his mind he wallowed once more in Lisa's touch, fresh from so long ago. Surely feelings were just as addictive as drugs or gambling or alcohol. "Yes, that would be nice. After all, what is the worst that could happen?"

❆ ❆ ❆

Morgan leaned over in his bed flopping his arm uncaringly over Holly.

What's the matter, dear?" she murmured.

"Just can't sleep!"

"I'm not surprised after what you have been through." She nudged him. "If you are going to be awake, I could take your mind off things and leave you very happy and sleepy."

He smiled, concentrating on moves he knew she lapped up. She was so special.

Afterwards they lay back, occasionally wiping the sweat from each other's bodies, too hot, too uncomfortable to touch.

"You know," Morgan said, "after all is said and done you just don't know what is going to happen. I may resign and look after you full time."

"Nope!" Holly denied him. "I couldn't stand you for twenty-four hours a day. But Lord knows, maybe your experience has changed you."

"Yes," he replied. He looked to the digital alarm clock and counted the days. "Just as a precaution, I think we all should increase our life insurance covers. Just in case I have changed."

www.ingramcontent.com/pod-product-compliance
Lightning Source LLC
Chambersburg PA
CBHW051051050726
47592CB00002B/486